THE TIME FETCH

THE
TIME
FETCH

Amy Herrick

SCHOLASTIC INC.

ISBN 978-0-545-66705-0

12 11 10 9 8 7 6 5 4 3 2 1   13 14 15 16 17 18/0

Printed in the U.S.A.   40

First Scholastic printing, November 2013

Design by Ben Mautner

To my mother,
who found the world
to be full of good hearts and useful things,
and who always had enough time.

THE
TIME
FETCH

The Fetch

First there was the doorway. It appeared high up in the back of a midsummer night. Round as a hoop, the rim glowing faintly, it stayed open only long enough to allow the Fetch to pass through. Then it was gone.

The Fetch itself was not made of anything you could hold in your hand, but was tiny and bright as a single ash blown out of a bonfire. It irritated and offended the darkness and the darkness began to coat it in a smooth pearly casing the way an oyster does when a grain of sand gets into its shell. This hardly solved the problem, for as the thing grew bigger it began to hum excitedly.

In annoyance, the night spat it out.

It shot across the sky in a swift arc. Unless you knew what you were looking for, you would have mistaken it for a shooting star. Its pearly shell was translucent. Its insides shone out a bloody gold, the color of your hand when you hold a flashlight against it in a dark room. The humming grew louder. Inside the Fetch, the Queen and her foragers had begun to awaken.

As they fell down from the cold glory of stars into the trembling air, the Queen sang out invitingly.

A hungry and half-cracked old owl heard the thing passing by. He plucked it out of the air. In his mouth, the warm Fetch took a nutlike shape. The owl perched on a branch and tried to open it with his beak, but to no avail. The thing was much too hard. The bird whacked the shimmering shell against the branch, but that didn't work either. At last, extremely frustrated, but too hungry to give it up, the owl swallowed the thing whole and flew off. The Fetch, of course, was indigestible and burned the owl's stomach. Restlessly, the bird flew over field and town and forest. For reasons he did not understand, he found himself heading toward the great city where he had been born. When he landed, at last, in the high branches of an oak in a small city garden, he tried to make himself comfortable. But he was miserable all night long.

At last toward morning, he passed the wretched thing, covering it in an excellent camouflage of green excrement.

Down it plummeted, humming with excitement, and landed in a tangled bed of ivy.

The owl, tremendously relieved, flew off to his destination feeling better than he had felt since he was a nestling.

Morning came. Inside the Fetch, the foragers and their Queen were wide awake and hungry.

The months that followed were rich and golden, and the Fetch was well hidden. The foragers were bound tightly to their Queen's authority. The Queen was an old one and knew full well that, left to their own devices, the foragers would eat until nothing remained. But as she commanded, they took only what was leftover or would not be noticed. This was plenty. The varieties of time are endless in a city in the summer. There was every kind of rhythm and heart-beat, from the quick and spicy, to the slow and sweet. So many different kinds of minutes going by, and who would notice a missing one here or there?

But all too soon, the days shortened and the air grew colder. The Queen sensed her own hour drawing close and she knew the law. Her final task must be completed soon. She shook out her green-charged wings and settled herself for the work ahead. She began to sing. The song she sang was an old one, and its notes could travel great heights and distances. She sang for three days and three nights, pausing neither to eat nor drink. Her foragers heard and came flying drunkenly home. By the time the last one was nestled in, the Queen's strength was almost spent. Still, she continued to sing until all were asleep. Then, at last, she came to the end. With the final note, her tiny heart burst open in a shower of sparks. A moment later, she was gone.

The Fetch, full of treasure, sealed itself shut. All that remained was the wait for the Keeper to open the doorway and call it back. Meanwhile, the Fetch was camouflaged in a shell of such commonplace dullness, none else could possibly be interested in it.

Part One

CHAPTER ONE
The Short End of the Year

On a Wednesday night toward the middle of December, the temperature dropped twenty degrees within a few hours. A wind came wolf-howling through the streets. Garbage cans were knocked over and tree branches splintered and snapped to the ground.

Edward slept through it all until the early morning, when he became aware of an incredible racket. It sounded like all the church bells in Brooklyn had gone crazy. But when he sat up, his heart pounding, he realized that it was just his aunt's windchimes jangling away out in her precious garden.

A cold and unmotivating dawn was just now beginning to break in at his window. He saw from the clock that it was a little after seven. He reminded himself that it was all dancing atoms. Nothing was solid.

Pulling the blankets over his head, he caught the tail end of a dream, something about an unfinished homework assignment. It slid by him like a snake into the woods, but the frantic windchimes clanged and clamored as if they were trying to give some sort of warning. Edward, who took his sleeping very seriously, tried to ignore them, but then he remembered. The rock. He was supposed to bring a rock to science class. Mr. Ross had given them two weeks to find a glacial moraine somewhere in New York City and bring back a rock from it.

Edward preferred to wait till the last minute to complete homework assignments. The last minute had arrived.

There must be a rock or two out in his aunt's little garden.

"Edward!"

The voice was surely addressing some other Edward.

"Edward, take that blanket off your head."

He pulled the blanket more tightly around himself.

"Taste the air!"

Taste the air? She was a certified fruit loop.

"It will make it easier to wake up. Taste the air."

He didn't want to wake up. He wanted to stay in this warm soft place at least until late spring or early summer.

"You're going to be late for school."

What kind of twisted, criminal mind had come up with this idea of school before noon?

Through the blanket he smelled something. There was a strong burning smell, but then something else brushed lightly against the inside of his nose—something powdery and sweet. It took him a moment to remember. He slid the blanket off his face just enough to be able to stick his tongue in the air. He thought he could taste it—a very, very faint trace of confectioner's sugar melting on his tongue.

Pfeffernusse. The little cinnamon-and-honey-flavored cookies his aunt always made at the start of the winter season. It was an illusion, of course, like everything else. Just little odor molecules firing off the neurons in his nose and then evaporating.

It was an illusion almost worth getting up for, but not quite. He snuggled back down.

There was a loud knock and the door flew open with a bang.

He heard her feet making a pathway through the treacherous swamp of dirty clothing and books and debris that covered the floor of his room. He felt her settle herself on the foot of his bed with a little *umph.*

"Why don't you just come on in?" he muttered. "Why don't you just come in and make yourself comfy?"

"Edward, there's no time to pussyfoot around here. I have received a warning. The first batch of pfeffernusse caught on fire. That is something that has not happened to me in over ten years and when that occurred . . . well, it was a very close call. I think it would be prudent to prepare the house now. I want you to come straight home today. We'll start hanging the evergreens and putting the lights in the windows. The sooner the better. We don't want to wait till the last minute. Time doesn't grow on trees."

"That's money," he muttered from inside his little nest.

"What?"

"Money. Money doesn't grow on trees."

"Yes, but money is piffle. And time is one of the great treasures."

If he asked her to explain herself, it would encourage her. He never encouraged her.

"Do you know why it is one of the great treasures?"

He didn't make a peep.

"Because without time everything would happen at once."

Whooooaaa. He always wondered where she got this stuff from.

"If everything happened at once," she continued, "there would be only darkness and chaos. Don't you wonder what the world would look like without it?"

Uh—no.

"Time is the One who gives birth to order, the One who makes the weaving of the Great Web possible."

No, no. Not the Great Web. Not this early in the morning.

The windchimes continued their demented clinking and clanging.

She paused and then, as was her way, she abruptly changed the subject. "Now, I have a wonderful idea," she said brightly. "Why don't you bring someone home from school today to give us a hand? There's lots of extra pfeffernusse. The second batch came out fine."

She was so obvious, he sometimes felt sorry for her. She wanted him to care about his state of lonely geekhood.

But he didn't. He was very close to perfecting his cloak of invisibility. Soon he would be able to walk straight across the school lunchroom without anyone seeing him, or snooze through an entire class without the teacher noticing a thing.

"Maybe you could invite that girl next door. She's in some of your classes, isn't she? She always seems so nice and . . . perky."

Edward snorted. Perky as a Cuisinart on high speed. About the very last thing he needed was Feenix sitting in his aunt's kitchen eating pfeffernusse.

"Was that a snort?" Aunt Kit asked. "Are you ready to emerge? I do hope so. Because it's getting late and if you don't start moving soon, I shall have to lift up the blanket and let this quite large spider go on your leg."

He took the blanket off his face and stared at her.

He thought about how it was hard to really see people you've been living with for a long time. He'd been living with her since before he could remember. She'd adopted him when his mother died. He'd been three. The only memory he had of his mother was her voice singing him to sleep. Sometimes, just as he was drifting off, he heard her again. But that was it. His father had apparently never been in the picture. All he'd been left with in the way of family was his aunt. Lately, he'd been feeling that she was way more than enough. When he tried to imagine what it would be like to have two parents and maybe even a brother or a sister, his mind boggled. Other people were such major energy suckers. He stared at her. Possibly others might regard her as not bad looking. He couldn't tell. He'd been looking at her for too many years. He warned himself not to make the mistake of thinking she was harmless. He'd made this error many times.

In her lap was a small plastic container with a lid on it. He looked at it uneasily. "What's that?"

"I told you. A spider. I saw it climbing up the outside of the bathroom window. I imagine it was trying to get warm, so I brought it inside. I'm going to let it make a little place for itself in my herb pots."

She grew oregano and parsley and thyme on the windowsill over the kitchen sink.

"Or I could let it go on your leg."

He sat up, keeping his eye on the container. "Do you think you might get up off my bed and remove yourself from this room? I have to dress."

"Good." She rose, holding the container in her hands. But then she didn't move. "I realize that what I'm about to say is probably a waste of perfectly good breath, but I want you to be careful. It's the short end of the year. The curtain between here and there grows thin. It would be much better if you didn't travel alone. Isn't there anyone you could walk to school with?"

He stared at her. "You think I'm gonna get mugged because it's almost the winter solstice?" She had a bee up her butt about the solstices.

She made a little *tcching* sound of impatience. "There are always dangerously powerful forces abroad when the shortest day draws near, but this time, I sense, one of those really loaded moments is going to arrive. A sneeze at one end of the world may change the whole course of things to come. At least do me a favor and try to stay awake. And probably best to stay away from the park for now. Too many ancient things astir in there."

He laughed at her. He hadn't gone walking in Prospect Park since back in the day when he used to play tee ball.

"And make sure you wear your winter jacket. It's hanging on the coatrack."

When she was gone, he lay down again and sighed. He couldn't have fallen back asleep if he'd wanted to. He wondered what she was going on about this time. The wind chimes tinkled and clanged away. With a start, he remembered the rock for science class. He would have to hurry.

By the time he got down to the kitchen, she was gone. She taught a pastry class in the city several mornings a week. He sat down on one of the tall stools and slowly ate a half dozen of the little confectioner sugar–coated cookie mounds at the counter. He had to admit, if nothing was really real, eating, at least, seemed sometimes worth the effort. He was about to take another when his aunt's cuckoo clock made its little whirring noise and then sounded the half hour. Edward rose with a sigh and took a deep breath. He opened the kitchen door, which led to her little garden, and stepped outside.

The wind nearly knocked him over. It had turned bitter cold.

Hurriedly, he poked around in the herb beds. Nothing. Not a rock in sight. The squirrels must have eaten them all.

He pushed at the rose bush and pricked himself on a thorn. Nothing there either. He sucked his thumb angrily. Why did everything have to be such a hassle? Was it so much to ask for, just one little glacial moraine rock?

In the western corner of the garden was an old oak tree. Its branches were whipping back and forth in the wind. Edward trotted along the brick path and stopped at the base of the tree. There were acorn shells and crunchy old brown leaves everywhere and a tangle of dying ivy. He kicked his way through this mess until his foot encountered something hard.

He bent to examine his find.

Hallelujah. A rock.

The windchimes jangled frantically.

The rock looked like a perfectly ordinary rock, rough and greenish gray. He reached out and grabbed hold of it. To his annoyance it didn't come free. It must have been partly buried. He scrabbled around it with his fingers and gave another heave. Again, the stupid thing resisted. This time he found a stick and jabbed it into the ground beneath the rock. A sharp sensation, like an electrical shock, went through his arm.

Now, he was ticked off. He dropped the stick and grabbed the stone with both hands and heaved mightily. This turned out not to be necessary. Like it was playing with him, the stone now seemed to fly up into his hand. He fell backward, with a *plunk,* onto his butt.

"Very funny," he said. The stone felt oddly warm in his hands. Weird. He stuck it in his pocket and went inside. He hoped it was the sort of thing you could find at a glacial moraine.

From behind the curtain, he saw Feenix come out of her house and go striding down the street in her cowboy boots and long black coat. The coat was open and flapped behind her. She tossed her black mane of hair as if she imagined cameras going off all around her. Her many earrings flashed once in the morning light and then she turned the corner and was gone.

Feenix. How could her parents have been so lame as to name her something like that?

Not that he couldn't handle her. Not that he couldn't use his mind's eye to turn her into a harmless mass of positive and negative electrical charges, but he waited a few careful minutes and then stepped out into the morning.

He moved slowly, keeping his head down and his shoulders hunched. Because he did not believe in exercise, Edward did not generally walk to school. But he knew that Feenix would take the bus on a day like this, so he figured he was safer staying on foot. The school was an entire seven blocks away, but in this case, it was worth the tremendous effort.

The street was busy as always at this time of morning, people emerging from the coffee shop, gingerly holding their steamy four-dollar caramel macchiatos out in front of themselves like little bombs that might go off at any second. They hurried along to the subway, trying not to blow themselves up. Little whiny kids got pushed in strollers to their daycares or wherever. Here and there, among the crowd were other prisoners of the state like him, heading toward their six-hour dates with unrelenting boredom. You could recognize them easily from the way they tried to keep their faces really blank and unreadable. He supposed he probably looked the same.

There were actually little patches of ice here and there on the ground. In spite of himself, he was glad his aunt had made him wear the jacket.

The sky was gray and low, and the wind blew in little bursts. Red and green plastic holiday decorations hung from wires strung over the street. They swung wildly. The store windows, still mostly locked behind steel gates at this time of the morning, were fully loaded with Christmas trees and electric menorahs and smiling snowmen.

Edward paid very little attention to the holiday stuff. As a kid, he'd gone along with all of his aunt's crazy winter solstice celebrations—the baking, the decorating, the singing, the big party, but now he no longer believed in it.

As a general rule, Edward didn't believe in anything. That is, he'd come to understand that reality was largely a hoax. One of the many useful things that Mr. Ross had taught them was that everything was made of atoms, and atoms were mostly empty space. Everything might appear solid. But it wasn't. It was 99 percent empty space.

When you took for granted that the floor you were standing on was solid, you were making a big mistake. When you put your butt down on a chair and didn't go through the chair and the chair didn't go through you, it was because of the magnetic repulsion of electrons against each other. You were really floating a minuscule fraction of an inch over the surface of the chair. If it weren't for that force of repulsion, everything would just pass right through everything else.

Other people looked like they were solid whole things. But they were really mostly full of emptiness. Most of what they had to say was just hot air, too. All this stuff they filled the store windows at this time of year with was worthless junk.

The things that people believed in, the things they kept themselves so busy with, were just ways of convincing themselves that their lives weren't completely random and unimportant.

Although he liked the smells. He breathed deeply and caught a whiff of the pfeffernusse that was traveling in his pocket and then that particular scent the air has when it's about to hit freezing. At the corner he nearly lost his way for a moment as he passed through the rows of pine trees for sale, but he was pulled out the other side by the smells of cinnamon and coffee that floated through the door of the donut shop.

He stopped there and gazed inside. It was always nice to check this window out, even if it was illusion. There was a row of donuts in the front decorated with bright wreaths of red and green icing. He felt someone's eyes upon him. Looking up, he saw a policeman with a donut halfway to his mouth, staring at him oddly. Edward preferred not to have policemen looking at him. He made his face as blank as possible and kept on moving.

Overhead a cloud of pigeons went scouting by, keeping their eyes open for any sort of edible garbage to make a miraculous appearance. At the corner, Edward waited for the light to change. He could see his breath in the air and stood there for a while, watching it. He got so busy looking at the little puffs of steam he was making, he didn't notice the light turn to green and then back to red again. Suddenly he felt something pulling on his jacket. Startled, he looked down and saw a little runny-nosed kid in a stroller who seemed to be trying to pick his pocket.

"Hey," Edward said indignantly. The light changed and the woman in charge of the stroller pushed forward. For a moment, the kid held tight to Edward's pocket, but then his hand was yanked away. The kid let out a loud scream of protest, but the woman, either deaf or very used to this sort of thing, just kept on going. Edward examined his jacket for damage, but it looked all right. He crossed the street.

The pigeons appeared to be following him. Ridiculous idea. They swooped down low, then settled overhead on a ledge and stared hungrily. Could they smell the pfeffer-nusse? Did pigeons have noses? A great gust of wind blew up the street. It knocked the pigeons off the ledge and they fluttered about like scraps of gray and white paper.

Edward felt a little tap, tap, tapping on his back.

"Excuse me."

He spun around. Standing in front of him was a man with very pale skin. Edward had never seen anybody with such white skin. It was practically the color of Ivory soap. Maybe he had some kind of disease. Edward stepped back. The man's eyes were a feverish, glittering, grassy green that stood out in contrast to the pale skin. In one hand the man was carrying a laundry bag, which clanked and clattered as if it were full of empty cans.

In the other hand, the man was holding up a beat-up

spiral notebook. "I beg your pardon for this intrusion. Is it possible that you dropped this?"

Edward looked more closely and saw that the man was holding his math notebook. It must have fallen out of his backpack. He reached out to take it, saying, "Oh, gee, thanks."

The man did not take his burning green eyes off of Edward and he did not release the notebook. "This is of value to you." It wasn't a question.

Edward stared. Homeless and, from the looks of it, crazy, too. "Well, it's my math notebook. My math teacher will probably make me suffer if I lose it."

"We will make a fair exchange then. You will give me what is in your pocket and I will give you this valuable book."

Now Edward noticed two things. The first was that the man's fingernails appeared to have algae or maybe moss growing on them.

The other was that one of those curious little whirlwinds that sometimes blow up along the streets on days like this was spinning along the sidewalk in their direction. Filled as it was with dust and leaves, you could easily make out its shape—narrow near the bottom and wide near the top. A couple of stray plastic bags caught up inside it took on different forms as they filled and deflated and filled again.

The man turned sharply to stare at this little tornado. He flapped the math notebook at it, as if he could shoo it away.

In Edward's experience these little twisters usually lasted

no longer than a few moments, taking off into the sky as soon as they had managed to pull off somebody's hat or turn an umbrella inside out. Now, indeed, this whirlwind came spinning right up to him and grabbed his hat from from his head. Edward reached out for it, but the wind tossed it higher and higher into the air.

"Hey," Edward said angrily. The gray sky seemed to press down upon the earth.

The little twister was growing bigger. Edward could feel it buffeting and tearing at his clothes. It threw a stinging cloud of black soot into his face. A high-pitched screaming rose from its center. Edward could no longer see his hat. With a stab of panic, he tried to back away, but the funnel came toward him, widening as if it had great batlike wings. It reached out and closed him inside its churning.

The Brooklyn street disappeared.

All around was a stinging, blinding wall of gray. Edward tried desperately to find something to hold on to, but there was nothing there. He took a step forward, but when he did, he felt no solid ground. Was he at the edge of the curb? He jumped back in confusion and turned around. But again when he took a step forward there seemed to be nothing solid underneath. It was as if he stood on a tiny island and all around him was a great howling nothing. What had happened to Brooklyn? Where were all the people?

"Help!" he cried. But his voice was sucked away by the wind.

"Help!" he called again, trying to balance on what was left of the solid world. "Help!"

He felt something grab onto his arm and give him a sharp yank. Over the edge he went.

"Let go!" he protested and tried to pull away, but whatever had him held him in an iron grip. Down he was dragged, through the howling and screaming and the blowing dust. He was falling so fast the pressure in his ears was painful. A gray light came rushing at him, filled with shapes and sound. In his confusion, he thought he saw the tops of trees and rooftops and then the sidewalk rising up. With a hard *thunk* he hit something and he found to his complete surprise that he was once again standing on Ninth Street. The morning river of people parted busily all around him as if nothing had happened.

The man with the green fingertips let go of him, but Edward hardly noticed this. He was busy watching the twister moving off, shrinking as it went. It picked up a pile of leaves and a Chinese takeout menu and disappeared down an alley.

Edward considered going home and getting back into bed. Certainly, this was way too much excitement for so early in the day and, besides, he had lost his lucky hat.

"What would you have done if I wasn't here? I cannot follow you everywhere."

Edward turned sharply and looked at the man. The guy's face was scary—so white and papery looking. Edward took a step backward, hoping the man wouldn't notice. "Yeah, well, thanks. Really. I'm sure I'll be fine. Could I have my notebook, please?"

"Every day closer to the Tipping Point you will become a sweeter and sweeter temptation."

Definitely nuts.

"I will give you the notebook for what's in your pocket."

Edward shook his head. "I haven't got any money. My allowance got finished off yesterday."

"I do not touch money. Give me whatever is in your pocket and I will give you your notebook."

Edward thought about it. "Okay, fine. But give me the notebook first."

The man hesitated. Then the green fingers let go of the beat-up object. Edward took the notebook and tucked it under his arm. The man watched closely as Edward reached into his jacket pocket.

Edward pulled out one of the little packets his aunt had made up for him and handed it over. Eagerly, the man unwrapped the packet.

When the paper fell open, he stared for a moment in puzzlement. Then, with an impatient shake of his head, he turned his glittering gaze back upon Edward. "Do you not understand? I am trying to help you. A Fetch should never be moved from its hiding place. You have made it into an irresistible temptation. Give it to me and I will do all I can to bring it safely back where it belongs. Don't you feel all the eyes upon us? "

Totally looney tunes. Paranoid, too.

Edward backed up slowly. "Those are cookies," he said soothingly. "Pfeffernusse. My aunt makes them. Try one. I gotta run. I'm gonna be late for school." He turned around and made a dash for it.

"Wait!" called the man. But Edward kept right on going.

CHAPTER TWO
Feenix

The minute hand still hadn't moved.

Those clocks were a scam. Everybody knew it. The prison guards told you they ran on real-world time, but this was an evil goblinslime lie. They ran on slugpower. And then they stared down at you with that look. Daring you to move. Great big no-blink eyeballs. She hated them. She hated not moving. It made her itch. She couldn't stand it, the thought of another dull and ordinary, dirty sock of a day. How could they waste her time like this?

Under the clock, Mr. Albers bobbled and bowed. Did his usual, wrote some numbers on the board, wrote some more numbers on the board. He looked exactly like Mr. Potato Head. Skinny little arms, short stubby legs, and no neck, just a little blip of a head perched over his middle. His voice sounded to Feenix like water going down the drain—*glug, glug, glug.* She had no chance of passing the test anyway.

She checked the pimple on the side of her nose with her finger. Still there.

When he turned to write something on the board she saw her chance. She slid from her seat and grabbed the eraser from his desk. She was back, sitting innocently, before he turned around.

People of all nations pelted each other with spitballs. Where were all these people from? Some were from countries that didn't even show up on the map. One of the principal's top ten schticks: Peace, diversity, makenicety. At the beginning of the year, she'd actually had everybody hold hands in a big circle around the school. UN-STONEAGECORNY-BELIEVABLE.

Feenix, herself, was one of those mixed-race people the principal was so crazy about. Her mother was half Jewish and half Italian, and her father was from Ecuador. He'd come over here with his family when he was fifteen. Both of her parents were short, but for whatever reason, she was taller than most of the other girls in her class. Nearly 5'11". She knew she was a freak. No point in fighting it. She had dark brown eyes, and one of them was slightly higher than the other. People looked at her once and then they looked at her again trying to figure out what was off. Some days she made up each eye in a different way, or inked a drawing around the outside of one and not the other—a smiling sun or a dancing blue devil. She was a good artist. She had wide cheekbones, dark brows, and, when she let it loose, a shoulder-length mane of dark hair. But depending on the mood of the day she might braid it, or twist it up high, or do a fifties-style bouffant. People stared at her. Let them look. Let the world take notice. Today she was riding easy with a nose stud and three sets of silver ear hoops, her favorite cowboy boots, and her Hello Kitty pink purse. She wore her noisy Scrabble tile bracelet.

Mr. Albers was too busy looking for the eraser to see Dweebo come into the room. But Feenix was watching for him. He was part of her mission. The way he tried to slip by without anybody noticing drove her nuts. He'd slide into his seat and go right back to sleep. If you tried to wake him up, he would just stare at you like you were a faintly annoying mosquito. He was such an ordinary little half-grown dweeb. Who did he think he was? This was a responsibility she took very seriously. Set his butt on fire.

She pitched the eraser into the air.

Yeess. Perfect landing.

"Behold, Mr. Albers!" she called in her ringing voice. "The treasure you seek has been found."

Edward stared at the eraser as if a bird had just pooped on his desk.

"Two points off your grade, Edward," proclaimed Potato Head, all red in his little face. "Bring me that eraser, if you please."

As Dweebo passed by glaring at her, she held up her

invisible force-field shield. *Ping, ping, ping.* His poisoned brain-wave darts fell uselessly to the ground. She smiled sweetly at him.

Science class. Feenix grabbed a seat by the window near Mr. Ross's treasure table. What a jumble of junk. Rocks and jars, squirrel skulls and dead insects. Venus flytraps and ferns and molds growing under lights.

No desks in here. Just high lab tables and tall stools, which gave you a good view of what was going on outside. Feenix stared out the window. She loved this kind of weather. The wind muttered. It groaned. It knocked things over like one of those old ladies looking through trash bins. The cold gray sky hung so low it nearly touched the rooftops. *Whooosh.* Papers and leaves and plastic bags flying by. Anything could come flying in.

Mr. Ross was in fine form. If Feenix could have found it in her heart to feel a fondness for just one of her teachers, Mr. Ross would have been the one. He was a hoot. Anything could get him excited. Frog intestines. The common cold. The speed of light. Rocks, for gods sakes. Rocks was what it was this term, but he was easily led astray.

He walked among them, beaming away. He was a small, compact man, with ears that stuck out. The more excited he was, the more they stuck out. They were pretty far out today.

"So are you guys feeling lucky today?" he asked.

What now, Feenix wondered. Their current subject was

geology and glacial moraines, but Mr. Ross loved to keep everybody on their toes, and he often started off the class with some kind of crazy question like this.

"Well, you should be," he said, "and here's why. Supposing that one summer evening, before your great-grandfather and your great-grandmother had first met, they were separately on their way home from work when a violent thunderstorm blew into town. They both happened to take refuge under the awning of the Regency Hotel. At the first clap of thunder, your great-grandfather, who was terrified of being killed by lightning, turned white as a sheet and his knees started to buckle. Your great-grandmother noticed this and quickly went over to him and took his arm. She asked him if he'd like to go inside the hotel and sit down and have a cup of tea. Your grandfather accepted. Imagine that that was the beginning of their romance."

Here Mr. Ross paused and allowed everybody to think about this.

"But now I want you to rewind and imagine that they were both on their way home from work that day and the timing was a little bit different. Your great-grandfather was just passing the library when the first bolt of lightning came, so he ran in there and your great-grandmother stood all alone under that awning. Thus, your great-grandparents did not meet. Imagine that therefore everything that happened afterward did not happen. Imagine, therefore, that you were never born."

He let everybody think this over for a half a minute, then continued. "How many great-grandparents did each of you have?"

"Eight," someone called out after a bit.

"Exactly," Mr. Ross nodded. "How many great-great-grandparents?"

This took a lot longer, but finally someone said, "Sixteen."

"How many great-great-great-great-great grandparents."

"A bazillion," Feenix offered.

"Correct in spirit. And if everybody all the way down the line didn't show up at the right moment and let romance proceed from there, you would not be here this morning. Correct?"

He waited while everybody took this in. "But here we are, my Young Seekers. Here we are. Against all the odds." His ears quivered and he leaned closer and lowered his voice. "Pure random chance, do you think? Or are there other forces involved?"

It got very quiet in the room.

Mr. Ross clapped his hands loudly. They all jumped in their seats. "Well, let us make good use of our improbable luck. Let us waste none of our precious time. Who can tell me where it was that we left off yesterday?"

But before somebody could remind him that they had been talking about glacial moraines, Feenix quickly gathered herself together and raised her hand. She had a responsibility to her game, after all.

"Yes, Feenix?"

She frowned as if she were thinking very hard. "You know how yesterday you said, like, the earth was a big round ball of rock spinning around sixteen hundred miles per hour?"

He nodded enthusiastically. "You remembered! It's kilometers, not miles, but that's terrific. What's the question?"

"Well, if what you're saying is true, how come when I jump up . . ." Here she slid down from her stool, threw her arms in the air, and jumped. All her earrings and silver charms jingled and clinked. "How come I still come down in the same place? According to my calculations, every second the earth should be turning about one half a mile."

Mr. Ross positively beamed. "You've been thinking!"

There was a rustling and murmuring in the seats around her. Apparently everybody, except Mr. Ross, knew what she was doing. She kept a record of how long she could keep him off topic for each period. His mind was always bubbling with so many ideas and theories, it was very easy to get him going on some completely unrelated subject.

"And you're almost right. At the equator, the earth turns a little less than a half *kilometer* every second. So how come you come down in the same place?"

"That's what I asked *you*."

"Ahhh—but you *already* know the answer. Everybody in here should know the answer. Think back. Why are you weightless in space and heavy on earth? Edward? How about you? What do you think?"

Dweebo, whose head was resting on his hand, eyes half closed, roused himself slowly.

"*Very dangerous. Very dangerous,*" Feenix whispered to the class. "*You're not supposed to wake a sleepwalker. You can give them a heart attack. Does anybody know CPR? Oh my God, imagine having to give Dweebo CPR! Eeew!*"

"Edward?" Mr. Ross persisted. "Why are you weightless in space and heavy on earth?"

Dweebo blinked. "Gravity?" he asked.

"Give that man an exploding cigar," Mr. Ross said happily.

Dweebo was glaring at her. Extra point for Feenix. "And, it's gravity," Mr. Ross said, "that pulls us back down into the same place after we jump in the air. And it's why, if you throw a stone into the air it doesn't just keep going, but eventually slows and falls back to earth. And speaking of which, who remembered today's assignment to bring in a rock?" He looked around the room expectantly.

But Feenix was ready. "Hey, Mr. Ross, look at this!" She had picked up one of the jars from his table. "The fruit flies have had babies."

He was such an easy mark. She almost felt a little guilty. But not really. He trotted right over and took the jar from her. He lifted it up for everybody to see. It was crammed with nasty little bitty flying bugs.

"Ah, drosophila. Amazing creatures. I was wondering when someone would notice. You know, first of all, they don't live much more than ten days."

"Ten days?" Feenix said, shaking her head, staring in wonder at the jar.

"Why bother?" someone else asked, "if you're only going to get ten days?"

"Maybe time is different for them," Feenix said. "Right, Mr. Ross? Maybe like each day is ten years to a fruit fly."

"Well, it's an excellent question from our point of view," Mr. Ross answered thoughtfully. "But to them, well I doubt they give it any more thought than they give anything else."

"Yes, but what I'd like to know," said Feenix, "is—what is time? Does time move? Or do we just move through it? Is it a made-up thing or does it really exist?"

Mr. Ross's ears were practically wiggling with excitement. Feenix could hear little snickers here and there, but Mr. Ross didn't notice a thing. "Time!" he crowed. "This lady would like to know what time is. Anybody want to take a stab at that one?"

"It's the past, the present, and the future," someone volunteered. "It's seconds and minutes and hours."

"Yes," Feenix insisted, "but what is it? Is it stuff? Is it something that physically exists? Or is it just one of those things people have made up to explain something like—like—lines of latitude on a globe?"

Seriously Detestable Robert raised his hand. He thought he was Einstein's second coming. He said in a bored voice, "It's the fourth dimension."

"Aha. The fourth dimension!" Mr. Ross exclaimed. "Remind us—what are the first three dimensions?"

"Length, width, height." Robert had this way of sniffing like the ignorance of the rest of the class smelled like a giant fart.

"Okay. So the length, the width, and the height give things their shape, right? Let's start with height. What would a world without height look like? Somebody else besides Robert, please."

There was a long, indifferent silence. Who cared? But then Danton spoke up. Naturally. Feenix could never believe how good-natured he was. He couldn't stand to see a teacher on the spot. "Flat? They'd be flat?'

"Exactly!" Mr. Ross smiled at him. "Without height we would have a two-dimensional world." He held up a piece of paper flat on his palm. "If there was no height, you wouldn't be able to look at this from the side, only the top. It would have no thickness. Things cannot really exist in space if they have no height, right? He gave everybody a moment to contemplate this. "But what about time?" he asked. "What if you had three dimensions and no time?"

Someone volunteered that everything would freeze in place.

"Aha. What do you think, people? Is that what would

happen? If time was suddenly removed from our universe, would everything freeze?"

"No," said Robert with annoyance. "You could never really make everything freeze because everything in the universe is made of atoms and atoms are little bits of energy that are always moving. If you took time away, then the atoms couldn't move forward either and everything would just collapse. According to the mathematician Hermann Minkowski you can't separate time from the other dimensions. They're woven together like a fabric. You can't have one without the other."

Mr. Ross was practically glowing. "Very, very interesting, Robert. Anybody else? Anybody else have any thoughts? Feel free to speculate. Theories abound in this field. What about you, Edward?"

Dweebo came in from whatever dimension he had drifted off to. Feenix often suspected that he was not as clueless as he looked. He blinked at her now like an old turtle and said, "What happened to rocks? I thought we were supposed to be talking about rocks."

For a moment Mr. Ross was confused. "Oh. Yes. You're right," he said pulling himself together. "How did we get off on that tangent?"

"Well, gee," Edward said, looking away from Feenix. "I haven't got a clue, but I have a rock."

"All righty then," said Mr. Ross. "Let's see it."

Dweebo reached into his pocket and pulled something

out. As he did, the windows rattled loudly and the wind gave a long low howl.

Dweebo got up. Slow as mud. He brought his rock to where Mr. Ross was standing.

Mr. Ross bent over and peered at it with interest. He reached out and Dweebo's fingers tightened around it protectively.

"It appears to be covered with some sort of matter," said Mr. Ross. "Why don't you go clean it at the sink?"

Dweebo did as he was told. He moved across the room at his own turtle-footed pace, looking at no one. When he brought the stone back, everyone could see that its surface was marbled, pearly gray and pink.

What was that smell? Feenix sat up, her bracelet clinking. It was wonderful. Familiar, somehow, but also very strange.

"Where, exactly, did you find this?" Mr. Ross asked. He tried to take the stone from Dweebo's hand, but Dweebo wouldn't let go. "Did you go to the park, as I asked you guys to do?"

"Well, uh, no. Not exactly. But I was like walking along and it was so interesting looking, I thought you would . . . um . . . appreciate it."

He was right. Mr. Ross couldn't take his eyes off the thing. "Well, what do you think? Igneous, sedimentary, or metamorphic? Let the rest of the class take a look. Let's see what they think."

Dweebo walked slowly to the front of the room and approached Danton first. Danton leaned forward curiously.

Feenix always thought that when Danton sat down he looked like a folded up grasshopper, his elbows and knees sticking out all over the place. When he stood up the story changed. Standing up, everything came together. On his feet he looked ready for everything. He was very tall. Taller than her, for sure, and he was getting taller every day. Humongous feet and hands and this unbelievable sunshiny smile. His skin was obviously the product of some ethnic funny business like in her own family. Though his was darker. It reminded her of shiny nutshells. She left him alone. Her mission was to wake people up and he was already wide awake. He moved easily from crowd to crowd, though he never quite seemed to settle anywhere. She could tell, too, that he didn't exactly approve of her. Well, many people didn't. So what? Most great minds were not appreciated in their own time.

As Dweebo approached him, Danton flashed his grin and then reached out and touched the rock.

"Igneous, sedimentary, or metamorphic?" Mr. Ross questioned.

"Uhh. Igneous?"

Mr. Ross didn't say anything. "Show the rest of the group, Edward."

Edward approached Brigit.

Oh boy. Feenix held her breath. Everybody held their breath. Brigit had shown up here at the Community Magnet Middle School for Misfits and Dimwits about three weeks ago. She had yet to say a word. She was red-haired and pale skinned, and she had this very colorful disability.

Feenix waited hopefully.

Brigit leaned forward and touched the stone. Odd, but the disability did not manifest itself.

Mr. Ross ignored the wind rattling at the window. "So what do you think?" he asked Brigit gently. Brigit pulled her hand back and gave a tiny shake of her head.

Feenix was next and Dweebo was slowly and reluctantly approaching her. Dweebo's expression was as coldly distant as the planet Pluto. She was about to tell him that his fly was down. Which it wasn't. Then her attention was distracted by the rock.

What was it? It looked like a regular rock, but also it didn't. And there was that smell again.

"Let me get a better look at it," she said. And her fingers curled around it, without waiting for his permission.

"Hey!" he objected.

She had the weirdest impression that the stone nearly jumped into her hand.

Now the wind gave a great wolf howl. It threw itself against the window and there was a loud shattering sound as glass exploded into the room.

CHAPTER THREE
Edward Loses It

Edward just stood where he was, watching all the commotion. Everyone else jumped up from their seats and moved away from the window, laughing and yelling. There was glass all over the floor and the wind was shooting around the room with a high-pitched whistling sound blowing papers into the air.

Feenix had stepped away from him, and Edward saw how amused she was by everybody else's excitement. She just loved it when people got discombobulated.

He had a feeling she knew perfectly well he was watching her, but she didn't turn in his direction. After a while she moved away and started searching for something on the floor. She bent down and when she came back up she had her ridiculous pink purse.

Meanwhile, Mr. Ross was calling for everyone to keep calm. "Into the hallway, please. One at a time. No pushing. Let's go. You over there, under that desk, let's not be ridiculous. Edward, you can move a little faster than that."

He managed to shepherd everyone out into the hallway and sit them down against the wall while he sent Danton to go get the custodian.

Calmly, Mr. Ross went up and down the line of kids to make sure no one had been hurt. Except for some minor scrapes everyone was fine. No sooner had he finished checking everyone out than the bell rang again.

In study hall Edward considered the problem of time. He'd actually been listening fairly closely to the discussion. He wondered what Mr. Ross would make of his aunt's theory that time was a great treasure and without it everything would happen at once. He would undoubtedly think she had marshmallows for brains. Her theories were generally without any scientific foundation. He had a brief, horrifying vision of her lecturing Mr. Ross about the Great Web of Being. Just the thought made him want to sink into the ground with mortification. He would have to be very careful to make sure they never met.

His thoughts went back to time. Would everything just collapse if there were no time? Edward's guess was that time was just another illusion like the illusion that things around us were solid. The past, after all, had already vanished and the future didn't exist yet. As for the present, how could you ever get hold of that, either? By the time you had the thought, "here is the present," that moment was already gone. Wasn't time another one of those things people invented just to get them through the day? Something that depended completely upon your point of view? What *did* fruit flies feel about living only ten days, he wondered? And what about rocks? Did a million years feel like a short time to a rock? If you were a rock—

It wasn't until that moment that he remembered. How could he have forgotten? His stone. He started to get up out of his chair, then wondered what he thought he was doing. Really. It was only an old rock and the science room was all the way up on the third floor. Way too much physical exertion. He sat back down. He tried to put it out of his mind.

The thought of the stone kept coming back to him.

Somehow he didn't like the idea of anybody else picking it up. The stone pulled at him. At last he found himself rising from his seat and heading toward the stairway.

When he got to the science room it was empty. Someone had swept up the glass and put a large sheet of cardboard over the broken window. The air was chilly, but the wind was gone.

He searched the floor. He searched the desks. He searched among the shelves and jars and boxes and terrariums that were Mr. Ross's pride and joy.

The stone was nowhere to be found.

• • •

At lunch Edward spotted an empty seat over by a couple of guys he knew. They were playing chess and they were so totally in another dimension, they probably wouldn't even look up.

The cafeteria was a minefield, but Edward's shield of invisibility was coming along well. Most people barely noticed him because they assumed that nobody was home. Which was exactly as he wanted it. He had a rich and busy interior life and he liked to keep it interruption-free.

As he headed toward the empty seat, Edward had to pass by two girls giggling and carefully dividing up a Twinkie with a plastic knife. Happily, they ignored him.

But then, just as he sat down, someone made a loud farting sound.

"Oh, that Dweebo, what a bean machine."

The person was attempting to change her voice, but it was a low, sandpapery voice that was impossible to disguise. Edward would have recognized it anywhere.

The two girls sawing at the Twinkie looked up and stared at him and burst into loud laughter. The two guys playing chess paused. They gazed at him curiously, then decided he was just some sort of temporary hologram projection or something. They returned to their playing.

Edward sat down. He pulled out the cheese and pickle sandwich on rye his aunt had made him. His favorite. She made the bread herself, too. He took a large bite and considered which entertainment to choose.

He could play the Change One Variable game. That was where you tried to imagine what would happen to the world if you changed just one small thing—like, what if people had three eyes instead of two? Or, what if there were eight days in the week, instead of seven?

Or he could work on one of his inventions. He had a lot of invention ideas he was always tossing around in his head, but he wasn't exactly in the mood for that amount of effort.

No. What he settled on was the game he called Imagine Different Ways to Make Feenix Suffer.

That was a reliable old favorite.

The first thing he did was have her trip and fall down the stairs. The second thing he did was have her deliver an English report without knowing that she had a piece of spinach stuck between her front teeth. The third thing he did was tie her to a stake and pile up lots of wood around her feet. Then he set fire to the wood. The little flames were just beginning to lick at her boots when he was startled out of his pleasant dreaming. Brigit, who had been carrying her lunch tray toward an empty seat, had stopped suddenly right where she was.

Brigit had first shown up at the school a few weeks ago in November. It was now the middle of December. No one had yet heard her speak a single word. There were many rumors about this. Some people decided she didn't speak English. Other people said she was deaf, but could read lips. Someone else claimed to have seen the inside of her mouth once when she yawned and that she didn't have a tongue.

Edward was sure that if anyone had given him a choice between starting at a new school three months into the year or disguising himself in a clown suit and joining a traveling circus, he would have chosen the clown-suit thing.

But apparently no one had offered Brigit this choice.

His theory was that she was extremely shy. Besides the fact that she never spoke, she was an insane blusher.

Right now she was staring at a spot on the ground right in front of her feet. Edward tried to figure out what she was staring at. He couldn't see anything remarkable, just the usual junk on the floor—an empty squashed milk carton, a couple of cupcake wrappers, and a grape.

Brigit took a hesitant step forward and, as she did, another grape appeared. It rolled out from underneath the table and hit her foot. She looked around nervously and another grape came shooting out from under the table. Unable to help herself, she stepped squarely onto it. The thing squished juicily. Now there was another and another—more and more, five, six, ten grapes rolling crazily across her path. Muffled laughter came from across the table.

Brigit stopped moving and kept her eyes fixed on the floor.

Here it comes. Oh no, Edward thought. He heard the laughter growing from behind them and watched Brigit with hopeless fascination.

She began to blush. Brigit had red hair, which she wore

in a long braid down her back. She was one of those red-headed people with that very milky, show-through kind of skin. The blush began slowly, like a match dropped into a dry forest. As the heat surged up into her neck and spread over her face, she turned a bright burning rose color. The blush was so intense it was hard to take your eyes off it. Although it was embarrassing to look at, too. Painful almost.

Brigit just stood there, paralyzed. You could tell she knew exactly what was happening and that everybody was watching.

A low, rough voice began to sing:

> Mine eyes have seen the glory of Brigit's burning blush.
> Just because a grape or two has turned the girl to mush.
> We have seen the red go creeping from her neck into her face.
> The grapes go rolling on.
> Glory, glory hallelujah,
> Glory, glory hallelujah
> Glory, glory what's it to ya?
> The grapes go rolling on.

Feenix's squad of evil henchwomen had gathered around her and joined in. Beatrice the Poisonous Toadstool and Alison the Hangnail stood at her side popping grapes in their mouths.

The thing that happened next happened very quickly. A hand appeared from out of nowhere, and snatched Feenix's little pink purse from off her shoulder.

Feenix stopped singing. For a moment she was too surprised to move. Then she gave a yell of fury.

"Eddie!" a voice called. "Heads up! Comin' to ya."

The little purse flew through the air and, without thinking, Edward put his hands up and caught it. It was a little pink-beaded affair, lumpy with personal junk.

"Hey!" Feenix called. She began to leap over chairs and around people in his direction.

Edward, his heart pounding, rose from his seat and began to run.

Around them, everyone else stopped singing and gave a cheer.

"Over here, Eddie!"

Danton was grinning happily, his hands up in the air, ready for the catch. Edward threw the bag toward him and Danton caught it easily.

Alison and Beatrice attempted to tackle Danton, but he laughed and eluded them smoothly. Feenix jumped on a chair and lunged for the purse.

"I'm open!" Edward yelled.

Danton threw the purse back to him and Edward tucked it under his arm like a football and began to run down the crowded aisle between the tables, heading for open space. Edward generally avoided any public physical activity since it might reveal that he had the hand, foot, and eye coordination of a sock puppet. To his surprise, the moment he had the purse in his grasp he found himself as light and swift as a deer. He held on to it tightly and felt the glorious pleasure of speed. Although shouting and laughing arms reached out to catch him, he was too slippery and too fast. He reached the open space by the water fountains and saw the exit door ahead of him. He put his head down and barreled through a knot of kids scattering them in all directions. When he looked up, there was Feenix, blocking his way.

He stopped short. She was, as always, taller than he was, and dressed to make other people stare at her. Today it was cowboy boots and pink leggings and some kind of lacy black skirt thing. He closed his eyes briefly, blinded and feeling the warm lightness in his veins swiftly leaving him, hissing away like air out of a balloon. She shook one finger at him as if he'd been a naughty child. She held out her hand.

Edward took the lumpy beaded purse out from under his arm and looked at it. It had a metal closure at the top. He started to hand it over to her and then stopped. With a quick snap, he twisted it open and, at the same moment, tossed the bag upside down in the air. A fountain of girly junk came flying out: eyeliners, Chapsticks, lipsticks, cell phone, snotty tissues, breath strips, half-eaten candy bars.

A low growl of fury came from her throat.

Girls hated it, he knew, when their purses spilled on the floor.

He watched with triumph while she scrabbled to pick it all up and stuff it back into the bag.

When she was done, she stood and snapped her bag closed. It had a thin pink strap, which she now slung over her shoulder, tucking the bag tight under her arm. She was breathing a tiny bit hard as she met his gaze with those unnerving eyes of hers. It was then that he spotted it, in the edge of his vision. On the floor near her foot.

His rock.

"Hey!" he exclaimed.

She followed his gaze and, quick as a snake striking, she bent down and snatched it up.

The wind rattled the windows of the lunchroom. It gave a low, hungry moan and dashed itself against the side of the old school building, like the waves throwing themselves against the rocks.

"Hey!" he repeated.

"I'm not happy with you, Edsel," she growled.

"That's my rock."

She lifted her eyebrow. "Your name is on it somewhere?"

"No, my name isn't on it."

"Then how do we know it's your rock?"

"I found it in my aunt's garden this morning and I put it my pocket."

"Well, then maybe your aunt's name is on it?"

"Nobody's name is on it, but that's the rock I brought in for science class."

"What if I told you that I picked up this rock last night when I went for a walk in the park?"

"You would be lying."

"It's just a rock. What are you popping your pimples about?"

"It's *my* rock." He felt how stupid this sounded, even as the words came out of his mouth.

The wind shrieked and Edward could have sworn he felt the building tremble.

"Whoa. Will you look at that?" someone whispered.

Edward turned.

The windows in the lunchroom rose nearly to the ceiling and looked out upon a gray afternoon. High up in the sky a gray object came falling toward them. It rushed down from the clouds in odd jerks and starts. Edward wanted to back up, but found that his feet were cemented to the floor.

The thing grew larger rapidly and now they could see the shape of a person with arms outstretched.

It was headed for their window, not in a straight line, but like a kite being pulled in, stopping and starting. Edward saw, with a very unpleasant drop in his stomach, that the thing had no head.

There were gasps and whispers. "*What is it?*"

The thing hit the glass with a thud and someone screamed. For a moment, it hung there, suspended. Its arms seemed to stretch up and reach toward them. Then, suddenly, it crumpled and twisted sideways.

"Look! It's just an old coat," someone shouted.

And with relief, Edward saw it was true. It looked like

an old gray raincoat. The wind must have snatched it up and puffed it full of air so that it only seemed alive. Now it spun away from them, jerking and turning, and then it fell out of sight.

For a moment the whole lunchroom was silent, then the silence was broken with loud laughter and gasps of relief.

Edward pulled himself away from staring out the window. He turned back to Feenix. "My rock, please."

Feenix's face showed nothing. "What rock?"

Edward turned his gaze to her hand. It was empty.

"What'd you do with it?" he demanded.

For a minute she was silent, then she said, "I think it's time for you to stop following me around and steaming up my space."

"What are you talking about?" It wasn't possible that she was saying what he thought she was saying.

"I see you in the morning, peering out your window curtain when I go by." Edward heard a few little snickers of delight break out around him.

He took a step back. "You are grossly mistaken."

She smiled. "Am I?" She adjusted her little purse on her shoulder and turned away.

CHAPTER FOUR
The Fog

Brigit slipped into a seat and felt the heat in her face and neck slowly recede. She saw Feenix head out of the lunchroom followed by her little gang. Edward sat down in his corner. Danton bounced back to his lunch, laughing and talking to the people around him. No one turned to look at her. That she had been forgotten was both a relief and a disappointment.

It hadn't always been like this. She was a quiet person, it was true, but back in her old school she had had friends and people to sit with at lunch. But then Leo, her baby brother, had died in his sleep and her parents had decided that it would be best to move to a new place. Somewhere in the shuffle, she stopped talking. Her mother, she knew, was worried about this and thought maybe it was because Brigit felt guilty or something and had brought her to doctors.

Brigit listened to the doctors politely and nodded her head yes and no, and returned to her silence. After a while her mother, who was so heavy with sadness, let her be. Her father seemed to spend more and more time at work, so she hardly ever saw him. Sometimes, though, he came to her room late at night when he thought she was asleep and just stood in the doorway. Only her grandad really tried to talk to her. He told her not to fret, that her voice had gone journeying and when she really needed it, it would come back to her. He was always saying things like this. He called her an Old Soul. He had been born in County Cork in Ireland and had come over here with his own mother and grandma when he was fifteen. He had an endless supply of stories about selkies and banshees and the little folk who lived in the hollow hills and could bring luck or ruin. He knew about the second sight and the songs that could make a person dance until they dropped. It used to be that most nights after dinner he'd sing her a song and tell her a story, but since Leo had gone, he had become more and more forgetful and withdrawn into his own past. Sometimes she imagined that they were all under some sort of enchantment and that if only she could find the right words she would call them all back. But whatever those words were, she had no idea and, of course, even if she did, she wasn't sure she would be able to speak them.

She finished her lunch and opened her book. She did not look up until the bell rang. She had been buried so deep in the wonderful story about the hobgoblin trying to protect the old English manor house where he has lived for centuries that she was confused for moment and not certain where she was.

She looked around the room and saw the stampede of kids rushing and pushing each other toward the exit doors. A tall boy whose head stuck up over the crowd turned and flashed her a grin. It was Danton again. She stared at him in surprise, but he was borne away by the rushing river of students before she could even begin to blush.

All afternoon Edward boiled with fury, as much at himself as at Feenix. To permit a mutant such as that girl to get under his skin was a violation of his most sacred principles.

He was so busy trying to calm himself down that the afternoon was gone before he knew it. When the bell rang at the end of the day, he almost couldn't believe it. He gathered his books without looking at anyone and slipped out of the building. He was certain that everyone was talking about what had happened, so he avoided going anywhere near the bus stop and decided to take a side street up the long hill. The wind had died down, but the afternoon was gray and damp.

He was about to turn the corner when a voice he recognized called his name. He could pretend deafness, he supposed. Although he was pretty sure that it would do him no good. He took a breath and turned around.

Edward watched Danton come bounding toward him. Where did the guy get all that energy from? All that snap, crackle, pop? It just radiated out of him. He sparkled with furious good health. His jacket was wide open like it was a lovely spring evening.

"Hey, man. Whassup?"

"Not much."

"You were really in the zone today."

Edward stared at him.

"In the lunchroom. With Feenix's pink beanbag. That was pretty awesome."

Edward didn't know what to say to this. They had had very little to do with each other in the past and Edward didn't see why they should start now. But Danton persisted. "Why don't you come along with me one Saturday and we'll shoot some baskets? I have some guys I meet up with."

Danton was not only a decent student but someone who moved with inexplicable ease between one social group and another. He was also the Lord of the Inflated Rubber Ball. If he didn't have a ball to throw, he was willing to use whatever was handy. Apples, oranges, and hard-boiled eggs were good lunchroom substitutes. That he imagined Edward would consider getting up early on a Saturday morning to meet some other guys and play basketball was dumbfounding. Edward decided the best strategy would be to just go along with him and then silently sneak away when the guy got distracted.

"Sure," Edward said. "Though I think I got something going on this weekend."

Danton laughed and put his arm around him like he knew just what Edward was thinking. "That's cool. We can talk about it next week. Right now we gotta figure out what we're going to do about today."

"What do you mean?" Edward asked sharply.

"You know what I mean. Your rock. Feenix's still got it. We need to get it back."

Edward's eyes gleamed for a moment. He thought about the rock. He thought about Feenix. Then he shook his head.

"Are you going to let her get away with this? You can't."

"It's only a rock."

"People shouldn't just go around just taking each other's rocks like that. What would happen to civilization if people just went around taking each other's rocks? If you let her get away with this today, who knows what she'll try to get away with tomorrow. It's for her own good. She's not a bad kid. She just thinks she is. We've got to go after her."

"Now? You want to go after her now?"

"Of course now. I saw her put it in her pocket, but if we don't stop her before she gets home, she'll hide it somewhere and then our mission will become seriously complicated."

Edward stared up at Danton. Surely, he was kidding. But the sunshiny grin was gone. The guy was serious. Before Edward could say another word, Danton had grabbed him by the arm.

"Come on, Eddie," he said. "I saw her back at the corner going into Mike's deli."

"All right," Edward said. "All right. Would you mind just letting go of the jacket, please? And the name's Edward."

Brigit, who was about to head up the hill toward home, saw the two boys pass by. She smiled to herself. They were such a comical looking pair, Danton with those ridiculously long arms and legs, bouncing around, practically levitating off the sidewalk. Edward, on the other hand, looked kind of like Winnie the Pooh, shuffling along, shaking his head "no" like a bear trying to get snow out of his eyes.

What could they be whispering about? A certainty came out of nowhere that they needed someone to watch over them. She knew better than to ignore a feeling like this. Quick as a sparrow, she flitted behind a parked car and watched to see where they headed.

When they entered the deli, Feenix was nowhere to be seen. Edward was relieved. Then he heard the voice of Beatrice the Poisonous Toadstool.

"And did you get a look at that hair, with that mousse or whatever it was? Somebody's got to tell her."

"I'll tell her," volunteered Alison the Hangnail. Edward thought of her that way because she was always biting at her cuticles. Also, that was exactly the kind of pain she was. Small and excruciating.

The girls were somewhere behind the magazine rack. There was a low, bored, answering murmur. Feenix.

"What is that scent you're wearing, FeeFee?" asked Beatrice. "It's so awesome."

"You're smelling things. I'm not wearing any scent."

Danton gestured to him and they edged down the aisle where the girls wouldn't see them, but could be spied upon.

Feenix was slinking along, now and then reaching out to touch a glossy magazine. Alison and Beatrice followed behind, chattering away.

The girls came out into the center aisle where the gum and candy were. Feenix darted a quick glance around, grabbed a Three Musketeers bar, and shoved it into her coat pocket. She headed casually toward the door, the other two following. A damp draft rushed in as the girls pushed their way out. Then they stopped and stood there, Beatrice and Alison blah, blah, blahhing away.

Danton and Edward waited inside, watching. Feenix gazed around herself, listening to the two other girls with a distant look on her face. After a couple of minutes she interrupted them, saying something that Danton and Edward couldn't hear. Alison and Beatrice headed off along the avenue, and Feenix stood there for a while, looking around. Then she reached into her pocket and took something out.

"There it is!" hissed Danton.

They watched her examine the rock, turning it around and around and even sniffing at it. Then she put it back in her pocket and seemed to make a decision. She began striding up the avenue into the wind, munching on the Three Musketeers bar as she went.

They watched, waiting a couple of minutes, and then Danton gestured to Edward. "Come on." He pushed the door open.

Edward couldn't believe he was actually doing this.

It was damp. It was cold. It was miserable. And here he was trying to keep up with Bigfoot. Up ahead, Feenix flapped along in her great black coat. What if she turned around and saw him?

He would be dead.

But she didn't turn until she got to Ninth Street. Then she made a left and headed up the hill. She seemed to be completely unaware that she was being followed.

Every time Edward tried to ask Danton what his plan was, Danton gestured for him to be quiet.

For a while, the holiday decorations were strung carnival-like over the streets—red and green and blue, bells and candles and stars. But when you hit Seventh Avenue where life was more upscale, the decorations became white snowflakes. Edward suddenly realized that it was already beginning to get dark. Boy, these December afternoons were really short. Overhead, the lights of the snowflakes began to blink on. They looked pretty nice, floating against the gray sky.

At the top of the hill, Feenix crossed the street and

reached the low stone wall that was the outer boundary of the park. She hesitated and half-turned around, looking behind herself.

Danton grabbed Edward and pulled him down behind a parked car. They crouched there waiting.

"I think she's going into the park," Danton said. "She'll climb over the wall. That's the way she does things."

Suddenly, Edward remembered what his aunt had said to him about the park. What had she meant? Something about dangerous things being astir.

"We'll watch and see where she's headed," Danton whispered. "Probably toward the swings in the playground. When we know where she's going, I'll circle around in front of her and you'll bring up the rear. We'll surprise her. Catch her with her defenses down."

"Her defenses don't *go* down. She's an armed warship."

Danton laughed. "That's just the way things look. Nothing's really solid like that. There's always a way around or through."

Edward was startled. It was exactly the kind of thought he often had. He stayed quiet for a moment, and then he said, "Okay. We surprise her. Then what?"

"And then, you know, we'll demand the rock. We'll, uh, reason with her."

"REASON WITH HER? REASON WITH FEENIX?"

Danton grinned. "Don't worry. You worry too much. C'mon. There she goes. She's over the wall. Let's see where she's going."

The boys darted across the street and crept up to the spot where Feenix had disappeared.

"You keep down," Danton ordered. "I'm going to take a look and just see which way she went." He periscoped his head up and peered over the wall into the park.

He was silent for so long that Edward finally asked him what was going on.

"Wow," Danton whispered. "This is so amazing. Look at this, will you?"

Very cautiously, Edward stuck his head up, too.

At first he couldn't figure out what he was seeing. The world he expected to find—the small woods and then the playground beyond—were gone. Instead, a dense gray fog met his eyes. Ghostly figures could be made out here and there, probably just trees and bushes and park benches muffled up in fog. The heavy mist went floating and sliding over the damp ground. Where had it come from so fast? Here and there, the globe-shaped street lamps could be seen. They looked like they hung suspended in the air.

"Was that fog there a few minutes ago?" Edward whispered.

Danton shook his head. "I don't know. I wasn't really paying attention. But it's wild, isn't it?"

As they watched, the mist began to creep over the walls of the park, poking blind and sluggy fingers into the air.

"Where'd it come from, you think?" Danton asked.

"Whaddaya mean? It came out of the sky, right? Fog is just like a low cloud."

Danton was watching the curling wisps as if he were hypnotized. "Maybe it came out of the lake," Danton whispered.

"Well, whatever," Edward said. "The question is, what do we do now?"

Danton didn't answer for a long time. Edward was beginning to think he hadn't heard the question, when finally Danton said, "What do we do about what?"

Edward stared at him. "Whaddaya mean? You're the one who wanted to go after the rock. And Feenix."

Danton looked puzzled for a moment. Then his face cleared. "Oh. Yeah. That's weird. I nearly forgot." He turned back to stare at the shrouded park. "Well, I don't think there's any point in going in there now. We'll never find her in that."

Edward didn't know what to make of this. The guy had been so wired up about his mission a few minutes ago. And he definitely didn't seem like the kind of person to retreat in the face of a little fog.

"What time is it?" Danton asked him. "I'm starving."

Edward checked his cell. "It's five," he reported.

"What?" Danton yelped. "Really? My mom will kill me, she'll boil me alive, she'll ground me for a year. I gotta go! Catch you tomorrow."

Before Edward could say a word, Danton took off running. Boy, he was fast. He ran in great bounding leaps. Just watching him made Edward want to lie down and take a nap. He gave his head a small shake and headed for home.

Neither of them noticed the little red-haired figure who slipped out from behind an oak tree. She stood in perfect silence, watching them. She waited till they were both gone from sight, and then she approached the stone wall and stared over it into the shifting fog. After a while she turned and she, too, headed for home.

CHAPTER FIVE
The Gingerbread House

Feenix stood outside the deli drinking in the cold air with relief. Escape from school. Escape from the big white-faced clock. Escape from Blabificent Beatrice who seemed to have almost nothing to talk about except other people's hair. Now if only something not boring would happen. If only some adventure would overtake her.

She reached into her pocket for the Three Musketeers bar, but her fingers brushed up against something else. What was this? Oh, yes. She pulled it out and smiled. Dweebo's stone. It was really a nice little stone—pearly pink and gray. About the size of a small potato, but much lighter than it looked. She brought it to her nose and sniffed at it again. *What was that smell?* She couldn't figure it out. Something that had been in Dweebo's pocket? But why would Dweebo's pocket smell like rain and rushing water and some kind of tree in flower?

She put the stone back in her pocket and found the Three Musketeers bar. She finished it in four bites as she strode into the wind. Now what? She couldn't go home. She'd gotten in trouble in French class for Krazy Glueing Mademoiselle Krigsman's teacup to her Larousse French-English dictionary. By now her mother would have gotten the call about the detention thing tomorrow, but detention was out. Detention was the same as Chinese water torture, since you had to sit at a desk without moving and you weren't allowed to do anything, not even homework or reading, just sit there and think about all the supposedly vicious things you had done like arriving after the first bell or glueing a teacup to a French dictionary.

Also, by now her mother might have opened the credit card bill and noticed the charge for the *Thousand and One Nights* Arabian Bazaar Bracelet she had ordered online. Feenix just wasn't ready to deal with the whole "what is wrong with you are you crazy?" tantrum. There were still a few hours left in the day. She would walk up to the park and see if anybody was hanging out by Ninth Street.

At Dizzy's restaurant, she paused to look in the window. Along the bottom of the glass someone had enthusiastically painted a wintry scene of people wearing back-in-the-day clothes and skating along an icy blue pond. On the other side of the glass you could see real people sitting in the warm interior of the restaurant. She recognized some kids from school drinking hot chocolate and laughing loudly. She felt a sharp pinch of envy. They looked so *comfortable* with each other. It would never be like that for her. She had friends, but most of them she couldn't stand.

Never mind. Everything could change in an instant. Comfort wasn't her zone. She needed . . . something else. An adventure. A great mission. Something to make the rest of the world sit up and stare at her in astonishment. The wind pushed at her back. Time tugged her forward. She flew up the hill. But then skidded to a halt. Something had snagged her attention.

Wowie zowie. It was a new yard ornament. She was sure she would have noticed it if it had been there before. It stood in the front garden of a brownstone building. A little man holding on to a lantern with one hand. Its other hand was upraised as if trying to give a warning about something. Its face was white as plaster and it was dressed all in green. What could it be trying to warn people about, she wondered? Maybe there was a dog inside the house or something.

While she stood there staring, she noted a darting movement from the corner of her eye. It was a sneaky movement. All her antennae went on the alert.

People didn't understand her. She was a sensitive girl.

Don't move. Act casual. Study lawn ornament. Now turn your head slowly.

It was Danton! She was sure of it. He was hiding behind that minivan parked at the curb.

Fabuloso! Something was happening. She cleaned an invisible speck of schmutz off her coat. To her delight, from the corner of her eye, she saw Dweebo's baseball cap bobbing alongside Danton.

Were they following her? Was it possible? Could Dweebo have such daring in him?

She nodded at the gnome, or whatever it was, and walked along whistling.

After half a block she reached into her pocket for her gloves and pretended to accidentally drop one. She bent to pick it up and peeked behind herself.

Yes! They were following her. Excellent. Awesome. Just when she had thought the afternoon was going to be a complete dead end.

She continued along slowly, heading toward the park, making sure she gave the boys plenty of time. She knew this park like the back of her hand. She'd lead them on a chase they wouldn't forget and then lose them in the woods up by the waterfall.

A low stone wall ran around the boundary of the park, with benches planted up against it here and there. On sunny days these benches were full of nannies with strollers, old people, and couples with their hands all over each other acting like they thought nobody could see what they were doing. But on this cold, damp afternoon, there was no one in sight all up and down the long tree-lined avenue. When Feenix reached the edge of the park she jumped up on a bench. For a few seconds she stood there, her long black coat blowing behind her. She waited to make sure that the boys would see exactly where she was going. Then she hopped up and over the stone wall.

She walked slowly so that they would have no trouble keeping up with her. The playground was empty and the swings all hung from their chains, straight and still. She sat down on one for a minute, just to give them a chance to catch up. Edsel, as always, would need a little extra time.

Down at the end, one of the swings began to creak back and forth ever so slightly, as if a person of very light weight were sitting on it, or as if a hand had pushed it. This gave her a start. It was the wind, of course.

She rose up and passed through the playground and onto the path that went by the band shell. For once, there were no skateboarders there. *Wow, it was getting dark fast.* Not that she hesitated. She knew how to take care of herself. There would be dogwalkers on the ball fields, and, after all, the boys would be right behind her. She didn't even need to turn to check on them. She was sure she heard their footsteps now and then.

Whistling, she crossed the roadway and stayed on the path that cut through the ball fields and led to the pond. When she reached the pond, she stopped by the dog beach, the small roped off area, which had been thoughtfully set aside for woofers. A skin of ice had begun to form on the water and there wasn't a beast or a master in sight. Feenix took a sneak peek behind herself.

Whooaa. Where had this mist come from? It was slinking across the ball fields, moving low along the grounds. It reminded her of a cat hunting something, sneaking along. If the boys were out there, she couldn't see them. She hesitated, wondering if it would be wiser to turn back. Then, right up close behind her, she heard something. A voice. She couldn't hear exactly what it said because it was trying to whisper, but it was grumbling. That had to be Dweebo.

Up she went, following the long curve. She could hear the sound of the waterfall that fed the pond below. The wooden bridge! Hooray. She crossed over it slowly, making as much noise as possible, running her hand along the smooth tree-log railing. At the far end of the small bridge was a large boulder, perfectly shaped for a little sit and a rest, but there was no resting tonight.

In a moment, Feenix found herself on the other side of the stream, back on the smooth path. She was high in the trees now. She listened for the sound of the boys' footsteps or their voices. But now there was nothing.

She strained her ears. All she could hear was the low soft shushing of wind through the old leaves. Very suddenly, she felt all alone in a way she did not like. With the mist pressing in, the darkness falling fast, and the sound of the water rushing by, it was like she was on a little ship far out to sea, a thousand miles from anywhere. She stopped whistling and held still, waiting for the sound of the boys behind her.

The silence, however, went on and on. All she could hear was the shushing of the trees. Crud buckets, where were the twerpy bleepsters?

To her relief, she heard a padding and a soft breathing. That had to be Edsel. He was so not in shape. She decided she would give them a great reward for their efforts and let them catch up with her. They could all walk back together and if he really wanted the stupid rock maybe she would give it to him.

Feenix waited until the footsteps were almost upon her. "Took you long enough," she called out.

A shape came out of the mist. "You have the advantage, your legs being longer."

Her breath caught in her throat. This was neither Dweebo nor Danton. Being accosted by strange people when you were alone in the park was not a good thing. And of course, it was her own fault. How come she never realized stuff like this till the last minute?

She couldn't see much of the person in front of her, but she could tell that whoever it was, was pretty small. He had switched on some kind of light and held it high so she couldn't see his face.

"Put that down," she said.

"Pardon me," he answered and lowered the light. "I did not mean to startle you."

"Do I know you?" The person looked weirdly pale in the falling darkness, but somehow familiar.

He shook his head. "I had hoped to catch up with you before the bridge, but the time is past for that now. We are all in great danger. "

She peered at him, trying to see if he was carrying some kind of weapon. From what she could make out he was small and kind of vegetarian looking. She was sure she had seen him somewhere before. In any case, she could probably give him a good kick and outrun him.

"The Fetch," he said urgently in a low voice. "You must give it to me now."

"Excuse me?"

"The Fetch. The stone you stole from the boy."

Whoa! How would this guy know about the stone? Could he have been following her, too? It was one thing to have a couple of yo-yos like Edsel and Danton sneaking up behind her, but some creepy little stranger?

"Do not be foolish. What you carry is dangerous to us all. If it gets into the wrong hands, we will all pay dearly. There are lesser powers who would make terrible mischief with it given half a chance, and already the Unraveler is on the loose. His strength increases with each day that we approach the solstice."

Lesser powers? An Unraveler? She imagined some kind of mutant X-Man whose power was making holes in people's sweaters. She giggled with sudden relief. Now she got it. "The boys put you up to this, didn't they?"

The little man made a gesture of impatience. "If your young friend had left the Fetch where it was meant to stay, we would not be in this peril. The Keeper would have collected the treasure at the appointed hour and no one would have been any the wiser. But a Fetch, once it is moved, is irresistible and the Keeper has little power to intervene. If some meddler wakes the foragers now, and any happen to get loose, we will be in the gravest danger. Who will call them in? Give it to me now. You cannot possibly hope to accomplish this task on your own." His lantern was half lifted and he held out his other hand commandingly. Suddenly she knew where she had seen him before.

A wind began to rise through the trees. It made a low moaning sound.

"Quick! Give me the Fetch!" the man repeated urgently.

The moaning grew to a shriek. A great gust of wind rammed into her from behind and the man's light vanished.

"Too late!" he yelled. "Keep it hidden. I will do my best to—"

But whatever he was going to say was cut off by the wind, which went howling through the branches overhead. Feenix heard a loud cracking sound.

Afraid she was going to be smashed to bits, she began to run down the path through the woods. The wind screamed angrily. She could hardly keep up with her own feet. The clattering of her boots was drowned out by the noise all around her.

Down and down she went, until at last the path spat her out of the trees and into the open meadow. She stumbled the last few yards and came to a stop. The wind tugged and pulled at her.

She looked around, confused. This space was called the Nethermead. She'd been here before, but only in the daytime, in the summer, when the place was open and calm and sunny, full of people playing Frisbee and soccer. Now, it was nearly night and nearly winter. Around the perimeter of the Nethermead ran a deserted road. The streetlamps with their long, curved goosenecks were just beginning to blink on. Their little pools of stuttering yellow light could only reach so far. The rolling surface of the meadow was covered in dry and flattened grass. Old leaves went spinning and tossing through the air. Beyond the encircling lamps, the branches of the trees lashed and whipped.

Feenix turned right, pretty sure this was the way to the main road. It had been quite a day. Really exciting. Much better than she had expected. Her mother would be having a heart attack right about now. Not a real one, of course. Her mother took a certain pleasure in having heart attacks. Although, oddly enough, Feenix realized her cellphone had not yet rung or buzzed with her mother's frantic text. Maybe the battery had died.

She pushed against the wind, which seemed to fight her, to want her to go in another direction entirely. She stumbled and then she stopped.

What was that over across the meadow by the hill? It looked like a small house made of stones. It couldn't be. There'd never been a house over there. How weird.

Well, whatever it was, she was going to ignore it. She'd had enough for the day.

She turned away and the wind rammed into her, spinning her around.

She was facing the house again. She stared at it. It had to be one of those historical museum things that popped up like mushrooms here and there in the park. The parks department was always doing stuff like this because they loved to educate and bore people to death at the same time. Then she noticed that there was smoke coming out of the steep, old-fashioned chimney. If it were a museum, why would somebody be inside cooking?

No, no, no, she argued with herself. She wasn't going over there. If she got up close to it there was going to be a plaque in front saying that So-and-So's Grandmother, who invented the first underpants or something, was born and died there in 17 B.C., and that the house was open to the public on Tuesdays between 2:00 and 2:25 P.M. She really didn't need to see this. Inside there was probably some really old beat-up wooden furniture and a spinning wheel.

A light came on in one of the windows.

The wind gleefully pushed her forward.

As she was pushed closer, another gust blew across the sky and a streetlamp standing beside the house came blinking on. Feenix stared in astonishment.

In the sudden flood of light, the house seemed to burst into color. It sparkled and glittered as if it were covered in pieces of glass and mirror.

She guessed she would have to take a look, after all. Just a quickie.

She set out across the rutted, rolling ground of the Nethermead and the closer she got to the house, the curiouser she became. Curiouser and curiouser. It couldn't really be what she was thinking it was.

But as Feenix tripped up the little path that led to the front door, she saw she was right. The house wasn't covered in glass and mirror. It was covered in candy.

Somebody had to be kidding. The walls were a fantastic arrangement of lollipops and sourballs, rock candy and jawbreakers, caramels and Gummi bears, red licorice and lemon drops. The steepled roof was glazed with a covering of shiny pink icing. Stuck into this icing were colored sugar violets and roses. The chimney, she saw, was constructed of blocks of fudge.

She'd never seen anything like it. Was it some sort of Christmas display gone off the deep end? Could this stuff all be real? She looked around. She looked at the house. With the tip of her finger she touched one of the caramels.

It gave slightly. Her finger came away with a little cap of stickiness. Before she could stop herself, she gave it a lick.

Delicious. Heavenly. Cautiously, she pried the whole caramel free and then popped it in her mouth.

It melted slowly, releasing an intense, creamy flavor like nothing she'd ever tasted before. She pulled another candy off and slid it onto her tongue.

The front door of the house blew open. A little old bubby lady wearing a red kerchief tied in a large knot under her chin stood there watching her. A faded print housedress fell loosely down below her knees. Navy blue kneesocks and white tennis sneakers finished the fashion statement. She tipped her face to the night air and smiled, revealing large yellow-stained teeth. It was impossible to tell how old she was. Her nose stuck out like a carrot on a snowman, but the rest of her face was worn and sunken. She could have been anywhere between eighty and three hundred years old. She sniffed the air and squinted at Feenix. Feenix stared at her.

"Believe it or not, dearie, I was considered a great beauty in my youth. Why don't you come in? Come in out of this damp and nasty bog-hole of a night."

"Excuse me," Feenix said. "I didn't mean to disturb anybody. The wind's just been crazy out here and I got lost."

From inside the house, a high eager voice called out, "Has she come?"

The woman leaned forward and seemed to sniff at Feenix. "Yes. It is the one we're waiting for."

"Well, why are you standing there? Bring her in and shut the door."

The woman reached out and took hold of Feenix's hand.

Feenix tried to step backward but found that her feet had gone funny on her. They had a rubbery feel.

"Oh, now," the woman chuckled. "Don't be shy. Come in. Come in." The voice was coming from far, far away. Long cold fingers enclosed her wrist. Unable to help herself, Feenix found herself stumbling forward across the doorway.

CHAPTER SIX
Forgetting

When Edward got to school the next morning, he stared at the wide front doors and had this uncomfortable feeling he had forgotten something. Before he could figure out what it was, a voice yelled out, "Heads up!" and a ball came flying through the air and landed in his hands.

"Over here! Over here! I'm open," Danton yelled. "Pass it back!"

Clumsily, Edward passed him the ball. No sooner had the ball landed safely in Danton's eager hands than the sound of the first bell drilled through the brick walls of the building and pierced the brain of any student still loitering around outside.

Mysteriously, it appeared that Danton had decided to adopt Edward. They were in most of the same morning classes together and in the ones where the teachers allowed them to choose their own seats, Danton chose to sit down right next to him. Edward did not pay much attention to this. He continued to be distracted by this feeling that he'd forgotten something. It was like trying to get hold of a dream or get at an itch that was in a really difficult-to-reach place.

He walked through the hallways, frowning, staring around him. Something was missing.

He combed the hallways and the classrooms. What was it? Had they taken a bulletin board down? Didn't there used to be a water fountain over there?

Well, whatever it was, it sure wasn't Danton. In gym class, he was on Edward's tail the whole time, pushing him to run and jump and catch. Edward's feet, of course, acted like they belonged to some distant relative in Australia, but when, now and then, he got it right, made a good pass or actually got the ball in the hoop, Danton would get all happy and excited and would yell, "You see? You see? That's what I'm telling you!"

He was such a nice guy that Edward couldn't help trying his best.

Danton's lunch tray was amazing.

There was a plateful of something that bore a distant resemblance to spaghetti and meatballs. Beside it was a sandwich wrapped in plastic wrap. Next to that was a styrofoam carton with chicken nuggets. Additionally, he had two bananas and a small plastic cup of applesauce. He began with the spaghetti. He plunged in with his spork as if he had been lost in the wilderness for days.

While he ate, he talked and asked Edward questions. He'd taken his little brother to Coney Island last weekend. Had Edward ever been on the Cyclone? Did Edward do any martial arts? No? It was the best discipline and good for coordination and the core. It was just what Edward needed. Maybe Edward would like to take a trial class at his dojo. Edward nodded and did not mention that he had no idea what a dojo was. Did Edward play World of Warcraft? Edward did not. He knew this was a video game, but he did not mention that his aunt allowed no video games. What *did* Edward do after school?

Edward hesitated. "Not much. You know, TV, the computer, homework, thinking about things."

Danton was eating the sandwich. It might have been bologna or might have been thin slices of rubber tire. When he was done he caught sight of the slice of bread that Edward hadn't eaten. "You gonna eat that?"

Edward handed it to him silently. Danton examined it, then took a large bite. Then he took another. He finished the rest, closing his eyes as he chewed. When he was finished he opened his eyes and gazed curiously at Edward.

"What was that?"

"Anadama bread with honey and butter. My aunt made the bread herself."

"Do you have any more?"

"That was the last piece."

"Is there more at her house?"

"Her house is my house. I live with her. She made a couple of loaves yesterday."

"She's a genius."

"I wouldn't say that. She's actually a wacko, but she's a good cook. She teaches baking and stuff."

"How's she a wacko?"

He sighed. This was not easy to talk about, but Edward did not believe in telling untruths. "She believes in solstices and nature and saving the souls of spiders and stuff."

"How come you live with her? Where are your parents?"

Edward paused again. The answer to this was always a conversational landmine. "Dead," he told Danton at last.

It was funny how the other person always looked so embarrassed at this news, like it was their own fault or something. "Oh, hey, I'm really sorry."

"It's okay. I don't remember much about them."

"You don't have any brothers or sisters or anything?"

"No." The look of sympathy on Danton's face made Edward irritable. What would he do with a little brother or sister? "Listen," Edward said, "Do you have the feeling that something's missing?"

"What?" Danton blinked.

They both looked around the lunchroom. There was shouting and laughter, chairs scraping across floors. The troll ladies who served the food yelled at people to move along. Paper airplanes and crumpled balls of aluminum foil sailed through the air.

At the same moment, they both realized that Brigit had been watching them. She was seated across the long table a little ways down.

"Don't stare at her like that," Danton ordered. "It makes it worse."

"It makes what worse?"

"That thing where she blushes. When you look right at her like that, it sets her off."

"But why is she looking at *us* like that?"

Danton shrugged and smiled his big smile. "'Cause we're so pretty?" He leaned over and grabbed a bruised apple that someone had left behind. "No point in wasting good food," he said, and then took a bite.

Since Brigit had stopped speaking, her ears had grown much sharper. It wasn't just that she heard the mice in the cabinets or her mother's muffled crying or the sadness of her father's footsteps when he returned late at night. Lately, she'd been hearing different sorts of things, strange things.

First, there had been that singing. It was high and silvery and vibrating, and Brigit hadn't been able to figure out where it was coming from. She had first heard it when she was walking home from school along Ninth Street. It was so strange and lovely she decided to try to follow the sound, but the wind caught the notes and carried them away. Late that night she heard it again. The singing woke her and she lay there listening to it until she fell back asleep. Then she heard it again, in the morning, when she'd been sitting in science class. It went on for several days, just little scraps of melody floating by, the words sung in some language she didn't recognize, and then it had stopped. No one else seemed to have noticed it at all.

Now today, there was something different. Not a song, just a girl's voice. It was driving her crazy. She was sure she knew the person it belonged to, but she couldn't think who it was. She'd been hearing it on and off all morning, but she could only catch a word or two, not enough to make any sense of. Whenever Brigit turned around to see who it could be, no one was there. Sometimes the girl sounded angry, but more often, she sounded afraid. Brigit found that every time silence fell, she was holding her breath, waiting to hear the voice again.

But when she waited, there was nothing.

At lunchtime—she wasn't sure why—she took a seat close to where Edward and Danton were. What a strange morning. She wondered what they were doing sitting next to each other. They were about the last two people you'd expect to find hanging out together.

Danton was one of those guys who had shot up overnight. His voice had grown deep already, too. He was impossible to miss. When he came into a room, he lit up every corner of it. She was pretty sure he knew who she was. He knew who everybody was and everybody knew him. He just nodded at her when he went by, but she had the feeling that he got it. He knew how hard it was for her when people tried to get her to speak and he wasn't interested in trying to get her to turn red. He probably wasn't interested in her, period. But at least he didn't torment her.

Edward never bothered her either, but that was because most of the time he seemed to be half asleep, like a bear trying to settle down into hibernation. He moved clumsily and he avoided talking, too. Maybe because his voice was still cracking all the time. In any case, today something was different about him. He appeared almost awake. He was sitting more or less upright and, every once in a while, he frowned and gazed around the room as if he, too, were looking for something.

She buried her nose in her book and when she looked up again, she saw Danton throwing grapes into the air and catching them in his mouth. Between swallows he talked to Edward, who looked like he was only half listening, though now and then he'd turn and stare at Danton. Then he'd start looking around the room again.

Brigit kept her eyes on the page, but she couldn't concentrate. Suddenly, she could have sworn she heard it. The girl's voice. She sat up with a start. It had come from somewhere in the back of the lunchroom. She knew the boys were staring at her, but she was too distracted to blush. She turned around quickly and searched the crowd, but, again, whoever she was looking for wasn't there.

Science was their last class of the day.

Edward decided that the safest thing to do would be to go into Advanced Level Chill Mode. He felt this was what was needed in order to protect his health and sanity. It was a little bit drastic and carried its own dangers, but there had been far too much excitement today. In this mode he made a conscious effort to bring all his bodily functions to a near halt. It was similar to what was done to people when they were going to travel through space for extended periods of time. In order for Advanced Level Chill Mode to work in school, you needed to find a seat at the back of the classroom where the teacher wouldn't notice that your body was no longer inhabited by a conscious human being. The danger was that you would be called upon and would, naturally, fail to hear a thing. Some teachers got all cranky when this happened.

He found a nice seat in the back corner by Mr. Ross's treasure table. He scrunched himself down and proceeded to slow his various support systems: first respiration and heartbeat, then sensory awareness. As he drifted off, he heard Mr. Ross blabbering on about the Paleolithic Era and ice ages. He had just reached a pleasant state of semi-consciousness when a loud bang brought him rudely back to reality.

His eyes flew open.

Mr. Ross was glaring at the class. He picked up the big geology textbook and dropped it on the table again.

"Wake up, people! You think that was so long ago, two hundred thousand years? Two hundred thousand years is only a second, a tiny tick, in the grander scale of things."

There was an uneasy shifting in seats.

"Okay! You people are way too comfortable for your own good! Hypothetical situation: Sudden time warp—we've been thrown back in time, say, around two hundred thousand years. We're nearing the winter solstice just as we are now. You are young hunter-gatherers. The days, you have noticed, are shorter and shorter, the nights longer and longer. The situation does not look good. It's cold. Nothing's growing. One of your tribe left the shelter the other night to relieve himself and never returned. Probably eaten by some wild beast . . ."

Mr. Ross seemed to be waiting for someone to say something. But there was only silence. He went on.

"You know nothing at all about the laws of nature and the movements of the planets, but you know enough to know that if something doesn't change soon, you will all be goners. What would you do?"

He waited again, expectantly, but still, there was no answer.

"C'mon, c'mon somebody. What do you think? What would you do?" Mr. Ross turned on Delilah.

"Delilah?"

She gave a bored shrug. "Pray?"

Everybody laughed.

Mr. Ross looked serious. "But she's right, you know. This was almost certainly one of the fears that made humans begin to look for the gods."

Edward noticed that several of the more marshmallow-brained glanced around nervously as if expecting some dude carrying a lightening bolt to jump out from under a chair.

Mr. Ross directed their gazes to the sky. "The sun will set even earlier today than yesterday. Tomorrow it will set even earlier. Dark will come on fast. What if the sun just vanishes? What then?"

Still no answer. Mr. Ross pointed to someone.

"We'd freeze to death?"

"Okay. Good. What else?" Mr. Ross pointed to Danton.

"Uh . . . since we wouldn't be able to grow anything, there'll be nothing to eat?"

"Yes." Mr. Ross nodded. "*Solstice.* Does anybody know what the word means?"

Edward knew. His aunt was very serious about celebrating the solstices, but he felt no need to share this embarrassing fact.

Mr. Ross, however, apparently read his mind. "Edward?"

Edward debated with himself about claiming ignorance, but again, there was his inconvenient belief in telling the truth. "Well, 'Sol' means 'sun.' 'Stice' means 'stop.'" That was as far as he would go.

But Mr. Ross nodded at him happily. "Exactly right. From the Latin. 'Sun stoppage.' The sun appears to stop in its tracks. There are two solstices each year. One occurs in December. One in June. In the northern hemisphere the days are now growing shorter and shorter. The ancient peoples considered this an extremely powerful time. In a few days the sun will appear to stop in its tracks and attempt to gather the strength it needs to begin its return. If things go wrong and we're all plunged into darkness, well then, good-bye, my young friends. Back in ancient times, as humans were growing more at home on earth, they came up with all sorts of tricks and stories and rituals to encourage the sun to gather the strength to win out over the darkness. Some were harmless enough. They decorated evergreens in the hopes of bringing back the green things that gave them food to eat. They hung wreaths to keep the circle of life going. They peered into the darkness watching for the enormous great-horned stag who they believed was strong enough to win the battle against winter.

"But other traditions evolved that were more—colorful. The Greeks, for instance, would choose a strong, handsome young man around this time of year and bring him to the handmaidens of their god Dionysus. The handmaidens would ply him with wine and send him running naked into the woods. They'd give him a good head start. Then they'd pray and burn incense, drink themselves into a fine madness, and strip themselves naked."

He had the class's attention. Edward was awake.

"They'd put little wreaths of ivy on their heads and go after him. The poor guy didn't have a chance. According to legend, they'd hunt him through the woods and when they caught him, they'd hold him down."

The class waited.

Mr. Ross narrowed his eyes. "Some say they'd then tear him apart and eat him. When they were done, they'd return to their temple, singing and chanting, and holding aloft an infant child. A great celebration of feasting and merrymaking would take place among the people then and, voilà, by great coincidence, the sun would be noticed to be growing stronger in the days that followed."

There was a long silence and an uncomfortable shuffling of feet.

"But where'd they get the baby from?" someone asked.

"Yes, indeed. Where *did* they get the baby from? Well, it was said that somehow it sprang from the blood of the one who was sacrificed."

Robert now piped up and asked with some impatience, "What does any of this have to do with science?"

Mr. Ross ran his hand through the hair on his head. He didn't have a lot of it and what he had now stuck up in uneven wisps. "Thank you, Robert. Where does science bring us? The ancient peoples didn't know what we know. Early on, many of them began to chart the regular movements of the sun across the sky, but they didn't understand *why* the sun moved as it did. They explained things with stories of wild women and Holly Kings and gods fighting the monsters of winter for twelve days. They could be pretty certain from the stories and observations they passed down from generation to generation that the cycle had been repeating itself over and over again. But at this time of the year, something appeared to be eating away at time itself, something that refused to make itself seen. The dark was so dark and the cold was so cold. How could they be sure that the end wasn't upon them? It seemed wise to continue doing whatever it was that their parents and grandparents had done in the years before.

"But now it's different, right? We have more information. We are able to look at things from the perspective of space and we can use telescopes. We can see that the seasons change because the earth orbits the sun at an angle. We can calculate the moment of the solstice to the second and we know that we have nothing to worry about. Right? This time of year is really no more dangerous than any other time of year. Winter vacation is in sight. We'll soon all be busy celebrating Christmas and Hanukkah and Kwaanza and the little bits of ritual which have floated down to us from the past—Christmas trees, flying reindeer, burning lights of various kinds—these are just leftovers from stories that were meant to explain things that no one understood.

The earth will tilt back toward the sun as it has always done and all will be well.

"But I just want you to remember that there are tipping points, when the balance of things gets so out of whack, there is no returning to the old cycles. Sometimes they arrive over what seem to be long periods of time. Sometimes they can arrive relatively quickly. There will be more ice ages. The earth's orbit will change. Those things will almost certainly happen somewhat slowly. But global warming, nuclear winters, oil spills, tornadoes, earthquakes that send out tsunamis—those happen relatively fast. And perhaps there are forces out there that we are not yet acquainted with. Forces within forces. A surprise or two. It may be that one day the solstice will arrive and the balance *won't* tip back. Who knows? It doesn't do to get too comfy, my young friends."

The end-of-the-period buzzer rang. For a moment nobody moved. Then there was a general stampede toward the exit, as if the whole class couldn't wait to get out of the room.

CHAPTER SEVEN
Inside

Her dreams were sickening and roller coasterish. Voices kept whispering over her head and she heard nonsensical words. And there was the smell—a foul and rotten stinking of something. She tried to open her eyes, but her lids seemed to have been Krazy Glued together. Then she heard an unpleasant sound, a sound like bones cracking and then a noisy sucking.

Slowly, it came back to her: the journey through Prospect Park, the pale little man, the wind, the candy house, and the kerchiefed old lady at the door. Whatever she was lying on, it was prickly and uncomfortable. She shifted a little and, without even realizing she was doing it, let out a groan.

Immediately the cracking and sucking sounds stopped.

With an enormous effort Feenix managed to open one eye and then the other.

There wasn't much light, but she saw right away that she was in a cage, the kind of cage you might keep a big dog in. She was lying curled up on some dusty straw. Next to her was where the smell was coming from. She could see the gristly white bones gleaming in the lamplight. A small mountain of them.

The inside of the house was not the same as the outside. It was a dark little dump of a place. The floors seemed to be dirt and the walls held up by bare wooden beams. There was a not-very-clean kitchen area and the only place to cook anything looked like the fireplace, which had a big iron pot hanging from a pole.

If this was a museum, it was a crummy one.

The old ladies were sitting at a wood-planked table eating with their fingers. There were three of them. Their only light was a single burning candle. At the sound of her groan, they had all stopped eating and turned to stare in her direction. The grease on their fingers glistened in the candlelight.

"She's awake," said one of them. Feenix thought it was the same voice that had greeted her at the door.

"Ooooh, goodie," said another voice, unpleasantly high and excited. "Let me have the spectacles."

"No," said the third. "I will examine her first. I will have the spectacles," and she snatched at something in the middle of the table and then rose and hobbled over to the cage. She bent down and examined Feenix, and Feenix examined her. The woman, if that's what she was, was wearing a pair of thick-lensed glasses and a long black gown. A bunch of keys hung from a twisted belt of yarn around her waist. She had long, gray hair, a long, horselike face, and most charming of all, only one nostril.

Feenix tried to sit up, but bumped her head on top of the cage. "All right!" she said angrily. "Let me out of here."

The old lady grinned.

"What is going on?" Feenix demanded. "What is this place?"

"The place is neither here nor there."

"Let me out of this thing." Feenix grabbed the sides of the cage and rattled the bars furiously.

The old lady with one nostril paid no attention to her demand, but stood there with her head tipped to one side. Meanwhile, the other two rose and made their way over to the cage. They peered down at her with interest. Red Kerchief, the one who had met her at the door, smiled and licked at her greasy fingers. The third one, who was very round, with tiny little pig's eyes and a soft, pudding face, smiled happily.

Feenix rattled the cage again. "Let me out of here immediately."

"She's a sparky one, isn't she?" said Piggy Face.

She came closer to the cage. Gingerly, she stuck out a

hard, wrinkled old finger and prodded Feenix through the bars, then nodded to herself.

"You crazy old prunes!" Feenix hollered. "Let me out immediately! My friends are right behind me. Do you have any idea what the penalty is for kidnapping? I don't know if they'll put you in jail or the loony bin, but either way they'll take your candy away."

One Nostril laughed. "No, no. No need to worry. Your friends never even crossed over the wall. By now they will have forgotten all about you. And we have been waiting for you so patiently. You have the most intriguing smell. Are you not flattered that we chose you? How many get to see the inside of our happy little home?"

"What are you talking about?" Feenix demanded angrily. "How could you have chosen me? And for what?"

Red Kerchief had stopped licking her fingers. She leaned forward and said softly, "Do you think it was just random chance that brought you to us? Do you think it was just improbable good luck?"

Something in these words reminded Feenix of Mr. Ross, but she was too angry to think about it. She rocked the cage furiously back and forth. "Let me out of here!"

One Nostril licked her lips and stared down at her through the thick glasses. Then she said, "Hasn't life been very dull? Have you not been seeking a great adventure?"

Feenix stopped shaking the cage for a moment. She stared at her with a terrible sinking feeling.

"You may call me Baba," One Nostril said. "I am the oldest."

As far as Feenix was concerned, they all looked about three hundred years old. "Okay, Baba. This is not funny. I need to get home before my mother has a coronary. You need to let me out of here."

"All in good time, little mortal. If we let you out now you would never find your way. The paths would all bring you right back to us."

Feenix laughed angrily. "What kind of joke is this? Who are you? What is going on?"

Baba smiled her pinched little smile again. "The stories told about us are countless. Surely your grandmother will have passed one or two on to you?"

"Did the Parks Department give you permission to put this house here?"

This made Baba laugh. "We are always here. It is just that at this time of year, the curtain between your side of the world and ours grows thin enough that some can see us."

Piggy Face leaned in closer now and sniffed. "I will open the cage, shall I?"

Baba nodded slowly, staring at Feenix. "Yes. Let us get a closer look at her." She lifted the latch on the cage and the door swung open by itself. Feenix climbed out stiffly. Then she stood up and stared at her captors. They were lined up in a row, peering at her, three old yentas bent and wrinkled like used candy bar wrappers.

Feenix crossed the room in two strides. She reached the front door and grabbed the knob. The door was locked. The key, Feenix had little doubt, was hanging from Baba's belt.

The next day and the days after passed in a terrible dream. How this place could exist inside the familiar and ordinary world, Feenix had no idea. But she was pretty sure it was Dweebo's stupid stone that had gotten her into this trouble. The old ladies could smell it. They were always sniffing at her—especially Piggy Face. Feenix had dropped it through the hole in her coat pocket, so that it fell deep down inside the lining. It was freezing in the cottage, and she never took her coat off. The witches seemed to think the scent was part of her own personal fragrance. Every time old Pudding Face got near Feenix, she groaned with anticipation.

Although the old ladies apparently had a sharp sense of smell, their eyesight was terrible and they only owned one pair of glasses, which they shared among themselves. They were always arguing about whose turn it was. Old Baba, who was clearly the boss, got them most of the time. The other two hobbled about the filthy place, bumping into the furniture and cursing and describing the horrible things they would do to each other if they were younger.

Feenix thought of ways she would get back at Edward for getting her into this mess.

During the day they let her out and made her work. Red

Kerchief, who was called Skuld, delighted in coming up with random, bat-brained chores for Feenix to do. Her favorite was making her unsnarl tangled up webs of old gray yarn and then roll them into balls. There were hundreds of these balls lining the dusty shelves of the cottage. Or she would make Feenix scrub the huge sink full of greasy pots with a toothbrush and then sweep the floor with a little bundle of sparrow feathers tied together with string. It was clear that she found this amusing and entertaining. If Feenix protested, Red Kerchief would grab her ear and twist it.

She had discovered on the first night that all three of them were unbelievably strong. When Feenix had lunged for the keys on old Baba's belt, Baba had lifted her up and thrown her clear across the room. Trying to fight with Skuld about stupid chores was equally useless.

"You dare to complain? Do you have any idea how few mortals are given this chance to enter the world in back of the world, especially in these days when the great forces are so little remembered? Here is the adventure you asked for. The very least you can do is perform these small tasks we give to you. Now, return to work or you will find yourself with something to complain about."

While she was working, Piggy Face, who was called Gorgo, often waddled over and pinched a piece of Feenix's face or arm between her fingers, rolling it and feeling it, snuffling like a congested pig as she did.

"Oh what a lovely, sweet-fleshed child you are. It is so nice of you to come and celebrate the Stoppage with us."

Only Baba One Nostril did not touch Feenix, but what she did was almost worse. She would come right up close to Feenix and then study her as if she was trying to figure something out. *"What is it? What are you hiding?"* she would whisper.

Feenix tried constantly to come up with an escape plan. The windows in the cottage were high up and very small and Feenix didn't think she could fit through any of them, but now and then one of the old ladies would open the front door and leave the house. She watched very carefully when this happened.

The one who went out would get to wear the glasses and the other two would stay behind, bickering and ordering Feenix around. When the third one returned, she would usually be carrying a small, limp animal—a squirrel or a bird or a rabbit. Once there was a poor cat. The old ladies would boil it, or make Feenix turn it on a spit over the fire and then they would sit down at the table and eat the meat with their hands, crunching and sucking away greedily. They would wash these meals down with what Feenix guessed was wine. After a couple of glasses they would begin to argue about who would get the last pieces of meat or whose turn it was with the spectacles. Generally, Baba won the argument, although occasionally, if she fell asleep,

Skuld and Gorgo would have a pinching match until one of them gave in.

The pile of old bones and bits of gristle in one corner of the room grew steadily higher. Luckily, they did not offer to share these delicacies with Feenix. They fed her, instead, bread and dried cheese. Feenix began to yearn desperately for an apple or a banana or a piece of celery, but there was nothing like that in the cottage.

How many days this went on for, Feenix was not sure. Time in the cottage seemed even more shifty than it did back in the real world. But she could see that the old ladies were growing more and more excited about this "Stoppage" thing. It was going to happen soon, whatever it was.

CHAPTER EIGHT
The Song and the Spider

For Edward, the next few days passed in the way days did in December. Everybody went rushing around, knocking each other over to buy gifts in crowded stores. There was that breathless feeling of anticipation. What was it for? He thought of Mr. Ross's paleolithic hunter-gatherers huddled around their little fires.

All week the house was filled with clouds of cinnamon and sugar. There were always cookies and pies and fruit-cakes baking. These were such good, comfortable smells. But when he tried to sit down on the sofa and watch some TV, his aunt appeared from out of nowhere and looked at him like he'd just committed a double felony.

"Are you kidding? Aren't you reading the signs? What

do you think you're doing? We've got work to do! Time's nearly up!"

She made him hang pine boughs over the doors and on the stairways to keep out evil spirits. She made him put candles in all the windows for lost travelers, and roll apples in peanut butter and birdseed and tie them up with ribbons in the little garden. Then she made him go back out and drag a tree home from the corner and set it up and decorate it with all her weird ornaments—her shark's teeth and animal skulls all wrapped around with gold ribbon and her many bizarre decorated cookie people. She wouldn't let him rest for a minute.

He pointed out to her that she was still living in the dark ages, when people didn't understand about the solstices and how the earth travels around the sun. "Darkness isn't going to swallow the world up just because you didn't hang your pine boughs. As it happens, we were actually discussing this in science class the other day."

She snorted. "Any scientist worth his suspenders know that every time you unravel one tangled ball of yarn, the universe sends you another. It is the nature of the Great Web."

Edward resolved again to make sure she never got anywhere near Mr. Ross. The thought of the humiliation that would follow was terrible.

"A great deal is known. But much more is not. There are

so many mysterious forces coming and going. Their names are always changing." She waved her hand at various invisible things floating around in the air between them. "No sooner does science get hold of one explanation than that explanation turns to dust and is replaced by another."

"So then why bother?" he said. "It's exactly what I'm always saying. Why bother if nothing is solid?"

She shook her head in exasperation. "It doesn't mean that things don't matter. A sneeze at one end of the world can change the whole course of things to come. What's important right now is the winter solstice, when we all look out and peer into the vasty dark. I suggest you humor me. If you'll just go into the kitchen and get my good shears, we can trim these branches a little."

Edward had wasted enough perfectly good energy on argument. In the kitchen he poked around in the drawers until he found the shears. Then, as he turned to go, his eye was caught by the gray spider on the windowsill. The one his aunt had rescued. The spider looked exceptionally busy this afternoon. It was running back and forth between the rosemary and the oregano and the thyme, leaving behind itself shimmering little spidery threads. It was exhausting just to watch, but Edward stood there in hypnotized fascination. What did the creature think it was accomplishing? It certainly wasn't going to be catching any flies at this time of year. Edward noticed a small silvery gray ball resting on the windowsill next to the herb pots. He leaned over to take a closer look and was baffled to realize it must be a ball of spider thread. Was his aunt actually collecting the stuff? He wouldn't put it past her.

"Edward! What's taking you so long?"

He wondered if it was something she used in some recipe or other. Edward shook himself. "Yuck," he said to the spider and turned away from the windowsill.

Danton took his little brother ice skating in Prospect Park one afternoon. They did at least one thing together every week. Danton loved his little brother and his little brother thought the sun rose and set at Danton's command. They walked over to the library and took the bus up Flatbush Avenue and entered the park through the gateway at the corner. As soon as they passed through, Danton was struck with a feeling that he was supposed to be doing something he had forgotten to do. What could it be? His brother, who was eight, danced around him with excitement.

"Stay close to me, Jay."

It was still light and the sky was filled with great streaks of gold and pink. But there was no one else on the path that wound through the trees. They went past the now-silent carousel, shut down for the winter, and soon found themselves crossing the road and approaching the rink.

"We'll get hot chocolate, too, right? And french fries?" Jay demanded anxiously.

"Sure," said Danton. This was what they always did.

What was it? Had their mother asked him to pick something up at the store for her? No. That wasn't it. He felt sure it was something he was supposed to do once he got into the park. But what could that be?

The rink was pretty empty at first, but as it grew dark and the lights twinkled on, other skaters came sliding in. The air was fresh and cold and full of the smell of the nearby lake, pine trees, and the clean scent of the ice. He and his brother raced in and out of the throng, chasing each other around, sneaking up on each other, shouting with glee when one managed to surprise the other. They were both excellent skaters. Danton found some other kids from school and they all went around together for a while, laughing and making snakes and showing off, until his brother begged him to stop so they could get their french fries and hot chocolate at the refreshment stand.

By the time they got back on the ice, the rink had really filled up. His little brother shot ahead and disappeared into the crowd. This didn't bother Danton too much. Where could Jay go? But Danton preferred to keep an eye on him. Looking for his brother's red wool hat, Danton glided confidently through the head-bobbing river of people. He caught a flash of something scarlet and thought he had found Jay, but when he got closer, he discovered this definitely was not his brother. It was, in fact, an amazingly old lady with a red kerchief tied tightly under her chin. The woman was skating around the rink with her hands locked behind her back, a little smile on her face, studying the crowd with a hungry look in her eye. And now her attention had been caught by something. Danton followed her gaze and saw that she was watching his little brother. Creepy, but she had to be harmless. He shot forward, cutting in front of her and grabbing hold of Jay's arm. Jay spun out for a moment, then caught his balance.

"Hey!" he gasped, laughing. Danton let go of him and shot forward again, making sure Jay was not far behind. They went around a few more times. Danton kept an eye out for the weird old woman, but he didn't see her again. She must have left the ice.

Soon afterward, Danton announced that he was starving and it was time to go home and have dinner. Jay did not argue; the french fries were beginning to wear off.

As they passed through the gate on the way to the bus stop, Danton again had the sudden sharp feeling that he had forgotten to do something. But a moment later the bus pulled into sight and the two boys ran for it.

Brigit continued to hear the girl's voice on and off all week, but that seemed to be mostly when she was in school. At home she heard other disturbing things. The wind kept her awake at night, keening and crying down the alleyway, knocking over the garbage cans as if it were looking for something. Then one night, when the wind fell silent, she heard her parents talking in the other room.

"Well? Is there any change? Has she spoken at all?" her father asked.

"No," her mother answered. Then she said coaxingly, "I wonder if it wouldn't help if you spent a little more time at home."

Brigit could hear the bristling in her father's answer. "Time is the problem, Celia. I don't know where the stuff goes. You know how busy we are at work. Most days I don't even have time for lunch."

Brigit wondered if this was true. Certainly, her father had grown very thin in the last few months.

"Come home for dinner one night, Al. I'll make the turnips and sausages you like."

"I'll try, Celia. But it won't be until this big project is finished and that's not going to happen for at least a few more days."

Brigit heard her mother sigh. Then there was only silence. She wished she could call out to them and, for just the briefest of moments, she thought she felt a fluttering in her throat. It felt like a bird stuck in a chimney, trying to get free. But then there was nothing.

Her grandad was the only one who was really around when she got home from school. But he was disturbed all that week, too. Sometimes he seemed to know her name (they all called her Birdie), but then other times he thought she was Irene, her grandmother, who had died ten years ago. They said she looked like her grandmother and that she had the same fiery red hair, so you could see why he might do this. But still, there was something unnerving about being confused with your own dead grandmother.

By Tuesday, her grandad started insisting that he needed to make brandy pudding. He spent hours looking through the old cookbooks. But when he couldn't find what he thought was the right recipe, he started to get agitated. Brigit soothed him and showed him how to look for a recipe on the Internet. Together they found something. She printed it out and he was excited, a little breathless, and he made her take him to the market. He hardly ever wanted to go out anymore, so she was pleased to do this, but when they got to the supermarket everybody was in such a mad rush, she knew the whole thing had been a bad idea. He stared fearfully at the people with their shopping carts stampeding up and down the aisles and asked her what was going on. Then a fight broke out on the line to the cash register. A woman with a two-year-old accused a man in a suit of cutting in line, and before you knew it, the two of them were screaming and cursing at each other. Her grandad grabbed hold of her arm so tightly, Brigit nearly cried out.

"What were you thinking of to bring me out here? 'Tis home we're going, lass," he hissed in her ear. "This is a dangerous time. Something has gotten loose that ought not to be."

And they went home without the things they needed to make the pudding.

But the next day, Brigit stopped at the market and bought the dates and the fruit and the brown sugar. They had a lovely afternoon in the kitchen, mixing and measuring and baking the pudding, which wasn't really a pudding, but a kind of cake. But then it came time to make the brandy sauce. Her grandad measured out the brandy and took a small glass for himself, and no sooner had he downed it than he started calling her Irene again. He took another small glass of brandy and then he began to sing. He had a beautiful Irish tenor and according to his own story, he had won Brigit's grandmother's heart with it by singing under her window. Brigit couldn't remember the last time he had sung. He used to belong to a chorus in Manhattan, but she didn't think he'd gone to rehearsals for months. This afternoon, though, he sang the song about the green growing rushes and then he sang "The Fiddler's Green." Then he had another glass of brandy and he sang the one about Mattie Grove who got caught in bed with Lord Darnell's wife.There seemed to be an awful lot of Irish songs about people getting caught in bed with other people's wives.

He went from one old tune to the next. She wished she could join in with him. She'd had a good voice, too. But that was before. Her mother and the doctors had told her many times that it wasn't her fault that her brother had died. She'd been taking care of him that night. She'd sung him to sleep and tiptoed out of the room. It wasn't till her mother went into the room later that anyone knew anything was wrong. It was just something that happened to some babies. She knew it was true, but lately she had been noticing that there were all kinds of ways of knowing things. You learned all kinds of things in school, but believing in them—really believing in them—was another matter. You could know the moon was thousands of miles away and that it was way bigger than a cantaloupe, but *believing* this was something else.

Her grandad had closed his eyes and was humming "Wee White Rose." When he was done, he fell silent and closed his eyes. Perhaps he had fallen asleep. The clock ticked on the wall and the scent of the baking cake filled the air. Outside, the wind went sighing down the alleyway. And then her grandad started to hum again. Brigit was thinking her own thoughts and only half listening. Then she was listening more closely. Where had she heard that melody before? It wasn't one of his usual songs, she thought. But still, it was familiar. She was sure she had heard it somewhere not too long ago.

Her grandad sat up in the chair with a groan and looked around the kitchen uncertainly, as if this was not where he had expected to find himself.

"Ah," he said sadly. "I was dreaming she'd come back."

Brigit went over and put her arms around him. He smiled then and tugged gently on her red braid. "There's no escaping it, lassie. She gave you this and the heart fire that comes with it." He frowned as if he were trying to remember something. "Ah, and she gave me something I was to give to you. Now what was it?"

There was silence in the fragrant kitchen, while outside they could hear the wind moaning and whistling through the alley as if it were looking for something it had lost.

"Ah, I remember now." He frowned at her, trying to puzzle something out. "It did not make a whole lot of sense then, did it? She said I was to warn you that time runs short. She said you must remember the girl in the long coat."

CHAPTER NINE
Nectar

One afternoon Red Kerchief gave Feenix an enormous basket of socks to pair. "Make sure they are matched up properly."

There must have been four hundred socks in there. Big socks, kneesocks, dirty white sneaker socks, nasty nylon black socks, green socks, striped socks, polka-dotted socks, and socks with little blue poodles printed on them. Where they had all come from, Feenix did not want to think. They didn't look like the sort of thing witches would wear.

"Forget it," she said. "I'm not touching those disgusting things."

Skuld picked Feenix up and shook her like a rag doll. Something fell out of Feenix's pocket and went clattering across the floor.

Feenix tried to reach for it, but Red Kerchief blocked her way.

"And what might this be?"

It was, of course, Dweebo's stone.

"Bring it here, girl," Baba One Nostril commanded. She was sitting at the table, sucking the marrow out of a small bone.

Feenix bent over reluctantly and picked up the rock and brought it to her.

Baba stopped eating. She stared at the stone without moving. She sniffed the air. She turned to Feenix. "Who gave this to you?"

This was an uncomfortable question. "Well, nobody *gave* it to me. I found it."

Baba eyed her coldly. "I believe you're lying. But that is of little importance." At first she touched the stone very cautiously with just the tips of her fingers. When it didn't blow up in her face, she lifted it into her palm and examined it more closely. She muttered to herself, "Here is the answer to the puzzle." Then she looked up at her sisters, but hardly seemed to see them. She gave a little grunt and leaned forward and blew out the lamp.

In the darkness the stone glowed in her hand.

"What is it?" Skuld asked.

Baba One Nostril did not seem to hear her. She kept turning the stone around and around, staring at it with a frown. She lifted it to her ear, then sniffed at it.

"I do not think this has been brought to us by chance," she said at last softly.

"Well, what is it?" repeated Skuld.

"I believe it is a Fetch."

A look of disbelief mixed with excitement came over Skuld's face. "A Fetch? How could this child have come into possession of such a thing? The last one was hundreds of years ago, wasn't it?"

"Yes. They keep themselves well hidden."

"Smell it!" Gorgo exclaimed. "Have you ever smelled anything more delicious!"

It was true. The smell that filled the room made Feenix shiver with delight. It didn't remind her of anything you would want to eat, but made her think of waking on the first day of summer vacation with the windows wide open and knowing she was going to live forever.

Baba One Nostril laid the stone carefully down on the table. She touched it with her fingertips and closed her eyes, inhaling deeply. When she opened them again, she spoke with decision. "Such a chance may never come our way again. The foragers will be sleeping now."

"But if you wake them?" Skuld asked sharply. "If any were to get loose—"

"Quiet! Do not presume to advise me! I am trying to think." Baba tapped very lightly on the stone with a long fingernail. "The treasure is protected with great cunning."

"I know!" cried Gorgo. She hobbled to the other side

of the room and brought out a small ladder that Feenix had not noticed before. She balanced it against the wall and climbed to the top. On a high shelf she found what she was looking for. She carried it down and brought it to the table and laid it in front of Baba One Nostril. A dusty wooden box.

Baba nodded, smiling. She unlatched the lid. She drew out a long black needle. Feenix shuddered. It was longer than a finger. "Yes," Baba said. "The Darning Needle. I had almost forgotten it. How many centuries since we have last taken this down?" She wiped the needle on her gown and then held it up to the light. "A bottle," she ordered. "Bring a bottle."

Gorgo hustled obediently and placed a small crystal bottle on the table.

"With great care," Skuld whispered. "Go slowly."

Old Baba's single nostril quivered with excitement. She lifted the needle over the stone then plunged it downward. It slid into the rock as if into a bar of soap. Feenix thought she saw two tiny sparks of light explode from the hole and then vanish.

"What was that? Did you see?" Skuld asked fearfully.

"It was nothing," One Nostril answered. "A release of gases. The nectar is volatile on the inside. Now let me concentrate. The thing will close itself up quickly."

She held the stone over the crystal bottle.

Feenix saw that a sticky golden substance had began to

ooze out of the small hole left by the needle. The scent that spilled into the room was nearly overpowering. To Feenix it was spicy, wild, and golden. It made her think of roses and fresh-cut grass and running horses.

"Oh, oh!" Gorgo whimpered ecstatically.

Everyone watched. Ten drops fell, only half filling the bottle, then the oozing clotted like blood and the honey stopped. They could see that a sticky crust had formed like a scab over the tiny hole.

Baba put the stone down with a sigh and lifted the bottle.

"Come, let us have a taste," Gorgo said eagerly.

Baba closed her eyes. "Yes. We will have a taste and I will go first." With great care, she lifted the bottle and tipped it so one single drop of the honey fell into her mouth.

They all waited.

For the first moment, she looked frightened. She shut her eyes tight and her single nostril quivered. Then she moaned and threw her head back.

"What is happening?" Skuld demanded, squinting furiously.

A soft and rosy pink began to creep across Baba One Nostril's old, ashy gray skin.

Her hair, which was steely gray and so thin it allowed her scalp to show through, thickened and darkened to a deep chestnut brown. Her face, loose and wrinkly like elephant skin, tightened and smoothed out. Her knobby, crooked fingers grew long and strong, and she flexed them as if they had been asleep for a long time and needed to be woken up. Her stooped skinny shoulders straightened, and she stood upright. She looked about two hundred years younger. She would have looked good, if it weren't for the bad nose thing.

The two sisters shuffled as close to her as they dared and stared at her openmouthed.

Skuld forgot her fears. "I will have my turn." She reached out for the bottle.

"No, no! I will go next," squealed Gorgo, trying to get in front of her.

Baba stopped her with a sharp gesture. "You are a greedy-fingered glutton. You will both have your turns, but I will hold the bottle."

Gorgo glared at her with fury, but held her hands at her sides.

Baba went first to Skuld and tipped a single drop into her mouth. Then she did the same to Gorgo. She put the bottle on the table, stoppered it, and stood back to watch.

In a few minutes the other two were transformed as Baba had been. Gorgo still looked doughy, but she was a young and pink-faced doughy. She had muscular arms and a round pumpkin-shaped body.

Skuld, to Feenix's surprise, was beautiful. She held herself like a ballerina, her head straight up, her shoulders back, her eyes glittering like little pieces of glass caught in a streetlight. Her red kerchief held back her long, flowing chestnut hair.

In every way—except eyesight—the three witches were stronger, healthier, and younger. To Feenix, it was not a happy improvement. They all took turns using the spectacles and peering at themselves in a little sliver of mirror that hung by the doorway.

"Let us have one more sip," breathed Gorgo. She turned her gaze greedily to the stone. "I've never tasted anything more delicious."

Baba One Nostril answered her scornfully. "What an infant you are. How long will it take you to learn when you have had enough? Besides, it would be prudent to save some for a later day, don't you think?"

"I suppose," said Gorgo sullenly.

"Let us turn our minds to other matters."

Baba looked at Feenix. "I think now would be the perfect time to reward our young visitor, don't you, my sisters?"

Skuld stopped examining herself in the mirror. "What do you mean?"

"She has brought us this great gift. We should let her go free."

Feenix's heart leaped up.

The two sisters stared at Baba. "Now?" asked Gorgo eagerly.

Baba tipped her head to one side and appeared to consider. "The time is ripe, don't you think? And it would seem only fair, wouldn't it?"

"Yes it would," replied Skuld chuckling. "In the words

of the great master, 'Fair is foul and foul is fair.' Let us be about the business. Darkness will fall soon."

"Yes!" sang young Gorgo. "Perfect, perfect, perfect."

Feenix couldn't believe her good luck. Bless Dweebo and his stupid stone.

"We'll even give her an extra good head start," Baba said with a smile.

"What do you mean?" Feenix asked alertly. "Why would I need a head start?"

Why were they all trying not to look at each other like they might burst out laughing?

Finally, Baba answered. "Well, we're going to invite you to play a game with us. It is like your game of Tag, but with a little Hide and Seek mixed in. We always celebrate in this way at the solstice. It is one of our favorites. And now, of course—" she glanced down at her youthful self—"we will especially enjoy ourselves." She met Feenix's eye. "You have brought us some extra time and we will give you some in return. All you need to do is cross over the wooden bridge. Once you are on the other side of the water, of course, we cannot follow and you will be free. If you don't cross over, well, then . . ." She grinned, but did not finish the sentence.

Feenix felt fear go racecar driving around her circulatory system, but she wasn't going to ask them for further explanations. Adrenaline would add to her speed. There was no way she couldn't outrace these poisonous prunes.

"How much time will you give me?" she demanded.

"Umm—what do you think, sisters? I propose an extra count of six hundred. Ten human minutes." She smiled again at Feenix. "We will unlock the door and permit you to go."

"You're going to close your eyes? You're not going to watch which way I go, right?"

"We will not watch you."

"And you'll keep your eyes closed till you get to six hundred?"

"We will."

"How do I know you won't cheat?"

"Our word is bound by law."

Feenix waited by the table staring at them. "Unlock the door."

Gorgo went over to the door and unlocked it. She smiled at Feenix as if she were a particularly delicious looking piece of chocolate cake.

"What are you waiting for?" Feenix asked. "Go to the other side of the room and turn your backs to me and close your eyes and start counting."

Baba laughed, but told her sisters to do as Feenix ordered.

As soon as they had turned to face the wall and were all counting out loud, Feenix lost no time doing what needed to be done.

She was out the door before the sisters had reached five.

CHAPTER TEN
Remembering

The morning dawned clear and bright, with a bite of coldness to it. Everyone and everything hurried along—the high, distant clouds, the people descending into the subway—as if a giant broom were sweeping everything in front of it. The buses and taxis raced each other through the yellow lights. *Where did they all think they were going*, Edward wondered? Were they just all excited about the holiday season, wanting to get to the end of the day where maybe there would be parties and singing and alcoholic beverages? Or were they just afraid, without really knowing it, that Mr. Ross's darkness was overtaking them?

Edward, for one, was not going to be suckered in by it. When he got to the bus stop, he was already late for school, but it was against everything he stood for to allow himself to be rushed. Rushing was stressful. He decided to wait for the next bus, although he knew he had just missed one and that walking would be faster.

When the bus finally arrived, Edward got on and saw that there was only one seat left. Before he could start in its direction, someone slipped past him and grabbed it—a small quick man with a ponytail, wearing a dark suit. The man looked up at Edward and smiled in an unpleasant way. Edward ignored him and grabbed onto a pole and gazed out the window at the morning world speeding by. He did his best to relax and slowly emptied his mind of all unnecessary junk. He was just shifting himself into a pleasant half sleep when the thought again came into his mind that he had forgotten something.

He tried to ignore it. But it wasn't any good. It whispered in his ear, it itched at his brain.

He found himself staring out the window, hunting for the answer. But whatever it was that was missing, it wasn't there. The problem nagged at him till he got off at his stop. It nagged at him till he reached the front steps of the school and he found Danton buzzing around worriedly like a bumblebee in basketball sneakers. He yelled at Edward when he saw him. "Eddie! What took you? You're slow as sludge. We're going to have to get late passes. C'mon!"

He moved Edward along, herding him down the hallway.

"Where, exactly, is the fire?" Edward demanded, but Danton ignored him and pushed him through the door into English class.

There were two seats left near the back of the room. Danton took one and Edward took the other. Just as Edward was snuggling himself down for a little nap, he saw, from the corner of his eye, a small hand reach over and drop a folded piece of paper onto Danton's desk. Edward turned his head curiously to see who had done this and he felt an unpleasant jolt of electricity go through his system when he realized it was Brigit.

What could it mean?

He watched Danton cautiously open the paper and stare at it. Danton stared at it for a very long time. Then he folded it up and passed it over to Edward.

Edward could not remember the last time he had been so curious about something. He waited until he was sure no one was looking and then he opened the paper.

It was a simple drawing, in pencil, of a tall girl in cowboy boots and a long dark coat. She seemed to be staring right out of the paper at them, almost accusingly.

Edward knew that he was waking up from a long dream. "Who is that?" he asked himself. Although, really, no sooner did the question shoot across his brain, than he knew the answer.

• • •

At lunchtime, Danton came over to Edward's table carrying a fully loaded tray of troll-lady food. He sat down with a grunt of pleasure and began eating. For several minutes he didn't say a word.

Edward didn't say anything either. He waited, putting off the inevitable. The big lunchroom was crowded and noisy. Everybody seemed to be excited and in a hurry. The troll ladies had framed their serving area with silver and gold tinsel garlands and dangling blue tinsel stars. Under this jolly display, they waved their ladles at the kids, yelling at them to move along.

Edward took a bite of his anadama bread, which his aunt had liberally smeared with cream cheese and strawberry jam. In the corner of his eye, he saw someone pass by him quietly. He caught the brief flash of red hair. There were a few empty seats to Danton's right, and Brigit took the third one down.

"Don't look at her," Danton said through a mouthful of chicken nuggets. "If you look at her that thing will happen."

Edward nodded.

When Danton had finished everything on his tray, he gazed at it sorrowfully. "You wouldn't happen to have any of that bread left, would you?"

Edward sighed and reached into his backpack and pulled out a package neatly wrapped in aluminum foil. It was a half a loaf of anadama bread, sliced and slathered in butter.

"When I told my aunt somebody at school liked it, she insisted I give this to you."

"What? She did? Really? She thought of me?" Danton took the package in excitement and opened it and tore off a hunk. He sniffed at it appreciatively and took a big bite. Mumbling through the bread, he said, "Tell her I love her! Tell her she's a genius! When are you going to bring me to meet her?"

Edward dreaded to think what would happen if he started bringing people home. It would not only lead to more stress but would give his aunt encouragement. It was against his principles to give his aunt encouragement. So Edward said nothing and Danton was too busy eating to notice. He looked like he was having an out-of-body experience. He kept sighing and closing his eyes. But when he got to the very last slice he appeared to have another thought.

He leaned down the table and extended his arm toward Brigit. He held out the bread.

"You've got to try this," Danton said to her. "It's really unbelievable." It was like he was trying to coax a little wild bird or something.

Brigit blushed faintly, but it didn't get any worse than that. Without looking at Danton, she took the bread.

"Taste it. C'mon. You've got to taste it. Eddie's aunt made it. She's a genius."

Brigit blinked and then she took a small bite. When she'd

swallowed it, she nodded. She threw Danton and Edward a shy smile and looked away. She nibbled at the bread.

"Listen," Danton said to her, "we wanted to talk to you." He slid, in a casual way, a couple of seats toward her. He beckoned to Edward, who reluctantly moved down, too.

Danton pulled the piece of paper out of his back pocket and unfolded it.

For a while they all just sat there staring at it as if the three of them were on their own little island. Edward found this kind of embarrassing.

"So who is she?" Danton asked.

"You don't remember?" Edward asked. "It's Feenix."

Brigit nodded at him.

"But—what happened to her—?" Danton looked confused. "Didn't she . . . ? Wasn't she . . . ?"

"Yeah . . ." said Edward, frowning. He was experiencing a sensation like the one you get when you put on someone else's glasses and take a few steps and the ground rises up to meet you. "We followed her to the park and there was that fog," he said. "When was that?"

Danton tried to count backward on his fingers. "Last Tuesday. No, it was Wednesday. But what happened to her?"

"Maybe she's been sick," Edward suggested.

"But why did we forget?" asked Danton. "It's like something wiped her clean out of our minds."

Edward, of course, had no answer to this.

Danton looked at Brigit, but she still had nothing to say. He moved his gaze around the noisy room, which was in constant motion like a pot of bubbling, boiling water. His eyes came to rest on the next table.

Alison the Hangnail and Beatrice the Poisonous Toadstool were sitting there as usual like they shared one marshmallow brain between them. They were giggling over some photos on a cellphone.

Without hesitating, Danton jumped up and bounded over to them.

"Hey, Beatrice. Hey, Ali. Whassup?" Danton said.

Now the two girls pretended they were trying to hide the pictures.

"Hey, what you looking at there, lovely ladies?" Before the girls could answer, Danton grabbed hold of the cellphone and examined the picture. Grinning, he held it out for any nearby spectators to see. From where Edward sat, it looked like it might have been a picture of Beatrice and Alison standing on the beach in bikinis. Edward had no desire to look any closer.

Danton, however, examined the photo with interest and said, "Cute babes." He handed it back to them with his shiny killer grin. Then he said. "So where's Feenix?"

Edward shivered. The air down here in the basement cafeteria had a special smell. This was mostly a mix of body odor and a hundred years of crumby lunches. But at this moment he caught a whiff of something more—a rotten, moldy, old-bone smell. Old teacher burying grounds under the school?

The girls looked at Danton expectantly, as if they were waiting for the punch line of a joke.

"So where's Feenix?" he asked again.

Toadstool cocked her head to the side. "Who's Feenix?"

"Funny."

The girls stared at him.

"Is she cutting?" Danton lowered his voice "You're covering for her?"

"Is who cutting?" Toadstool asked suspiciously.

"Feenix. You know who I mean. Tall girl, wears a lot of noisy jewelry. She sits right here every day, bringing sunshine and light into the lunchroom. You know who I mean." He was getting impatient.

Beatrice looked at Alison. "Do you know what he's talking about?"

"Not a clue. This your dream girl, Danton? She sounds very special."

"No, she's not my dream girl," he said. "You know who I'm talking about. *Feenix.* She usually sits right here between the two of you."

The girls, Edward could see, were confused. It wasn't like Danton to make fun of people, but the girls were beginning to decide that this was what was going on. It was a death warrant to allow someone else to make a fool of you in a public place. Alison's little close-together ape eyes squinted at him coldly. "Why don't you go find a basketball hoop and throw yourself through it?"

Danton stared at the two of them dumbly for a minute and Edward felt sort of sorry for him. Danton shook his head like a horse trying to get the flies out of its ears. Then he turned around and came back to Edward and Brigit.

The bell rang. No one was ready. There was a great outcry and then the crowd began rushing toward the exits.

Now that he had remembered, Edward was afraid. He could see it in Danton, too. His usual cheery I-can't-wait-for-whatever-is-going-to-come-next face was shadowed with worry. Brigit still didn't make a sound, but you could tell that she was thinking hard.

Health and Hygiene class, which generally seemed like a ten-year prison sentence, passed like a comet. Ms. Mankeweiz barely had time to describe the slow, painful death caused by not eating enough leafy greens, when the bell rang again.

In history, Mr. Channer rushed through the Boston Massacre, the Intolerable Acts, and Boston Tea Party. The buzzer drilled straight into everyone's brain. The mob rose and stampeded to the door.

"Tomorrow the Revolutionary War! Read chapter eight!" Mr. Channer roared at them.

Danton whispered loudly in Edward's ear. "Distract him. I want to check the roll book."

Edward knew what he was up to right away. He did what

Danton ordered and stopped by Mr. Channer's desk to ask him if the whole Tea Party thing was what got people drinking coffee. Mr. Channer told him way more than he ever wanted to know in answer to this question. When he finally escaped, Danton was waiting for him in the hallway. His face was grim.

"She's not in the rollbook," he said. "It's like she was never there."

They walked silently to science class.

Edward sat down in the back row and tried to think things through. A few days ago Feenix was a terror, a plague, a human tsunami, and now she was gone. Not only was she gone; it was like she had never existed. No one even remembered her, except Danton, Brigit, and him. Why? How could such a thing be? Rack his brain as he might, there were no good answers. What if it turned out that his aunt's rantings about mysteries and balls of yarn had some truth to them? Was it possible that mysterious forces could make people just disappear off the face of the earth? Where would they disappear to? Could it happen to just anybody?

Mr. Ross was standing in the middle of the room holding the fruit-fly jar aloft. It was now absolutely, totally jammed with fruit flies.

"As I said the other day, they get ten days to grow up, breed, and die. Each female lays about four hundred eggs. Let's say there's a hundred females in here right now and each one lays four hundred eggs in the next few days. How many new fruit flies will be in here by the end of next week?

"A million," someone offered.

"What's important for you to understand," said Mr. Ross, "is that the growth of the population is exponential. It doesn't merely double in size. Every ten days it is four hundred times bigger than it was ten days earlier. In theory, in ten days there will be forty thousand fruit flies in here. In twenty days, there will be sixteen million. If we let them out of here, by the end of next month they will have taken over the world, won't they?"

A confused look of worry appeared on a couple of faces, but Robert said, "No, of course they won't take over the world."

"And why would that be, Robert?"

"Because they've got to find fruit to eat. When they run out of food, they'll stop reproducing."

"Excellent. There are many checks and balances built into ecosystems. One check of a population is how much food it has to eat. It can only keep on growing for as long as it has adequate nutrition. So when these guys run out of food they will start dying. Can you think of any other things that might keep this population from growing out of control?"

"Not enough room?" someone offered.

"Sure," said Mr. Ross. "If this population keeps exploding in here, they soon won't have enough room to breathe or move."

"Not enough to drink?"

"Right, again. Drought is a very effective way to keep populations in check. What about disease? And predators? If we let these fruit flies go in a nice sunny meadow full of swallows, they'd probably be mostly eaten up in an hour. In other words, a population can keep on growing only if no other checks are put upon it. In our world, the checks and balances are part of an extremely delicate and complicated system. Human beings, as we are continually discovering, are generally the worst offenders when it comes to messing with the balance of things.

"Let me remind you, my dear young friends, that you will soon inherit the guardianship of our beloved planet, a planet that is in the midst of a mass extinction event such as has not been seen since the Cretaceous-Tertiary extinction event sixty-five million years ago when the dinosaurs were wiped out. There are predictions that if we continue in our greedy and shortsighted ways, half of all currently living species will be extinct within a hundred years. Remember what I have said to you many times. Entropy is one of the busiest and most powerful of forces at work in the world around us. Entropy, anybody?"

Robert answered in a bored voice: "The tendency of systems to move from order to disorder."

"Right. All the things in a closed system—cars, people, animal species, the solar system—everything tends to run down, fall apart, die, lose available energy. Human beings, in their willful ignorance, generally seem eager to help the process along. But think about it, my young seekers. There may be ways to slow entropy down. Even reverse its progress. You can align yourself to fight alongside the powers of order and creation. You can battle to keep things going, even join the ranks of those who devote their lives to making greater harmony and knowledge. Or you can sit back and allow things to run down."

There was one of those long pauses where everybody waited for something to happen. Only Edward and Danton and Brigit knew that they were all waiting for Feenix, who no longer existed, to interrupt and send the discussion shooting off on some other tangent. Since she couldn't do this, the silence grew until Mr. Ross suddenly remembered that they were actually supposed to be talking about rocks.

"So," he said. "Back to mineral formations. Let's turn to chapter four."

Edward's locker was on the other side of the building from Danton's. Perhaps he could give him the slip. It had really been an exhausting day. He used a side door and kept his head down. He exited out into the gray afternoon and immediately slammed right into some dingbat who was standing still in the middle of the sidewalk.

The person made no sound, merely stood there, unmoving, blocking his way. When he looked up he was somehow not particularly surprised to see that it was Brigit. It wasn't quite freezing, but the wind was cold. She had pulled up the hood on her down jacket and wound a very long green scarf around her neck several times. She looked directly into his eyes. He knew that this was hard for her to do, so he refrained from making any sarcastic remarks.

As he stood there, pinned in place by her clear gaze, someone else came bounding along and then braked to a stop by Edward's side.

"I figured it out, Eddie! It's the rock."

Edward turned and found Danton bouncing excitedly up and down.

"What?"

"It's that crazy rock you found."

"What do you mean?"

"We all touched it. That's why we remember her and nobody else does. And the reason she's disappeared has something to do with the rock, too."

"That doesn't make any sense."

"None of this makes any sense. But we've got to find her."

"Why?" Edward said crabbily. "She was a ten-foot headache."

"What if she's in some kind of trouble?"

A little gust of wind came curling around the corner. It carried some old leaves with it and a restaurant flyer and a beat-up baseball hat. It dropped the hat at Edward's feet. He bent down to look at the hat more closely.

"Hey!" he said, outraged. He picked it up and brushed it

off. "This is mine. I don't believe it. I lost this the other day when—" He stopped himself just in time.

"When what?" Danton asked.

But Edward knew he needed time to think this over. "Never mind. It's not important." He shook out his hat and put it on his head. He looked at Danton and Brigit. They looked at him.

"Fine." He gave in with a sigh. "Fine. But where are we going to look for her?"

"In the park," Danton said without hesitation. "Let's go to the place where we last saw her. Maybe we'll find some sort of clue."

As the threesome headed up Ninth Street, Edward asked Danton what exactly he planned to do once they got to the park.

"Well, we'll have to see if we can find any traces of her. Ask people if they've seen her. That kind of thing. But we'd better hurry. It's already starting to get dark."

When they reached the park, Brigit went right to the spot where the boys had last seen Feenix.

"Hey," Danton said suspiciously, "how did you know—?"

But, of course, she didn't wait to make an answer. She climbed up on the park bench and jumped over the stone wall. It wasn't quite dark yet, but the light was rapidly draining from the day.

"Hey," exclaimed Danton again, "wait up." And he scrambled after her.

Edward followed them, grumbling to himself.

The playground, when they got to it, was empty. All of the little diaper-wearers were safe in their nice, warm homes watching cartoons, while Edward was out here in the damp cold chasing after a missing person no one missed.

They walked past the swings, which all hung perfectly straight and still. Then suddenly, one of the swings began to creak gently back and forth, as if someone on soundless feet had run swiftly by and given it a quick push.

Brigit went over and stared at it, her head tipped thoughtfully to the side. She put her hand on it and it stopped moving.

"Hey, look at that!" yelled Danton. He was pointing to something standing outside the back gate of the playground. The other two followed him to take a closer look.

They stood there staring at a plaster gnome dressed in green. It was strung all around with little white holiday lights, which were just beginning to shine out now that the daylight was nearly gone. He looked like he'd been put there to catch people's attention as they went in and out.

Around the statue's neck was hung a sign with some red letters neatly printed on it:

> Volunteers needed.
> Time is nearly ticked out. The short end of the
> year draws near.
> Meet at the Fallkill Bridge.

"Must be a park clean-up thing," Danton said.

"At this time of day?" Edward said. "It's got to be a joke." But *the short end of the year.* Hadn't he heard that one too many times in the last week?

"Look!" Danton said. He was pointing across the ball fields, over in the direction of where the pond and the dog beach were. A shadowy crowd of people was bustling around. Some appeared to be holding flashlights.

"See. There they are. The volunteers. Let's go talk to them. Maybe they'll have seen some sign of Feenix. And if they haven't, well, maybe we can give them a hand or something."

"Are you serious?" Edward moaned. "You want us to go help a bunch of green peacenik hippies pick up aluminum cans in the dark?"

But Brigit had already set off in the direction of the flickering lights and Danton was close behind. Edward, muttering curses under his breath, followed slowly.

Across the main road they all went. They hurried over the frozen ball fields, not speaking much. Only Danton, every now and then, would say aloud, "This way," or, "There they are—over there."

It was getting late and all color had drained from the sky. The park lamps began to come on, pale and wan at first, but gradually growing stronger.

The crowd over by the dog beach seemed to keep getting bigger. But now you could see them only by their flickering flashlights. They looked like a very enthusiastic bunch, constantly moving and weaving about. Edward wondered what they could be doing. How many aluminum cans could there be lying around over there at this time of year? Maybe the dogs had been having a beer party.

"Come on, Eddie, speed it up a little," Danton said. "They're on the move."

It was true. Now the crowd was breaking up. The flashlights scattered into the woods. In and out of the trees they wove, some up the hill, some twinkling around the edges of the pond.

The three young people reached the dog beach just as a last beam of light went flickering along the ground and disappeared into the shadows.

"Oh, no," Edward announced, coming to a full stop. "I'm not going up into those creepy woods now. There are all kinds of voodoo worshippers and ax murderers in there."

Brigit did not even pause. She turned and stepped onto the path and dove into the trees without checking to see if they followed.

"Wow," Danton said. "She's awesome, isn't she?"

Edward looked at him sharply to see if he was kidding. No. Apparently he wasn't.

"C'mon," Danton urged him. "We can't let her go in there alone." He leaped onto the path.

Edward gazed back longingly at where they'd come from. But the ball fields were deserted and it would be a long way to travel all by himself. A white, unblinking moon was rising over the trees. It stared at him. It stared at him the way his aunt would sometimes stare at him when he was trying to chill out on the sofa and she wanted him to do some completely pointless chore like pick up his clothes from the floor or do his homework.

Yeah, yeah, yeah. He sighed and trotted up the hill after Danton and Brigit.

CHAPTER ELEVEN
The Bridge

Feenix was off and running before the door had clicked shut behind her. She did not take time to enjoy the view. The wide open space of the Nethermead stretched out around her. It was twilight. Darkness was approaching quickly.

Directly across the meadow she was sure she could make out the two boulders that marked the entrance to the path. Once she got there, it would be a short run up the hill to the bridge. Ten minutes should be more than enough time.

How many days had she been cooped up in that nursing home for the criminally senile? She had forgotten what it felt like to stretch her arms and legs. Oh, joy, to have escaped their creepy clutches. The last frost had turned the grass brown and the ground was hard. It was perfect for running on. Over the rolling meadow, she flew. Her coat billowed out behind her as she raced toward the hill and the line of trees.

Around the edges of the meadow ran the necklace of streetlamps. Each one cast a steady soft dandelion head of light out into the falling darkness. She reached the two boulders in no time. The path sloped up to the left and disappeared into the dark twilight beneath the trees. She turned back to check on the house. It sat there, its jewel-like colors shining poisonously. There was no sign of movement. She leaped onto the path.

It was a steep climb and she was out of shape, but as she neared the top of the hill she clearly heard the sound of the little brook. Hooray! The bridge could not be far ahead. Panting and sweating, she leaped forward and, to her surprise, the path took a sharp turn to the right. This was not the way she remembered it. She tried to stop so she could get her bearings and listen for the water, but to her horror, she found that her feet would not obey her. They continued to hurry along the path as if she were on a treadmill at the gym, forcing her forward.

Abruptly, the path hairpinned around and she realized that she was now trotting back down the hill.

"No!" she screamed. "No way!" In the next moment, the path became slick as ice. She skidded and her feet went out from under her. Down she went onto her butt and she began to slide. It was like a nightmare game of Chutes and Ladders.

Faster and faster she slid. Desperately she tried to grab on to something, but the branches she took hold of broke off in her hands. She closed her eyes not wanting to see what she might be about to smash her skull into. Down she went, bouncing, bumping, scraping helplessly along. The path spit her out at the bottom of the hill. It took her a few seconds to understand that she had come to a stop. She opened her eyes. She was back where she had started.

The empty Nethermead lay in front of her. Up from behind the tops of the trees a nearly round yellow moon came into view. It was huge. It looked like a moon you would see in a play. Across the open space, the door of the house stood wide open. Not good. She remembered with a sickening lurch what Old Baba had said about the spell they had put on the paths.

She crept back into the shadows and searched the area, but didn't see any sign of the witches.

Blast the old loonies. There was no point in climbing up the path again. She was going to have to cut straight through the woods.

Making as little noise as possible, Feenix rose to her feet and stepped into the underbrush. She hesitated only a moment and then began to make her way up the hill again, this time picking her way through the trees. The temperature was dropping and she pulled her coat tightly around herself. Under her feet the blanket of fallen leaves hid treacherous stones and frozen ruts, but she made her way as quickly as she could, staying on the lookout for any signs of move-ment in the forest around her, and always listening for the sound of the brook.

The moon kept showing up here and there between the branches of the trees. She was happy to have its light, but she didn't like the way it made the shadows slide and shift. All around her were small noises—rustlings, patterings, creakings. In the corner of her eye, something seemed to run by. She turned, but there was nothing there.

Would the witches have spread out, she wondered? Or would they hunt her in a pack? She climbed upward, stop-ping now and then to look and listen. There was no sign of them, though once she peered upward and caught sight of what she could have sworn was a tiny face, all wrinkled like a crushed paper bag, staring down at her from a tree trunk. The face didn't move, and it certainly didn't look like any of the witches. She hurried past it quickly. She looked behind herself once or twice, but nothing seemed to be following.

How long it had been since she left the house, she had no idea, but she felt pretty sure she had gone past the ten-minute count. She stopped to listen and she thought she could hear faintly, a little off to the right, the sound of run-ning water. She adjusted her direction and found her way blocked by a fallen trunk and a tangle of branches and leaves. A storm must have knocked this tree down and there seemed no good way around it, so she climbed up and over, panting and sweating, stopping to get her scarf untangled from a brittle old branch.

When she reached the other side, she stopped again to listen. She could have sworn the sound of the water was now coming from her left. How had that happened? She must have lost her bearings when she climbed over the tree. She adjusted her direction. Up she went and up. But now, when she stopped to make sure she was going right, the water seemed to be coming from behind her.

It wasn't possible. She hadn't even reached the top of the hill.

It had to be the old phelgm wads trying to confuse her, but no way was she going to start going back down. She would ignore the sounds and just climb. Sooner or later she would reach the top and find the water or another way through the woods. She took a deep breath, plunged forward, and then stopped short.

Someone was standing in front of her, giggling and snuffling.

"Ahh," snortled a familiar voice. "Sweet victory. That I should be the first!"

Feenix tried to dart around her, but young Piggy Face was swifter than any ball of witch lard had a right to be. Feenix faked a turn to the left and then reversed direction and tried to dive past her the other way. No good. No matter what she did, the doughball was always standing right in front of her, laughing and thoroughly enjoying herself.

"Did you really think you could outrun us, foolish girl? Even in our old age we would eventually have caught up with you. In the end none escape. Stop wasting your energy. I merely await my sisters. It is best to do the rending together."

Feenix stared at the greasy creature. The getting younger thing was not an improvement in her case. She had a moist, big-pored complexion and her skin shone whitely, like one of those mushrooms that springs up in the park after the rain.

"Do you know how different you look now?" Feenix asked her. "I love your hair."

The bloated Gorgo patted at her hair. It was tangled in dark curly rats' nests all around her head.

"And you look almost young," Feenix went on. "Why, another drop or two of that stuff and you'd definitely be the prettiest of the three."

Gorgo frowned and narrowed her eyes.

"Right now, of course, Skuld is the winner. But that's not because she's a natural beauty like you. It's because she stole an extra sip."

"You are lying. She had no chance to do so."

"Sure she did. When you and Baba were looking at yourselves in the mirror, she took a couple of nips. You know what she's like. She thinks she's the big queen of everybody."

Doughball got even redder in the face. "She is a thieving, two-faced, maggot-breathing deceiver. It is always thus with her. When she arrives here I will—I will—"

"You'll what? There's really nothing you can do. The only thing that would really give you the power would be if you could get hold of that bottle."

"Yes. When we have completed the ritual and returned to the house I will find a way to get hold of it."

"That won't be possible."

Gorgo frowned. "What do you mean? Why not?"

"Because it's not in the house anymore." Feenix took the bottle out of her pocket.

Gorgo started toward her with a yelp, but Feenix held the bottle higher and uncorked it. "Stay where you are. If you come a step closer, I will turn it upside down and spill the stuff onto the ground."

Piggy Face stopped moving. Again, a wonderful smell filled the air. Curiously, the smell was completely different than it had been before. This time it made Feenix think of turning leaves and crisp apples. It filled her with courage like a strong cup of coffee and renewed her spirits.

Gorgo eyed her furiously, but stayed where she was.

"I'll make a deal with you," Feenix said calmly. "You undo the spell on the woods so that I can reach the bridge. Then I will give you the bottle."

Gorgo thought about it. "How do I know you will keep your side of the bargain?"

"You don't, but you've got five seconds to undo the spell and then I spill this stuff onto the ground. One . . . two . . ." Feenix started to tip the bottle.

"Stop!" Gorgo said. "I want that bottle before the others get here. I will do what you ask." She held her palms out flat over the ground and spoke three unpleasant sounding words in a language Feenix did not recognize.

"Done," said Gorgo. "Now give me the nectar."

"First tell me the way to the bridge."

The witch pointed. "Right up there, beyond that ridge."

In the stillness, Feenix was positive she heard the water.

"Catch," she said, and she tossed the bottle to the waiting hands.

Feenix knew she shouldn't hang around—the other two could show up any minute, but she couldn't help herself. She just had to see what happened next. Piggy Face lifted the bottle to her mouth.

What happened, happened fast. The witch took one swallow and immediately she began to grow younger. First the lines in her face changed. Now there wasn't a wrinkle in sight and her face grew tight and pink like an almost too-ripe peach. Her mouth was a bright fat strawberry. Feenix thought she must have been around seventeen. She had big shoulders and ginormous breasts and she looked strong. She was looking down at herself with excitement.

She decided to take another another sip. Big mistake. In the very next moment she began to shrink. It was like a *Twilight Zone*–Discovery Channel nature film run backward. She went right from being a round-faced teenager to being a piggy-faced kid. Before Feenix's eyes, she grew shorter and shorter until her long black gown swam around her. Her face shrank into a childish moon and her mouth turned into a little button. Her eyes filled up with terror. Her hair, which had been long and scraggly, tightened into short greasy curls. Now she was only as high as Feenix's waist and then she was only up to her knees. She tottered forward in her way-too-big black witchy shoes and fell to the ground. She landed on her hands and knees. She tried to crawl forward, and immediately got tangled in her robes. The doughball baby flopped down on her belly and let out a long howl of fury.

Feenix turned and plunged up the hill in the direction that the witch had pointed. The sound of the water grew louder and louder. In just a few yards she stepped out of the woods and there was the wooden bridge.

"Yes!" She leaped onto the path. In a few moments, she would be back in the "real" world, running through the park's ball fields, passing regular non-witch people walking their dogs. The little stream chattered to her, encouraging her to keep moving.

As she was about to step onto the wooden planks, a glinting down near her foot caught her eye. She bent down to see what it was.

She drew in her breath. It was a bracelet.

And what a bracelet. She could tell, even without touching it, that it was real gold. It was a wide, heavy looking hammered band with some sort of dark engraving running around its surface.

Why did she hesitate? What could be the harm? She'd pick it up and put it on and she'd be over the bridge in two shakes of a rat's tail. And standing here undecided like this was certainly the stupidest thing she could be doing.

She looked around to make sure that there was no one watching and leaned down and picked up the bracelet. She slid the hoop up her wrist. The thing was so heavy. Awesome. She examined the engraving curiously with her fingertips, but couldn't make out what it looked like in the dim light.

Then, at that moment, she heard a sound—a faint whispering and scuffling carried along in a stray snatch of wind.

No. There was no way she was going to let them catch up with her. Just a few steps and she would be over. She lifted her foot and brought it down. Her boot made a satisfying hollow *thunk* on the first plank of the bridge.

Next step. But now a dreamlike feeling came over her limbs. She tried to bring her next foot forward, but before she could do anything, she felt something take hold of her wrist and yank her backward.

No! Had the other two caught up with her already?

She prepared to bite and kick and scream.

But when she whirled around, there was no one there.

What the . . . She looked down. It must be her sleeve caught on a branch or something.

She gave an experimental tug, and something tugged back. She pulled harder and whatever it was pulled back sharply.

Anxiously feeling with her fingertips, she found what seemed to be a slender chain attached to the bracelet. It was being pulled straight and taut into the darkness behind her.

She knew with an absolute dead certainty that someone was holding on to it at the other end, playing with her, preparing to reel her in.

The Old Flea Bags again! They had set a trap and she had fallen straight into it.

Furiously, she yanked at the chain, trying to snap it, but whatever it was made of, it wasn't snappable. And now when she tried to slide the gold band off, she found it was so tight it was digging into her arm. It had seemed so big when she pulled it on.

She gripped hard at the thing, trying to force it back down. But the harder she pulled, the tighter the bracelet seemed to become. It bit painfully into her flesh. This was no good; her circulation would soon be cut off.

She stared at the bridge in front of her. If only she could get herself over and across the middle of it, she felt sure all enchantments would be called off. She grabbed hold of the railing, and straining and heaving, she managed a step forward. The railing was a thick wooden log, damp and slippery in the cold. With both hands, she held on as tightly as she could and tried to drag herself forward. She was able to win a few inches, but then whatever was holding on to the chain gave a long hard yank and she lost the ground that she had made.

They were playing Tug-of-War with her.

Her heart sank. Even if it was just one of them, she knew she could never hope to win. And then she saw that it wasn't just one of them, because now a hooded figure slid out of the darkness on the other side of the bridge, the side she had been trying to reach. They had surrounded her. The figure walked toward her with silent purpose.

Well, she would not go down without a fight. She had her teeth. She had her boots. She got ready.

The dark shape drew nearer without a word and Feenix, stuck where she was, made herself steady her breathing. When the shape was within kicking distance, Feenix kicked. Her boot met bone and the shadow wordlessly retreated for a moment. Then it came toward Feenix again, this time with one hand outstretched.

Feenix lifted her foot for another good kick, then stopped. What was it about the way that this hand was held out?

The world seemed to turn upside down and then right itself again.

"You!" she cried. "What are you doing here?"

Behind the small hooded figure came another one, very tall and gangly. Then, unmistakably, bringing up the rear was Dweebo.

"I do not believe this," Feenix said in a strangled voice. Then she screamed, "I'm stuck! Pull me over! Hurry or I'm dead!"

Brigit asked no questions, but grabbed hold of Feenix's outstretched arm and pulled. Danton grabbed hold of Brigit. Dweebo hesitated, but then grabbed hold of Danton. The three leaned backward and heaved and strained and pulled. Feenix slid forward a few inches. The bracelet dug into her arm, making a ring of fiery pain. She knew the witches would never let go. They would rip her arm out of its socket and eat it raw.

Well, then, fine. Let them have it.

"Pull, you guys! Pull!" Feenix yelled.

"All right, everybody," Danton commanded. "We're going to pull together on the count of three. Eddie, brace your feet where the plank sticks up there. That's it. Everybody ready? Altogether then—one—two—three!"

They gave a tremendous heave.

"That's it!" Danton yelled out. "One more time. Keep it up, Brigit. You're magnificent!"

They gave another enormous pull. Feenix screamed from the pain. She slid forward another few inches. She thrust her leg out. She stretched it and stretched it and somehow got the toe of her boot over the middle plank of the bridge.

The moment she did so, there was an angry *pwopping* sound and the bracelet let go of her arm. It was like the sucker of some evil creature releasing itself. It slid off her arm.

As the chain went slack, Brigit, Danton, and Dweebo all

tumbled backward in a heap on top of each other. Feenix wasted no time, and in a single, furious leap landed safely on the other side of the bridge.

The bracelet fell to the ground and rolled away like a hoop into the darkness.

Part Two

CHAPTER TWELVE
The Disappearing Pumpkin

"Little Bird, Little Bird, are you awake then?"

Brigit opened her eyes and saw her grandad standing by her bed with a mug of tea. She smiled at him. How happy she was to be in her nice, warm bed. She stretched and made half an effort to remember what it was that had happened last night. There was a scary, unpleasant part, but there was something very nice, too. Something someone had said. She went after it, but it darted off like a dragonfly into the leaves.

The scary, unpleasant part didn't move. It stayed half-hidden, but she could see its head sticking out. She made herself go after it. It seemed like it was important to remember. She went back in her mind to yesterday at school. Slowly it came to her how Edward, Danton, and she had decided to look for Feenix, how they had walked up the hill and through the park. She shivered at the memory. When they had found Feenix caught on the bridge, Brigit had known right away that the other girl was in great danger. She couldn't have said how she knew this, but she was sure that there was something hungry and not human trying to pull Feenix back into the shadows. It took all three of them heaving together to drag her forward. Then, as soon as she crossed the middle of the bridge, the thing on her arm—a bracelet it looked like—went flying away. From the way she screamed you could tell that it hurt her terribly.

Afterward, Feenix went around kissing everybody. Brigit felt herself turning red when it happened, but she didn't think anybody could see that in the dark. When Feenix got to Edward, he pulled back the way he always did when she got near him. Brigit understood, although under the circumstances she thought it was a little impolite. When Danton asked Feenix to tell them what had happened, she said it was all too horrible to think about right now. She'd tell them the story tomorrow. The rest of the trip home was still fuzzy in Brigit's mind, but it seemed to her they'd all been very quiet and in a hurry.

Her grandad handed her the tea and let her take a sip. The sweet, milky warmth spread through her and she took another sip and looked at him over the rim, trying to decide if it was going to be one of his good days or one of his bad days. He was in his red tartan flannel robe and his little wisps of white hair stood up uncombed from his head. He put his fingers to his lips. "Up with you, lassie," he whispered. "Time is running out. Let today be the day. You must look for the doorway."

What could he mean, she wondered? His watery blue eyes watched her. Then he seemed to be distracted by something over his head. He frowned and hit fiercely at the air, as if he were brushing away invisible flies.

Would they all be together again, the four of them? If they did come together, it would be because of Danton. That's what his talent was, although he didn't really know it. He thought he was an athlete and, of course, he *was* an athlete. But what he *really* was, was a Bringer Together. It was his gift. She'd been watching him since she'd started at the new school. It was hard not to watch him. It was amazing that he had noticed her at all.

Her grandad was speaking softly. "I cannot find your gran," he told her in a whisper. "I've looked and looked, but she's been misplaced. I want you to go downtown now and see what it is that's keeping her. 'Tis the short end of the year. The days go shrinking smaller and smaller. *You know* the sort who will go wandering abroad and I'm afraid. Help me find my shoes." He batted his hand at the invisible flies again.

She saw that her grandad was barefoot and she could feel the cold coming up out of the floor, although the sun was shining. She jumped out of bed to go look for his slippers.

In the hallway she nearly bumped into her mother, who was just emerging from her bedroom. She stopped where she was, looking only half awake.

"I was having the strangest dream," she said slowly. "Shouldn't you be in school?"

Brigit gave her a quick hug and then dashed into her grandad's room and picked up his slippers. In the hallway, she passed her mother who was still standing there, maybe thinking about her dream.

When she got back to her grandad and bent over to help him put on the slippers, she glanced at the alarm clock. It was true! Eight fifteen! How had that happened? As she started to rise, her grandad grabbed hold of her braid.

"Your grandmother gave this to you, you know. Red as the devil's tailcoat. Not many knew her well. She was meek as milk seven days of the week, but on the eighth day she was a great, brave fury of a woman, magnificent to behold."

Brigit felt a shock go through her. That was it! The thing she couldn't remember. This was what Danton had said to her on the bridge—that she was magnificent. Not that it meant anything, really. He was always saying things like that to people. He seemed to believe it was his mission to encourage everybody.

Her grandad was blathering on. "You'd better get your-self out there, lassie. We are all counting on you."

Counting on her? Counting on her for what? It wasn't going to be one of his clear days. But there was no time now.

She kissed him and hurried into her clothes. Her mother was no longer on the landing and she assumed her father must already be at work. She decided she would have to skip breakfast. She ran nearly all the way to school.

She was still late.

Feenix woke slowly, too, rising up from her sleep, feeling oddly free and safe at the same time. She was aware of the drowsy pleasure of being able to stretch her legs and toes out to their fullest length. Mr. Pearlmutter, her orange and white striped cat, had snuck under the covers. He shape-shifted contentedly against her back. He was like a big bag of flour covered in fur. For some time she stayed behind her closed lids, not wanting to think about anything. When she did finally open her eyes, she was met with an unpleasant surprise. Her mother was standing over her bed, gazing down at her with a frown of confusion.

"What?" Feenix asked her, wishing she would go away.

"I thought—I thought you were— "

"You thought I was what?"

"I thought you were—sleeping over at—"

"Mom, let me sleep. Why are you here clogging up my airspace? Here I am."

With her eyes closed, she could feel her mother's suspicion. Almost all of her mother's body mass and time was given over to worry about and criticism of Feenix. Right now she would be running down the list: Homework?

Inappropriate friends? Test grades? Last meal taken? Constipation? Etc., etc.

"Mom, let . . . me . . . breathe," Feenix hissed. "Go away."

"You need to get up right now, Edith! Do you know what time it is?"

"Time for me to get five more minutes of sleep and don't call me Edith! I've told you a million times. Nobody in their right mind would name their kid Edith. My name is Feenix."

"Edith is a perfectly beautiful name. How can you dishonor your own grandmother like that? You will always be Edith to me. And it's eight twenty."

"What?" Feenix opened her eyes to see if her mother was lying.

"You think I'm kidding? Look." Her mother lifted the alarm clock and pushed it right in her face. Sure enough, it said eight twenty. "You forgot to set it again."

Feenix sat up with a loud groan. She felt Mr. Pearlmutter's disapproval. He stayed under the covers. "Out! Please get out! I'd like to dress in private."

Her mother stood there for a few more seconds running her paranoid gaze around the room and then up and down the part of Feenix that was sticking out of the covers. Then she shook her head and retreated with the words, "Five minutes! I'm going to make you some oatmeal!"

"Do *not* make me oatmeal. I will not eat it. I'm not hungry."

But her mother had gone deaf, spurred by the certainty that her daughter would be dead of starvation by noon if she didn't force oatmeal into her.

Feenix lay back down and felt around for Mr. Pearlmutter and took him in her arms. She tried to remember what had happened yesterday. She had the feeling it was important, but it lay just beyond her reach, and she kept drifting back into a soothing sleep.

"Are you moving up there, Edith?" her mother yelled. "I don't hear anything!"

With a great effort, Feenix made herself sit up. Why did she have the sensation that the morning was waiting impatiently, holding its doors open for her like a train in a subway station?

Danton's little brother woke him by throwing a wet towel on his face and announcing that their mother had said he could have Danton's share of the pancakes.

"No way!" Danton yelled.

"Yes way! You're real late!"

Danton leaped out of bed and wrestled the little dude to the floor and made him say, "Eat my socks," three times backward. When Danton let him up, Jay asked if they could shoot some baskets together later.

"It'll probably be too late for that by the time I get home. I've got some people I've got to see."

"Who?" his brother asked, disappointed.

"Some friends."

"A girl? It's a girl, isn't it?"

"What? No way. A girl? Are you kidding?"

Jay shook his head and smiled knowingly. Danton grabbed him by the armpits, lifted him up, turned him upside down, and threw him on the bed so that he bounced. "We'll play something when I get home. Stratego, maybe. But get your homework done and stay in the house. Help Mom. Be careful and stay out of trouble."

Something in Danton's tone seemed to catch at his attention. "Why would I get in trouble?"

"Because it's the shortest day of the year today. A dangerous time."

"Why? Why's it a dangerous time?"

"Because Santa Claus is coming to town, that's why, little dude. Stop asking so many questions."

Danton dressed in record time and raced his brother to breakfast. He was in too much of a hurry to notice the cloud of bright things, smaller than gnats, flickering in and out of existence in the sunny kitchen.

Edward's aunt woke him in five-alarm panic mode. She had overslept. Apparently the clock hadn't gone off and she had a pie crust class at eight forty-five. She pulled the pillow off his head and flew around the room tweeting and screeching. Words fell like little scraps of paper: School! Train! Butter! Flour! Time! Armed robbery!

"What are you talking about? Give me five minutes." Edward snuggled deeper under the covers. He was feeling very contented and pleased with himself, but he couldn't remember why. As he sleepily searched for the answer, she yanked the blanket off of him.

"Don't you understand? Your five minutes have been stolen right out from under your nose. We're running out of time. I can feel it."

"You can't run out time," he muttered. "It's the fourth dimension."

"Where did you hear such nonsense? Everything runs out eventually. But this is too soon. Doorways open at this time of year. Something's been set loose that shouldn't have been. You'd better get up. Your help may be needed."

"What? Who's going to need my help?"

"The battle's going to be terrible this year. I can feel it."

He was not going to ask her what battle she was referring to. When he was little he'd assumed this was the way everybody's aunt talked, but now that he could see what a basket case she was, the thought of bringing anybody home after school had become mortifying. According to Aunt Kit, there were beings, forces, and influences messing around in everybody's business everywhere. Some days there were fairies fiddling with the barometric pressure and making her cakes fall. Another day there were six-armed goddesses interfering with the Stock Exchange. Last month there was a planet in retrograde stirring up hurricanes. And she was always changing her story so he was never sure she was serious about any of it. He was visited again by the terrible vision of Mr. Ross meeting up with her. He'd never be able to show his face in science class again. He sat up with a groan and looked around. She was gone. Where had she got to? He glanced at the clock. It was eight thirty! How was this possible? American History started in twenty minutes, and Mr. Channer had threatened to fail him if he was late again. He was a dead man.

To Edward's surprise, when he got to class, Mr. Channer wasn't even there yet. There was an empty seat right near the door and he slid into it with a sigh of relief. He spotted Feenix, but she made no sign that she had seen him. A moment later, Mr. Channer arrived breathless and apologizing. Something had gone wrong with his alarm clock. He was all bent out of shape. How they had fallen so far behind he didn't know, but in order to complete this section of the curriculum before the holiday break, they would have to move doubletime. For today, he would have to shelve all debate and discussion and simply move them through the material as quickly as possible.

"Please open to page one hundred and three. Elise, would you read the first section out loud and, Edward, in order to ensure that you stay awake today, we'll have you outline the material at the board as she reads."

Mr. Channer was a freak about outlining. He claimed it was the number-one most-important skill that you needed to learn to prepare you for college. Usually he just made the students do this at their seats, but every once in a while he selected a victim to experience the special torture of having to do it at the board in front of everyone else. Until today, he had never called on Edward, but Edward's luck had run out. Edward quickly considered his options. He didn't see that he had any unless he was willing to lie and claim that he had a sprained wrist, which he wasn't willing to do. He rose and walked to the front of the room—a man going to his doom. Feenix, he knew, would be without mercy. She would keep up a running peanut gallery commentary about his handwriting, his clothes, and his general nerdiness. It would be worse than those dreams where you found yourself riding the subway without any clothes on. It would be worse because you weren't going to wake up and the torture would seem to last forever. He steeled himself and picked up the whiteboard marker.

Elise began to read. Edward began to write:

THE REVOLUTIONARY WAR
I. Causes
    a. the French and Indian War
    b. British legislation
        1. taxes
        2. quartering act

To Edward's surprise, Feenix said nothing. The rest of the class got bored waiting for the entertainment to begin, and there was a lot of shifting and whispering. Mr. Channer interrupted Elise every other minute or so to make sure Edward got the right stuff on the board. Edward prepared himself for the period to go on into eternity. But then another surprising thing happened.

The end-of-the-period warning bell went off.

Was it possible? Edward didn't think he'd been up there more than five minutes. They'd only gotten to page 104. Maybe he had arrived later to class than he'd realized. Mr. Channer must have been even later.

But Mr. Channer seemed astounded, too. He looked up at the loudspeaker in confusion, then at the class. "Hold it!" he said angrily to the class. "Hold it. It's got to be a mistake."

The second bell went off. Everybody grabbed their books, laughing and shouting, and stampeded from the room.

Science class was next.

Mr. Ross once again took up his investigations into the fascinating world of rock life. Edward put his brain on hold. Now and then, he became aware of Feenix interrupting. But her attempts seemed uninspired and half-hearted, and the class was soothingly boring.

Was it an hour or a second later that he felt the small wet thwack on the side of his head? His attention was aroused briefly, then fell back into nowhere.

Another thwack and then another.

Deeply annoyed, he opened his eyes and looked around. Danton had just propelled another small wad of wet paper in Edward's direction, and it hit him on the side of the nose. Edward glared at him, but Danton was clearly all worked up about something new. He jerked his head sharply, trying to get Edward to look at something.

Edward turned sleepily in the direction indicated.

On the table under the windows there was a large pumpkin that Mr. Ross had cut open and placed where everybody could make observations of what happened to it as it began to decay. They were supposed to be keeping journals to sharpen their observation skills. Yesterday, the pumpkin, a handsome orange globe, had just begun to grow a faint, fuzzy mold on its insides. Edward hadn't looked at it yet today, but what he immediately noticed was that it seemed to be surrounded by a strange flickering sort of mist. No. It wasn't a mist at all. It was a more like a cloud of glitter or teensy shards of glass. The cloud stayed where it was, but the sparkling things, whatever they were, were in constant motion—darting, dropping, climbing.

Edward shifted his chair closer. He still couldn't figure out what the sparkly things were, but now he noticed something else. Before his very eyes, like a speeded-up clip on the Nature channel, the pumpkin was falling into an advanced state of decay. Its insides had been entirely taken over by the velvety black mold. The pumpkin softened and sank inward like an old lady's mouth with her teeth taken out. An unpleasant yellowy liquid leaked out onto the tray and the stench that curled toward his nostrils made him want to gag. In a few moments the pumpkin had collapsed. It lay in a flattened ring of rusty orange. He met Danton's eyes. Danton shook his head worriedly.

Edward felt resentful. He didn't want to think about all this. He really needed a break. He turned away and did his best to sink back down into oblivion. But it was no good. In a few minutes, driven by nervous curiosity, he looked back at the pumpkin. What he saw was not possible.

The pumpkin was gone. The stink was gone. The cloud of shivering glitter had vanished, too.

CHAPTER THIRTEEN
Room 219

Lunchtime. Feenix led the way. Alison and Beatrice came behind. Feenix was still trying very hard to think. She let Alison and Beatrice do the snickering.

Noise filled the room. Two hundred half-baked human beings eating and shouting and banging things without any consideration for the feelings of others. Normally, she liked this noise. It kind of cocooned around you. It made you feel enclosed and protected from the adults who all wanted to suck your blood. But today she wished it would go away. It made it hard to concentrate. And it didn't sound right somehow. It seemed to her that it kept sort of stopping and catching like a bad CD. Then it would start up again.

She was tired. Her memory of the last few days grew blurrier and blurrier the more she tried to catch hold of it.

And if she did manage to catch hold of some little sound or picture, it was very nasty. Much nicer to maybe just let go of the whole thing.

Alison and Beatrice sat down in their usual spot at a table right in the middle of the lunchroom. This was a good spot, because you could see everything and everybody. Alison patted the seat next to her, and Feenix sat down, too.

Feenix batted at the air. "What's with these flies?"

"What flies?" Beatrice replied, frowning.

Feenix started to point to them, but now they were nowhere to be seen.

Across the room Feenix saw Danton and Brigit, who, for some reason, were actually seated side by side.

"Are those new earrings?" Alison asked her.

Feenix didn't answer. She was trying to think. They'd come to her rescue last night, hadn't they—the three of them? It was too bizarre for her to have made it up.

She felt Beatrice and Alison eyeing her curiously.

"What is your problem?" she demanded, irritably.

They shrugged and ate their chips.

"Did you get through that math test?" Alison asked after a pause. "I only finished about two-thirds of it. I'm gonna have to see if I can get Mr. Albers to let me do some extra credit. Did you hear what happened to Fiamma? No? Oh my God—she was late and she was running down the steps to catch the train and she was wearing flip-flops even though it's only two degrees out because she hadn't been able to find her shoes and she fell and she broke her nose. She's gonna have to get surgery."

"Well, it's a golden opportunity," Beatrice said. "That nose could certainly use some work." Beatrice nudged Alison in the ribs. "Look at that," she said loudly, pointing to a girl at the next table. "Look at that sweater. Did you ever see anything so old?"

Feenix looked at the sweater. It was blue and it looked like it might have been hand-knitted by somebody. Actually, she thought, it was kind of amazing looking.

"Yeah, and look at the skirt," Alison fake-whispered.

"Don't you have anything better to do?" Feenix found herself saying. "I mean, don't you get bored with that stuff?"

The two girls stared at her. "What's with you, today?" Beatrice asked. "You okay?"

From the corner of her eye, Feenix saw Danton stand up and wave at somebody. It was Dweebo. You could see that Dweebo was thinking about turning and running, but Danton waved at him insistently. Dweebo moved slowly toward Danton and Brigit.

At this moment the loudspeaker crackled on again, and Ms. Riccio in the front office made a long announcement about some period changes. Feenix did not pay much attention. She had taken out her little jewel-encrusted mirror and snapped it open. She studied herself, then snapped the mirror shut.

"Did you hear that?" Alison asked in a tone of jubilation. "No eighth period!"

There were those tiny green gnats again. Where could they be coming from? "What's with these little buzzy things all over the place?" Feenix said again.

"What buzzy things?" Beatrice looked around, puzzled. "I don't see anything."

"You don't see that?" Feenix pointed at the glittering cloud.

She remembered, suddenly, two little green sparks. Where had she seen them? Didn't they look just like these things? Then she knew.

"Are you all right, Fee? You're so pale."

When Feenix looked again, the cloud was gone.

She pushed her chair back and stood.

"Where are you going?" both girls asked, but she didn't answer.

When Edward arrived in the lunchroom, Danton immediately waved him over. There was no sense in Edward's trying to pretend he didn't see this. Danton was an inescapable force of nature. But Edward moved as slowly as he could. By the time he reached the table, Danton had resumed eating. "Slow as rust," he said, his mouth full of fish sandwich.

Although Brigit was sitting right next to him, she seemed, as always, a little ways apart, sort of camouflaged, like a bird hiding in the leaves. But she nodded at Edward. He gave her as tiny and nonthreatening a nod as possible in return.

"You're not actually eating that?" he said to Danton.

Danton swallowed. "Listen," he said. "Did you see what happened in science—" He was interrupted by a voice over the loudspeaker.

"Attention, please. Because of unexpected scheduling conflicts, the holiday singing performance has been moved forward to this evening at seven o'clock. Eighth period today is canceled. All band members, chorus performers, and stage crew will report for rehearsal during this time. Any exams scheduled for eighth period will be given Monday morning at seven thirty."

As far as Edward could tell, this made no sense, but since not making sense was certainly nothing new at this school, and since he wasn't in the holiday performance and had no exams during eighth period, he just rode right over it like he would ride a little wave at the beach. He sat back, watching the rest of the lunchroom acting confused and delighted.

Danton put his sandwich down. He gave Brigit a quick look. He looked at Edward. "So what do you think?"

"I don't want to think. I want to be left in peace."

"But that pumpkin . . ."

Edward shook his head. "Just some weird kind of mutating mold. Who knows? This is the twenty-first century. Everything mutates fast in the twenty-first century."

"No. There's something going on with time. I'm telling you, it's not working right. The bells are going off too fast. History couldn't have lasted more than ten minutes. And now there's this business with the holiday performance being moved to tonight and last period cancelled."

"It's the holiday season. Everybody gets weird at this time of year."

"Oh yeah? Then what about this?" Danton was holding up the last remnant of his sandwich and waving it around.

Edward stared at him.

"Don't you see? Fish sandwich! Fish sandwich is only ever served on Friday. It's a leftover from holier times. Somehow it's gotten to be Friday already."

Was this true? Edward really didn't know. But he was fairly sure that when he'd gotten up this morning it was Wednesday.

"I didn't dream it, did I? It was actually you last night, wasn't it?"

It took Edward a few seconds to realize who had said this. He turned around and there she was. Feenix. Looming over him.

Edward knew enough to neither flinch nor blink. He met the enemy's eyes straight on. She stared at him and then looked at the other two and nodded.

Edward was deeply distressed to see her actually pull out a chair and sit down. He looked at Danton and Brigit to see what they made of this. They were both watching Feenix as if hypnotized.

"It was that stupid stone you picked up, you know. If you'd gone into the park to find one the way we were supposed to do, this would never have happened. Where'd you get it from, anyway?"

"What are you talking about?" Edward asked.

"The stone. It's what's messing everything up."

"That's what *I* said!" Danton interrupted. "That's what I said yesterday when we were trying to figure out why nobody else remembered you! I said it had to have something to do with that rock."

"Come on," Edward said. "It was just an old rock."

Danton didn't seem to hear him. He was staring at Feenix. "All right. What happened to you? Where did you disappear to the last few days? It's time to tell us."

Feenix didn't answer for a long moment. Then she said, "Yes. I'd better tell you. I've been having a hard time getting it all together in my mind. But I think I've got most of the pieces straight now."

She paused and looked around at them all. "I warn you, it's going to be hard to believe."

"Try us," Danton said impatiently.

"You have to promise to keep your minds way open."

"C'mon," said Edward. "You're not really going to sit here and seriously listen to whatever nutjob line she's going to try to feed us, are you?"

Feenix glared at him. "You can always leave. It's a free country."

Edward sighed. He looked at the other two. They didn't move. He stayed where he was, too.

Feenix began her story.

As he listened, Edward found himself more and more troubled. He knew it wasn't the kind of story you would invent to make fools out of other people. It was too unbelievable. If you wanted to make fools out of other people, you had to make up a story that seemed possible. This wasn't possible. But then, again, the way she had disappeared last week wasn't possible, either. He wondered if maybe they'd all gone crazy, if maybe something had gotten into the water supply—mushrooms perhaps, or maybe terrorists had dropped some kind of hallucinogen into the cafeteria food.

She finished with how she'd tricked the pig-faced witch into getting shrunk down into a baby, and then how she got herself to the bridge and picked up the bracelet. "And then you guys showed up and rescued me, which I don't think was a coincidence. I somehow think you were meant to find me."

Edward saw how the other two were watching her, fascinated. Feenix was pale with excitement. Her eyes glittered. The diamond stud in her nose caught the light from overhead.

"Why you three of all people, I have no clue. But now we're in it together."

"In *what* together?" Edward asked sharply.

"In this mess that we've made."

"What mess?" Danton persisted.

"Those little flies all over the place—haven't you seen them?"

They all stared at her. "Yes," Danton said uncertainly. "Do you know what they are?"

"Unfortunately, I think I do."

They waited. But before she could spit it out, whatever it was, the end-of-lunch bell went off.

A great wave of noise rolled across the lunchroom—outrage, swearing, and laughter. Nobody was ready. It seemed much too soon. But that was nothing new, Edward argued to himself. Lunch period always seemed shorter than the others.

Feenix looked around in frustration and shouted, "MEET ME—" But wherever it was that she wanted them to meet, the words were lost in the thunder and racket of youths rushing and pushing each other down in their eagerness to get educated.

Edward knew this might be his last chance to escape. He gathered up his books and allowed himself to be carried off by the crowd.

He felt that he needed to think. His next class was a study hall, but he was too disturbed to sit still. As his fellow students settled themselves into their classrooms, he found himself wandering along the second floor hallway. He did not see Mr. Pomerance as he was emerging from his room. They almost bumped into each other.

"Ahh. Edward. Just the man I need. Would you be so

kind as to deliver this to Ms. Granger in room 219?" Mr. Pomerance held out a folded piece of paper.

Edward began explaining that he'd already had a very rough day and that any further unnecessary activity was probably not a good idea, but Mr. Pomerance cut him off.

"Unless you've got a doctor's note, get moving."

Edward sighed and took the folded piece of paper and headed down the hallway, looking at the room numbers as he went: 201, 203, 205 . . . He thought he knew who Miss Granger was—wasn't she that little round French teacher with the braid? He certainly hoped that Mr. Pomerance wasn't using him to carry any hanky-panky love letters. Room 219 was probably down there around the corner where that singing was coming from. It must be the school chorus practicing. They were singing something that sounded like Latin, maybe. His aunt was always listening to old hymns and things in Latin. He couldn't recognize any of the words. He turned and ambled down to the end of the corridor. Room 215. Room 217. The singing had stopped. There was a big window here and, to his alarm, he saw another swarm of the flickering gnats hovering in its wintry light. Edward swatted his hand at them and they were gone.

He had reached the end of the hallway. He had been sure that it turned right here and that were some more rooms around the corner. But he must have been mistaken.

He looked around himself uneasily. Where had that other hallway gotten to? This was very confusing. He had noticed before that whoever had numbered these rooms had apparently been dropped on his head when he was a baby. He headed back in the other direction, thinking that perhaps 219 had somehow made its way around to the beginning somewhere.

But when he got to the beginning of the hallway, there was no 219 there, either.

He decided that under the circumstances, he had done all he could do. He trudged slowly back to Mr. Pomerance's class. Mr. Pomerance sat at his desk in an empty classroom. He appeared to be marking papers and he looked like he was doing it in a great hurry.

"Uh, Mr. Pomerance?"

The teacher looked up from his labors irritably. "Yes? Make it snappy. I've got another class in a few minutes."

"Well, uh, there doesn't seem to be any room 219." Edward fished in his pocket for the note. He pulled out a stub of a pencil and a shoelace, his MetroCard, a piece of orange peel, and a Canadian quarter. "Ah . . . gee . . . sorry. I think I may have dropped it."

Mr. Pomerance watched this whole performance with a look of wondering impatience. "Dropped what?"

"Well . . . uh, you know, the note you gave me for room 219."

Mr. Pomerance frowned at something invisible in the air just beyond Edward's shoulder. Then he gave his head a quick shake as if to clear it and returned his gaze to Edward.

"For fifteen years, you people have been trying to drive me mad, but I assure you, you're wasting your time. I was insane to take this job to begin with. Go to class, Edward. And take my word for it, time flies. Make the most of it."

Edward looked at the junk in his hands and then stuffed it back in his pockets.

At the end of day, Edward slid out the side door and scanned the area carefully. Avoidance mode. When in doubt, it was always the best way to go.

The wind slapped him in the face. The sun had gone out of the afternoon, and it was colder. He pulled on his hat, descended the steps, and headed toward the bus stop.

When he got to the corner, a bus was just pulling in. The driver seemed to be in a terrible hurry. Before the bus had even finished braking to a screeching halt, the door folded open.

"Let's go, buddy! You think you might speed it up a bit? I got a schedule I got to keep to."

Edward mounted the stairs and nearly lost his balance as the bus lurched forward with a hiss. What was with this dude? He fumbled for his MetroCard, dipped it, and found a seat.

It was an unusual bus ride. The driver raced in and out of the traffic as if the Terminator were on his tail. The pizzeria, the Dunkin' Donuts, and the YMCA went by in a blur. At the next stop, a woman stepped into the street with her hand out, and the bus driver shot by her without slowing down. Edward turned to see the woman's surprise turn to fury. But then he was distracted by the sound of loud horns as the bus accelerated through a light turning red and barely missed colliding with a Chinese food delivery guy barreling along Sixth Avenue on his bicycle.

At the stop before Edward's, two women stood waiting. Edward didn't know much about women's clothes, but he could see that they were oddly dressed. One of them was holding a squirming baby. As the bus approached them, the one with the red kerchief around her hair stepped into the street and planted herself right in the path of the bus with her hand up.

The driver screeched to a halt, swearing under his breath. The women mounted the steps with the squalling baby and took the first seats they could find. Edward watched them. The baby had a red and puffy face. It was screaming its head off. The two ladies peered out the window, watching fixedly for something. A building address maybe?

Edward pressed the tape between the windows of the bus, and stood as the STOP REQUESTED light blinked on. He half-expected the driver to ignore the request, but the brakes squealed again, the doors flew open, and Edward tumbled out onto the pavement.

He walked the last couple of blocks slowly, feeling glad to be alive, glad to have escaped from school, and mighty relieved to have avoided whatever unnecessary expenditure of energy Feenix and the others were going to try to get him to go along with.

It wasn't until he had nearly reached his house that he noticed the three shapes huddled on his front steps. They looked up at him expectantly as he swung the gate open.

CHAPTER FOURTEEN
Time Eaters

"What took you so long?" Feenix demanded.

Edward sighed.

"Feenix wouldn't tell us her theory until you got here," Danton said impatiently.

"How considerate of her." He unlocked the front door and let them all in.

The house smelled wonderful. There was always the fragrance of fresh bread rising or baking, but now there was also all the combined deliciousness of cinnamon and vanilla and cherry pies and pfeffernusse and pine boughs and the big tree. Danton let out a small *yip* of happiness. Edward flicked on the lights as they made their way toward the kitchen, but when Brigit stopped to examine the tree with his aunt's weird collection of ornaments, the others stopped with her.

"This is incredible," Feenix exclaimed. There were tiny birds' eggs, seashells, cicada shells, sharks' teeth, small animal skulls, polished stones, earrings that had lost their mates, autumn leaves that had been dipped in wax, and little wizened figures whose heads were made from dried shrunken apples. But most eye-catching were the cookies. They were cut into all sorts of shapes and sizes, and each one had been carefully iced and decorated. There were ginger-bread boys and gingerbread girls and stars and reindeer, of course. But there was also a mermaid, a minotaur, and a three-headed dog. There were birds and lions, trolls and unicorns, and a woman with six arms.

"I've never seen a Christmas tree like this," Feenix said. She touched a cookie in the shape of a golden slipper, mak-ing it turn slowly on its golden thread.

"We don't exactly celebrate Christmas. We celebrate the winter solstice."

"Your aunt made all these?"

Edward looked at her sharply. "How did you know I lived with my aunt?"

Feenix laughed. "Edsel, that's what I love about you. You are so clueless. I know so much more than you realize."

"I'm starving," Danton interrupted. "You think maybe your aunt has some of that bread lying around?"

They all followed Edward into his aunt's holy kingdom. Edward hadn't really looked at it in years, but now that he was bringing company in, he couldn't help seeing it with fresh eyes. She had painted the kitchen in bright Mexican-rug kinds of colors, and the floor was a dark red tile. One wall was hung with shiny copper pots and pans. There were windows all around and a glass door leading into the little garden. Sitting on all the windowsills were pots of basil and oregano and rosemary. Edward saw the spider busy at work in one corner, but he didn't point it out. He led them over to the green granite counter in the middle of the kitchen where there were tall stools so you could sit and eat and talk while his aunt cooked. They each took a stool. Over their heads was an upside-down forest of drying herbs and flowers and bulbs of garlic.

"Awesome," Danton breathed happily. "Let's eat. Then Feenix will tell us what she wants to tell us."

Edward peered into the big refrigerator. He saw with relief that his aunt, as always, had left him a snack that would feed a small army in case there was an invasion. He took out the plate that was loaded with carefully cut triangles of pita bread spread with olive oil, goat cheese, and black olives.

MICROWAVE FIFTY SECONDS, said the little paper taped to the top.

He did as directed. A good garlicky, cheesy fragrance filled the room. Edward brought the plate over. It wasn't just Danton but all three of them who lit up in their own peculiar ways.

"I'll make hot chocolate," Edward offered. He was surprised

at himself, but he prepared the hot chocolate carefully, with milk and real cocoa, and hunted down the bowl of whipped cream hiding in the back of the fridge.

Edward found himself enjoying the snack in a way he hadn't enjoyed a snack in a long time. The olive oil tasted peppery and sharp, and the cheese was perfect on top of it. Outside, the gray sky grew dark and the wind rattled at the windows. Inside, there was warmth and contentment.

Well, this wasn't so bad, after all, Edward reflected. Everyone was quiet while they ate.

Then Feenix, of course, had to open her mouth. "All right," she said. "That's enough feeding our faces." She looked around at all of them.

Edward thought with irritation that he'd never seen anybody who liked having all eyes upon herself more than this girl.

"Here's the thing," Feenix said in a low voice. "Remember I told you that when old Baba poked that needle into the stone these little spark things came shooting out?"

"Your point?" said Edward.

"Well, they looked just like those little things flying all around the school today."

Edward couldn't help remembering the tiny glittering wizzits hanging around the pumpkin and then the cloud of them in the hallway later when he was trying to find that missing room. "Yeah, but you said there were only a couple of them," he objected. "They're hard to see, but there must have been hundreds of them today. Maybe more."

"Exactly," she replied. "Don't you get it?"

"Uh . . . no," Edward said.

"Oh my God!" exploded Danton. "You mean they're reproducing! Like Mr. Ross's fruit flies!"

Feenix nodded her head solemnly. "It started out there was just two of them and now they're all over the place."

"But what are they?" Danton asked.

"I don't know. I tried to catch one under a glass a few times, but it's like they vanish whenever you try to get near them."

Edward knew this was going nowhere he wanted anything to do with. It was a Feenix version of one his aunt's delusions. Brigit looked distant, as if she were listening to something far away. Danton, he could see, was concentrating very hard.

"So you think they're some kind of insect?" Danton asked. "Maybe like a bee kind of thing? And the stone thing wasn't really a stone, but some kind of hive? If they're reproducing that fast, they must be feeding on something. But what?"

"Isn't it obvious?" Feenix said.

Before anyone could say anything, Aunt Kit's clock began to give its warning sound.

The clock was a crazy business. It had a large round face

like any old clock, but it had a boxlike wooden frame. This frame was carved all over with a snaky vine full of leaves and out of the leaves peered a number of small, curious wooden faces—sun, moon, fox. Before the clock went off it always made a faint whirring sound, which it was doing now. As they stared at it, a door on its side snapped open. Out popped a wooden gingerbread man. He began to jerk along the track that ran around the base. Behind him came a wooden baker holding a rolling pin in the air. Then came his wife, followed by a cow and a horse and then some peasant people. They all ran around the circle and then disappeared inside the door at the other side of the clock. Both doors snapped shut. The clock chimed five times.

"That!" whispered Feenix. "That's what they collect. You see what I mean?"

"No," said Edward. "We do not see what you mean. And why are you whispering?"

"Think about it! How could it be five o'clock already? We just got out of school."

Edward considered this uneasily. It was true. How *could* it be five o'clock already? Danton and Brigit were nodding.

"And what about those missing periods? And everybody being late for everything?" she continued. "And did you see the way people were driving and how everybody was rushing in and out of the stores bumping into each other?"

"You're not saying what I think you're saying, are you?" asked Danton.

"Yes. Yes, I am. Old Baba called the Stone a 'Fetch.' And I think that's exactly what those little insects are doing. They're fetching our time. They're stealing our time like bees steal pollen. Then they must turn it into that honey stuff."

"You can't be serious?" Edward said.

"I'm perfectly serious."

"Actually," Danton said, "it would explain a lot. I mean, think about it. Think about that pumpkin. I bet that's why that pumpkin just shriveled up and disappeared. They sucked all the time right out of it."

Edward now remembered the missing room.

"What?" Feenix said to him sharply. "What? You're thinking something. What is it?"

He considered not sharing, but he knew that really would not be fair. "Well, this afternoon, Mr. Pomerance sent me with a message to room 219, but when I got to where room 219 should be, it was gone. If it was your snitcher bees—and I'm not saying it was—but if it was, it would be kind of like what Mr. Ross was saying about space and time all being part of the same fabric. If you take all the time away from a thing, then the thing can't exist in space anymore."

Everybody looked fearfully around the bright, warm kitchen. The clock ticked loudly. The wind banged at the windows and moaned.

"Does anybody mind if I take this last piece?" Danton

said. When nobody said anything, he took the last piece of cheesy pita bread and munched on it with great concentration.

Edward pointed at Feenix. "You know, if any of this is true—and I'm not saying it is, because it's crazy—but if it is, it's all your fault. Possibly this will teach you to stop picking up things that don't belong to you." Somewhat to his surprise she remained silent.

Danton said loudly, "I don't see that it's really anybody's fault. I mean, how could we have known and what does it matter? We have to figure out what to do. What if these things *are* reproducing, you know, like Mr. Ross's fruit flies? Remember how he said they would just keep on reproducing until they ran out of food? What if these things just keep multiplying until they've eaten up all our time?"

There was a long, unpleasant silence while everyone thought about this.

"If only there was some way to get them all back into the stone thingy," Feenix said. "Then maybe we could stop it up with a cork or something."

"That's a brilliant plan," Edward said. "Especially considering that, thanks to you, we don't even have the stupid thing."

"Exactly what is it that makes you think you're so much smarter than everybody else, Dweebo?"

"The name is Edward."

"Whatever. In any case, you should really try working on that negative-thinking problem." She lifted up her pink sequined purse and snapped it open. She rummaged around until she found what she was looking for and laid it on the counter.

"Oh, no," Edward whispered.

"Oh, yes," Feenix said.

They all stared at the stone.

Outside the kitchen the wind rattled and whimpered at the windows.

No one moved. Then Brigit leaned in to take a closer look. Danton did the same. Edward really wanted no part of it, but he couldn't help himself. He leaned forward, too.

Then there was a terrific bang and a rush of cold air.

Feenix let out a loud scream and they all spun around toward the source of the sound.

Aunt Kit stood in the doorway, her arms loaded with bags and parcels and evergreen branches.

There was a long pause as she took in the four of them sitting around the counter.

"Well," she said. "Well."

She laid her pine branches and red holly berries on the counter and let her bags down onto the red-tiled floor.

"I'm Kit," she said. "Welcome. I hope Edward's given you something to eat? Please excuse my breathlessness, it's been a wild ride of a day. Such a dangerous time of year."

Edward watched her nervously. If she said anything about how absolutely delighted she was that he'd finally brought home some friends, he would be a marked man for life.

"Introduce me, please," she said.

Before Edward could say a word, Feenix stepped forward with her hand out, her bracelets jingling. "I'm Feenix."

Aunt Kit took the hand and held it. "Yes, it's time we met. I've seen you going by many times." His aunt held her gaze for a long searching moment. Then she let go with a nod. She turned to Danton.

"And you must be the fellow who admires my bread."

Danton took her hand and kissed it. "It's an honor. It was one of the best breads I ever tasted. Is it a secret recipe? My dad makes bread sometimes, but never anything like yours."

"The secret to good bread, and most everything else, is taking your time. But I'll be glad to share the recipe with you and your dad."

"Oh, wow! That'd be great."

Aunt Kit bowed her head and turned her attention to Brigit.

"I've met this young lady before," she said. "Brigit, I believe."

The others looked at Brigit in surprise.

"It was in the city at one of our concerts. The West of the Moon Chorus. Your grandfather sings with us, doesn't he? And you came to hear us."

Brigit nodded.

"I've been thinking about him. He hasn't been at our last few rehearsals. I've missed his voice."

She was studying Brigit intently. "I was so sorry to hear about the loss in your family. It would be good for your grandfather to sing with other people again. Why don't you give me his number and I'll call and invite him to our celebration tomorrow and your parents, too, of course. You'll bring them with you when you come."

Edward felt bad for Brigit. It was never easy when his aunt got someone in her laser beam, and Brigit was so easily embarrassed. He wondered, too, what her loss could have been. There was a longish uncomfortable silence, while Aunt Kit gave her a piece of paper and a pencil. Brigit wrote her number down. Then Feenix, being Feenix, opened her mouth and changed the subject. "What did you mean about it being such a dangerous time of year?"

Aunt Kit turned to her and seemed to think about how to answer this. At last she said, "The Tipping Point is upon us."

"What's the Tipping Point?" Feenix asked.

"We have reached the Great Turn, the winter solstice."

"Yes," said Danton, looking at the others meaningfully. "Mr. Ross, our science teacher, was talking about that."

"So what's supposed to happen?" Feenix asked.

"Time grows short, and chaos and disorder threaten. The curtain between here and there grows thin and things we do not understand may cross back and forth," Aunt Kit told her.

Edward could not help chiming in. "Mr. Ross also pointed

out to us that all that superstitious stuff was made up way back in the cave days. Back when people didn't know what we know now."

"And, remind me, what exactly is it that we know?" Aunt Kit asked.

"Well, now we have telescopes. We can see that the seasons are changing because of the way the earth is tilted as it goes around the sun."

"I have nothing against telescopes, Edward. They are wonderful inventions. But the best telescope is useless to a blind man."

What was the point? The day could hardly get any worse. He made no further attempt to argue with her.

"But enough talking," Aunt Kit declared. "There are things to be done! It's supposed to snow, did you hear? Edward, would you hang these branches over the fireplace? I don't want anything coming down the chimney in the night." She lifted the branches so she could hand them to Edward. Then she stopped.

She had uncovered the stone lying on the green granite counter. "What—?" She stood there staring at it. She leaned down and peered at it more closely.

She looked up at the young people. "Where on earth—?" She gazed back down at the stone. "Is this—?" She shook her head. His aunt appeared shaken. This was a rare thing for his aunt. She reached out slowly, but at the last moment seemed to think better of it and drew her hand back.

She lifted her head. "Who brought that in here?"

Everybody looked at Feenix.

"Yes—well, I did," she said uncomfortably.

"And where exactly did you get it from?"

"I got it from him," she said, pointing at Edward.

"Edward? You got it from Edward?"

Before Edward could make a retort, a high, thin wailing came winding down the alleyway. Aunt Kit turned sharply toward the window. They all turned with her. There wasn't anything there that anybody could see, but she quickly stepped over and closed the curtains.

"It's just the wind," she said. "Pick that dirty thing up off my clean counter and put it in your pocket."

Not very happily, Edward picked the stone up and stuck it in his pocket.

She watched him closely as he did it, then said, "Well, there isn't much time then, is there?"

"What do you mean, Kit?' Feenix asked.

"Speak softly. If there is to be a celebration tomorrow, what needs to be done must be done." The way she had fixed them all with her steely gaze seemed to imply that they all ought to know exactly what she was talking about.

"You're going to have to go down to the grocery store for me."

"What?!" Edward protested. "You want us to go back out there in the cold?"

"You must keep your voice down!" she hissed at him

glancing at the window. "You want the whole neighborhood to hear you?"

"What difference does it make who hears—"

But she had turned on him The Gaze That Freezes Blood to Ice. "I've forgotten a couple of indispensable items," she said softly. "You will go quickly and quietly and stay close together. If the supermarket is closed, find an open fruit and vegetable store. They stay open late and with luck they'll have what we need. You don't mind, do you?" she asked the others.

"We'll be happy to go to the store for you," Danton said. "Just write down what you need." He gave Edward a look while she quickly scribbled her list.

"Thank you," Aunt Kit said. She didn't smile. "Tomorrow, if time keeps ticking and the sun returns, we will celebrate together. Now, there's not a moment to waste. You must all dress very warmly. It's getting cold. If you don't have gloves and scarves, I will lend you some."

No one dared to object. She watched them closely as they put on their coats and hats and buttoned themselves up.

"Edward, where are your gloves?"

Before he could answer, she had slid her hand into his coat pocket, not the one that had the stone in it, the other one. He thought he would die of embarrassment. "Hey!" he protested loudly, but she fumbled around in there until she brought out a pair of gloves. She handed them to him with a weird look of satisfaction.

"I could have done that myself, you know," he said angrily, but she had already turned away and was now looking at Brigit.

Brigit, without blushing, met her gaze steadily. She was all buttoned up, and she was wearing a bright green wool hat that stood out in contrast to her red hair. Edward braced himself for whatever weird advice Aunt Kit would now deliver, but she merely said, "Your hood is stuck inside your coat. May I?"

Brigit nodded and Aunt Kit gently, with a little fumbling, pulled the hood out. "If it gets too cold, put it on."

Brigit nodded again. Aunt Kit handed her the shopping list. "Take care of one another and hurry!" she said. "If the warp and the woof hold true, I expect all of you at the celebration tomorrow. Bring anyone you want. And whatever you do, stay clear of the Unraveler."

Part Three

CHAPTER FIFTEEN
The Green Man

A minute later they were all standing breathlessly on the sidewalk in front of the house. Nobody was quite sure how they had gotten there, it had all happened so fast. When they turned to look back they found the front door firmly shut. There was no sign of Aunt Kit.

"She's a pistol," Danton said admiringly. "But what was she talking about? What's an Unraveler?"

Edward muttered, "Sorry about that. Pay no attention. She's not all there."

"Don't be such a pea brain," Feenix said to him. "She's obviously got way more going on than most grown-ups. I'm sure she recognized the stone. Didn't you see? She was totally blown away. And she was worried somebody was going to see it. That's why she made you put it in your pocket. And all that stuff about keeping our voices down. She was afraid somebody was going to hear. I think she wanted to tell us something, but she couldn't come right out and say it."

"You're right," Danton said, lowering his voice nervously. "That stuff about the 'warp' and the 'woof.' What did that mean? Does anybody have a clue?"

Brigit nodded eagerly. She took a pen out of her pocket, and standing under the street lamp, she drew a little picture on the back of Aunt Kit's shopping list. It looked sort of like a tic-tac-toe board, only with lots more up and down lines.

"Oh, of course!" Feenix exploded.

"*Shhh!*" Danton warned.

"Right, right. Sorry." Feenix brought her voice down. "The woof and the warp are what's on a loom. You know, like when you're weaving something. One is the threads that go up and down. The other is the threads that go across. I forget which is which."

"Like Mr. Ross's space-time fabric!" Danton whispered excitedly. "Maybe Eddie's aunt thinks the woof and the warp are unraveling and she's sending us out to do something about it?"

"You're right!" agreed Feenix. "That's got to be it. She's sent us on a mission. But what is it, what does she want us to do?"

They all looked at Edward.

"What? You think I have some special insight into the

way her mind works? Don't you understand I pay as little attention to her as possible?"

For a long minute, they all just stood there looking at each other and now each of them noticed how much colder it had gotten and how the wind was going up and down the alleys, hunting and crying. The air tasted like snow, but there was no snow yet.

Finally, Brigit gave a little start and held up the piece of paper with the shopping list on it.

"Right!" said Danton. "Of course. The first thing we've got to do is go to the store."

Since nobody else had any better ideas, they started down the hill. Danton hurried them. The other people on the sidewalk were in a big rush, too. Everyone was huddled inside their coats, intent on getting done whatever it was they thought they needed to get done. Nobody paid any attention to anybody else. Then Feenix stopped abruptly.

"What's with the library?" she said staring.

Everybody followed her gaze. The library was a brick building that had been old to begin with, but now it looked *really* old. Its windows were broken and its front steps were crumbling.

"What happened to it?" Feenix said. "I was in there just the other day."

"You read books?" Edward asked.

Feenix looked at him with disgust. "Don't be pathetic. As it happens, I love reading."

"Holy tamales!" cried Danton. He lowerd his voice to a hoarse whisper. "Get back, get back. Look what's coming through the window."

Everyone looked where he pointed. Streaming out of the broken window into the night was a cloud of the glittering electric bees.

"Get back! Get back!" Danton whispered again. He dragged them down a narrow alley. They peered out fearfully. The cloud of sparkling things paused at the entrance to the alley. None of the young people dared to breathe. In the silence they heard a sound like a million soda bubbles popping and fizzing.

A stray cat slid out from behind a garbage can a few yards down by the entrance to the alley, heading toward the sidewalk. The cat's ears were pricked alertly. Maybe it, too, had heard the sound of the bees. The cat looked around, sensing danger, but before it could turn, the bees were upon it. The animal let out a single yowl of protest and then was swallowed up by the hungry swarm. When the swarm finally lifted and disappeared into the darkness, Danton wasted no time, but unfolded himself and slipped silently over to where the cat had been. Now there was just a small heap of dust. A gust of wind sent this dust scattering in a hundred directions.

"Let's get out of here before they come back," Danton urged, but Feenix didn't seem to have even heard him. She stood staring at where the cat had been.

Danton grabbed her arm. "Come on!" he urged.

"What are *you* looking at?" Feenix snapped at Edward as she wiped at her eyes.

They went along as fast as they could, nobody speaking. Any people they passed on the street paid no attention to them, they were all in such a hurry.

"Look at that traffic light," Danton whispered sharply, pointing to the next intersection. The light blinked red, green, yellow, red. It was blinking much too quickly, going through its cycle with hardly seconds between one color and the next.

The traffic light drew their eyes farther down Ninth Street. They saw now how many places had been visited by the insects. The work they were doing was weirdly uneven. Things that were still moving, moved way too fast. Cars went past as if their accelerator pedals were stuck to their floors. Up ahead, on the elevated tracks, the brightly lit windows of a train shot by like the streak of a meteor. A bundled-up mother pushed a stroller in front of her like she was being chased by a pack of wild wolves. She did not seem to notice that the face of the baby in the stroller was ancient and wrinkled. Things that stood still, stone steps and sidewalks, buildings and chimneys, were in various stages of crumbling and disrepair. In some places the aging was hardly noticeable. In others, the work was nearly done.

When they reached the supermarket they saw that the cheerful red awning was torn and tattered. There were no posters advertising the not-to-be-missed specials on pork chops and paper towels. The windows were broken. It didn't look as if the store had been in operation for years.

Even as they stood staring, they could see the building aging before their eyes. The bricks crumbled. Rust grew over the metal doors. They heard a great crash as part of the roof gave way. Then another thing began to happen. A thin tear ran up the front of the wall facing the street, like a dark flame racing up a curtain. The tear grew taller and wider. They all watched in horrified fascination. Whatever was inside of it was neither dark nor light, solid nor gas, up nor down.

"What is that?" Feenix whispered. "It's making me dizzy."

"Look away! Look away!" Danton ordered everyone. "The bees must have eaten away everything that's in there. It's like a rip in the time fabric."

Before he could finish, they all saw what he meant. The flickering cloud of bees came swarming and humming out through the horrible crack.

Danton didn't need to tell them to run.

They raced after him down to the next corner where he made them turn right. They kept going for a few blocks along Fifth Avenue. Then Danton turned right again up a side street.

"This way! This way!" he urged. By the time he stopped, they were all panting.

"Where are we?" Feenix demanded.

"I think we're on Sixth Street," Danton said. "I just wanted to get us away from those things."

They all looked around nervously. "Listen," Edward said. "I think we should all go home. It's not safe wandering around out here."

"I know how you feel, Eddie, but I don't see how that's really an option," Danton replied.

"Of course it's not an option," Feenix replied. "Everything's crumbling into dust and the time fabric is starting to rip just like we saw back there at the supermarket. Who knows if any of our houses will even be there if we go home? Your aunt sent us out here to stop the bees. There's something we have to do. But what is it?"

Brigit held up the shopping list.

"Right," said Danton. "She wanted us to go shopping. Let's start with that. The supermarket is obviously out of the question. Is there a fruit and vegetable store around here?"

Edward stared at him grumpily. "I'm not even sure where we are, you've been so busy dragging us around in circles." Brigit held up her hand as if she were asking for quiet.

She seemed to be listening.

"What is it?" Danton asked her.

They all watched her under the streetlamp. She was concentrating very hard, frowning and looking around herself. At last, she appeared to make up her mind about something. She nodded at them, and then crossed the street and started walking quickly up toward the next corner.

"Wait!" Danton called. "What's up? Where you going?" He hurried after her, and the other two followed.

They hadn't gone far when they all heard it.

There was music coming from somewhere, a little melody, silvery and beckoning, like someone was playing on a flute or a recorder.

"There!" Feenix cried. "It's coming from up there. Do you ever remember seeing that before? It looks like a little bodega."

When they caught up with Brigit, she was waiting for them at the entrance to the store.

In front of the store two wooden display stands were piled high with glistening mounds of apples, pears, and grapes.

"You'd think they'd take them inside in weather like this," remarked Danton.

The silvery piping music came floating out the door, curling around them like invisible tendrils, tugging on them. Brigit stepped up the little incline and walked inside, not looking to see if they followed.

Inside, there was hardly room to turn around. Buckets full of daffodils and tulips, pots of primroses and hyacinths crowded every inch of floor space. Arranged in the display stands along the wall were all the green-leafed things you could and couldn't name—lettuces, spinach, dill, scallions, basil—dozens more. It must have been these that gave the room its moist green light. There wasn't anybody standing behind the front counter.

The music went curling and winding through the aisles.

"But where's it coming from?" Danton whispered.

"Must be a radio or something," Edward said.

"Where are your ears?" Feenix retorted. "There's some-body playing in here somewhere."

Before they could start arguing again, Brigit pulled out the shopping list. They watched her as she stood there reading it.

"Well?" Feenix demanded. "What does it say?" When Brigit didn't answer, Feenix tugged it out of her hand.

"One red apple, vanilla beans, and anchovy paste," Feenix read. She turned to Edward. "What does she do with anchovy paste?"

He shrugged. "Haven't a clue. It's not even vegetarian."

"Is she a vegetarian?" Danton asked.

"Generally," Edward replied. "Though with her, you never know."

"All right," Danton said. "It's all we've got to go on. Let's find the stuff."

They all stuck close together, nobody wanting to be left alone. There were several cramped and mazelike aisles. Feenix found the apples and chose a nice shiny red one. Edward discovered the spices and found a thin plastic container with two vanilla beans rattling around inside. They went deeper toward the back of the store, and then Brigit stopped abruptly and picked up a toothpastelike tube from one of the shelves. She held it aloft. ANCHOVY PASTE was printed on its gaily colored side.

"Okay," Danton said. "I guess that's it. But now what?"

There was silence and they all realized that the music had stopped.

A voice spoke from somewhere over their heads. "I had nearly given up hope."

The man was sitting at the top of a ladder. It was one of those ladders that slide along a track. The man was very pale and very old, and he held a strangely shaped instrument of some kind. It looked like several wooden pipes of different lengths tied together. His coat had been sewn together out of patches of different colored green silks. Since each patch caught or reflected the light in a different way, the coat looked almost alive like a snakeskin or like the leaves on a tree. The man pointed at Edward. "Step forward," he commanded.

Edward looked around nervously.

"Yes, you. Step forward."

With great reluctance Edward stepped forward.

"You don't recognize me."

Edward frowned and peered up at him more closely. The others watched.

Edward hesitated. "You're not the guy who—?"

"Yes, and you can see how my strength has waned. Now, it falls to you to carry what I would gladly have carried. How did you find your way to me?"

"Well, uh, Aunt Kit sent us," he answered. "She needed anchovy paste and some other stuff."

The man stared at Edward. Edward squirmed beneath his piercing gaze. At last the green man nodded. "I see. This would be Aunt Kit, the baker, I presume. You understand that if I leave this place unprotected now, it will be destroyed. There will be nothing green to arise again. What must be done is up to you." The man's eyes burned fiercely. His skin was still creepily pale, like marble that was trying with only half success to come alive.

"You have the Fetch upon you?" he asked

Danton was the first to speak. "Yes. Show it to him, Eddie."

Edward took the stone from his pocket and held it up for inspection.

The green man did not move from his perch. He leaned forward to look at it hungrily. Then he said with a sigh, "You do realize that if you'd given it to me when I offered to take it for you, none of this would have happened."

"What's he mean, Eddie?" Danton asked. "What's he talking about?"

Edward said defensively, "I met him on the street, on my way to school last week. I thought he was—uh—I didn't understand what he wanted." He waited for Feenix to say something sarcastic, but she remained quiet.

"And I offered to carry it for you, as well, did I not?" said the green man, turning to her.

Feenix merely looked unhappy. "It was you, wasn't it . . . that night on the . . . hill?"

"Of course."

"So, there we go, Ms. High and Mighty," Edward said.

"All right, all right," said Danton. "And if I hadn't convinced Edward to follow you up to the park that day, none of this would have happened either. I'm to blame, too, but what's the difference now?" He looked back up at the green man. "Tell us what this thing is and what we have to do?"

"You carry a Time Fetch."

"Yes, we figured out that much," Edward said impatiently. He was still holding the stone in his open palm. "But what is it? What's it doing? How'd it get here? Don't tell me it's one of the Old Ones my aunt is always going on about?"

The green man laughed. "Your Aunt Kit would probably call *me* one of those, but the Time Fetches are not of this world and it would be incorrect to describe them as young or old. The Keeper sends them out so the foragers may gather time."

A small gust of wind blew past them and made the green man's patches flutter like leaves. He looked around sharply. Perhaps someone had opened the door at the front of the store.

"But what do you mean?" Feenix demanded. "What's it doing here?"

The green man shook his head impatiently. "To explain the way one thing works means we must understand the way everything else works. Nothing stands on its own. There is no time now for an explanation."

Edward made a small choking sound at these words, but the green man ignored him.

"But this I will tell you. The Keeper sends the Fetches and their foragers out to gather time. The law permits a Fetch to stay in a world only long enough to take the bits of time that will not be missed, the seconds and minutes that no one notices—or hardly notices. Have you not felt how some hours go faster than others?" He gazed at them and they nodded uncertainly.

"Yes, well . . . it is said that the Keeper is able to gather time in this way and use it where it is needed, sometimes even to begin new worlds. Naturally, such a treasure is prized from one end of the Great Web to the other. Not least, of course, by the ones whose work it is to undo it."

At these words, the little wind that had somehow gotten loose in the store went racing impishly around the shelves, knocking jars and cans onto the floor.

"Something, of course, has gone very wrong here . . ."

The green man looked accusingly at the four young people. "Someone moved the Fetch from its hiding place. In the ensuing confusion some of the foragers managed to escape." Now the man's gaze came to rest upon Feenix. "You know how this happened, I think."

"Well, it wasn't me! It was those criminally insane bag ladies! They were the ones who opened the thing up."

"But you took it when it was not yours to take, did you not? You brought it to them. Willingly or not, you aligned yourself with their power. Nothing you do is without consequence. In this case, because of your carelessness, the foragers have been able to multiply and feed until our world is nearly gone."

"But there's got to be something we can do!" Danton said.

The green man turned his glittering eyes upon him. "Of course there is something you can do. There is always something. But it will require courage and cunning and speed."

"That's us!" Danton cried. "We'll give it our best, won't we, guys?"

Brigit nodded solemnly.

"A mission," Feenix agreed.

Edward groaned.

"Tell us what to do," said Danton.

"You must prevent the Fetch from falling into the wrong hands and find the doorway where the Keeper waits."

"And if we can find the doorway, the Keeper will save our world?" Danton asked.

The man shook his head. "It may be, but we cannot presume to know what the Keeper will do. What is for certain is that if an Unraveler wins this prize, it is more than our own world that will suffer. Now waste no more of the time left to us. Make for the Weaver's Hill."

The gust of wind should have played itself out by now. Instead it was gathering strength. It ricocheted from shelf to shelf, knocking boxes and cans over.

"Watch out!" Feenix warned. "Remember what happened that day in science class. Dweebo, I think you ought to—" But before she could say what she thought he should do, the wind gave a triumphant shriek and pounced and the stone was knocked from Edward's grasp. Instead of tumbling to the floor, it went spinning like a top toward the ceiling.

"No! No! No!" the green man cried. "Catch it! Catch it!"

They all watched paralyzed, except for Danton, who gave a little grunt, bent his knees, and took a flying leap. He flew through the air with his arms outstretched as if to intercept a pass. Up he went, up and up, his face clear and calm and concentrated. His huge hand opened and closed and he plucked the stone from the air.

"Well done!" called the man, although they couldn't see him anymore. He was surrounded by a whirling and tossing storm of lettuces and radishes and flowers flying through the air. "Hurry! The Keeper draws near!" he cried out. "If there is help to be found, it will be on the Weaver's Hill. Enter through the Cat Gate. It is the shortest way and there is no time to lose. I will do what I can to hold this one off. Edward, hang a holly bough over the door. Run!"

They all ran to the front and tumbled out the door onto the sidewalk.

"Where's the holly? Where's the holly!" Feenix yelled.

"Keep your hat on. It's right here." Edward bent over the bucket of branches with their bright red berries. He grabbed a long sturdy one and passed it through the latch of the door.

Brigit nodded at him, smiling.

"Now," said Danton, "which way do we go? Where's this Cat Gate and this Weaver's Hill?"

"He's got to be talking about the Third Street entrance to the park," Feenix said. "You know—where those big bronze panthers are."

"Right!" exclaimed Danton. "Third Street is this way." He began to move them along. "And what about the Weaver's Hill? Anybody got any ideas on that one?"

"My aunt's talked about it," Edward said. "Slow down a little, will ya? Let's pace ourselves or we'll all be wiped out before we get there."

Danton ignored him. "So where is it?"

"I never paid much attention,"Edward panted. "Supposedly, it's a big mound of a hill in the Long Meadow. It's one of her magical hot spots. I think she meets up with her pals there on Midsummer's Eve."

"Some Midsummer's Eve," Danton said. "Do you know where it is?"

"Vaguely."

"We'll find it," Danton said without stopping.

It was only then that they all noticed that it had begun to snow.

CHAPTER SIXTEEN
Older

It was a terrible journey. It didn't take long before Danton realized how lucky they were that Eddie's aunt had wrapped them up so well. The wind blew from every direction at once and in what seemed only a matter of minutes—though who could really be sure anymore?—the ground was covered and the snow began piling up. The streets were empty of people and many of the old brownstones no longer looked lived in; their front stoops were crumbling, their windows boarded up. The snow came harder and there were few lights burning, but just when they thought complete darkness had taken over, they would spot a lit-up plastic snowman, or a menorah, or a candle burning in a window. Other than these occasional lights, there was an empty end-of-the-world feeling to the windblown streets. Danton tried not to, but he couldn't help thinking about his little brother and his mom and dad. What if the forager things had found them? What would that mean? Crazy pictures of his brother crowded into his imagination, pictures of a little withered-up old man. He tried to do what he did when he was playing a game, pull in his focus so that all that existed was the world of the game—the ball, the other players, the boundaries of the field—but his heart was full of doubt.

It was Brigit who spotted the next rip in the fabric. She grabbed Danton's arm and stopped him before he could step into it.

He looked down and saw how the foragers were eating their way through the earth, leaving behind a growing snakelike crevasse. He teetered at its edge and saw how, sickeningly, the whole world seemed to fall away into a bottomless nothing. It appeared that once you fell into this, you would fall forever. If only there were some color in there. Even blackness would have been a relief. But its un-ness was sickening. Brigit's small mittened hand held onto him tightly and pulled him backward and away from the chasm. Dizzy, he fell on his knees in the snow and, for a long moment, he kneeled there, breathing deeply till the nausea passed.

"C'mon," he said, standing up. "We've got to get past them before they cut us off. Hurry."

They ran alongside it as fast as they could, but the snow and the wind slowed them down, while the lengthening crack seemed heedless of the weather. "The other way! Go back the other way!" he ordered them.

But this did no good either, for a swarm was now working hungrily away at the other end. It occurred to Danton that the foragers knew exactly what the four of them aimed to do and were trying to head them off. The time rip was always just ahead, devouring the ground into nothingness.

Feenix was the one who stopped first. "We'll have to jump over it," she announced. "It's the only way."

"You're right," agreed Danton, swallowing his fear. He turned to the others. "Don't look down," he commanded. "You lose your sense of direction when you stare into it. Look up, or close your eyes if you have to. I'll go first. Watch me. Get a good running start." He backed up a little way. "One, two, three!" He ran forward. Just before the edge, he launched himself into the air.

For the first few moments he flew into the cold sting of snow and wind. Then just as he reached the top of what should have been his arc, Danton felt a slight jolt. He had stopped moving. What was going on? He risked a brief look down and saw that he was suspended in the air. There was a weird tingling in his toes, as if thousands of bubbles were bursting open inside of them. He struggled desperately to get himself loose, but he was caught. The foragers were surging up through his feet and ankles, past his knees. What were they doing to him? They were feeding on him. He could feel his heart rate accelerating madly.

Then something exploded up against him from behind. Something like a voice that wasn't a voice firmly ordered him to MOVE. Then there was a slight tearing sensation, as if he were being pushed through a barrier no thicker than a skin of milk on a cup of boiled cocoa.

He fell in a heap onto a snowbank, and someone fell on top of him.

When he opened his eyes he found that he was lying on his back, staring into the face of a familiar-looking young woman. Who was she? This was embarrassing, not just because she was lying on top of him, but also because he knew he ought to know her name, but for the life of him, he couldn't remember it.

She rolled off of him and stood up awkwardly, brushing at her coat. She was slender and graceful like a little tree. He lay there for a moment watching her, trying to figure out what had just happened. Behind him, he heard Feenix say, "Dweebo? Is that you?"

The voice that answered her was deep and sleepy. "No, it's Santa Claus, who do think—" The voice stopped, surprised by itself.

Danton rose slowly. He had a second's trouble catching his balance. His feet seemed very far away. A light fell from overhead, a single street lamp still burning. Snowflakes tumbled and danced out of the darkness into its illumination. "Jeez, Danton! Weren't you tall enough already?"

He turned to look at Feenix, but it was not Feenix. Her

voice was the same, but her face was different. What was it? Her jaw was stronger, her cheekbones wider. And that weird thing with her eyes wasn't gone, but you didn't notice it in the same way.

"We're older," Danton said to them all and shook his head, trying to clear it.

Feenix was holding out her arms and legs, trying to see what had happened. "How much? How many years do you think?" she asked excitedly. Nobody answered. She looked around at the other three. She reached up and grabbed Danton's jaw, turning his face from side to side. "Around three or four, I think. You don't look bad at all. How do I look?"

"What does it matter how you look?" Danton cried. "We're in big trouble here! Everybody get up. C'mon, Eddie. We've got to get moving." But Eddie was still sitting in the snow, testing his arms and then his legs, each one separately, like he wasn't sure where the old Eddie ended and the new one began.

"Let's go," said Feenix and she offered him her hand.

He looked at it suspiciously, but didn't take it. He hauled himself awkwardly to his feet.

Feenix fell quiet, staring at him.

Eddie was now much taller than Feenix was. A few days' growth of dark beard shadowed his jaw. "Huh," he said in a wondering voice, staring down at his distant feet.

The snow was hissing and blowing around them. Danton

understood who the other young woman was—the one who had pushed him through to other side. What he wanted to do more than anything else was to turn and take a look at her. But he didn't have the nerve. Besides, there wasn't time for everybody to stand around and stare at each other.

"Heads up!" he yelled.

The wall of foragers had lifted itself into the air and was forming into a massive angry-sounding cloud. Although each one moved more swiftly than the eye could see, as a swarm they were clumsy and slow. Nevertheless, Danton knew there was no time to waste. "They're coming toward us. We've got to move."

He pushed and bullied them along. The storm was now so wild, the landscape around them was nearly unrecognizable. But here and there Danton would catch sight of a familiar landmark. At Third Street, he turned them up the hill toward Seventh Avenue. In places they passed great humped drifts of snow under which lay abandoned cars. In other places were huge gaps where buildings had crumbled and fallen into ruins. Streetlamps would appear suddenly out of the blowing storm, dark now and rusting away. But as they neared Seventh Avenue, a small circle of light appeared, floating low in the sky.

"Careful!" Feenix called out. "There's something up ahead!"

"Keep going forward!" Danton shouted. "If it's another swarm, it's pretty small. We can duck under it." He took a breath and plunged forward, resisting the urge to look behind him, wanting to appear more confident than he felt.

The circle in the air grew steadily brighter. When they had nearly reached it, Feenix called out, "It's not the bee thingies! It's only one of those big electric snowflakes!"

With a rush of relief, they all saw she was right. It hung overhead from a lamppost. All of the restaurants and stores were dark and empty, buildings crumbling into ruins. But this one snowflake continued shining into the darkness.

"Look, that's where the fish store must have been!" Danton yelled. "Two more blocks and we'll hit the Third Street entrance to the park!" This time he turned to the others to make sure they were with him and he found himself almost face-to-face with Brigit. She looked right back at him. Beneath the faint light falling down upon them, he could see how she had changed. Her freckles were nearly gone, her mouth wider, a little catlike. Her green eyes were still shy, but met his gaze without flinching. She smiled at him. It was her, but not exactly her. He experienced an unfamiliar sensation, like he'd spilled a cup of hot soup on his chest. The sensation spread upward against the force of gravity. It traveled into his neck and then into his face.

He turned away from her quickly. "C'mon, everybody!" he called. "Let's pick it up. Just two more blocks and we're there! We need to get some space between us and that thing back there."

They all doubled their pace, although Eddie, as usual, tagged along at the rear.

When they were halfway to the next corner, Danton paused and took a deep breath. He turned to check for the foragers. There was no sign of them or their great wave of nothingness. It probably didn't mean much, since the snowstorm made it impossible to see beyond a half block or so, but he felt a rush of hope. Maybe they'd be able to outrun the ravenous swarm. "Let's go, people! We're nearly there. Hurry up, Eddie, move your sorry behind!"

Danton plunged ahead.

The wind picked up again. It came from all directions at once, and in the howling and the whiteness, it was difficult to tell how long it took to get to the corner. Danton, of course, was the first to arrive. He stopped and waited for the others to catch up. Whether the foragers were far behind or close on their tails, it was impossible to tell, but in only one more block they would reach the park. Brigit stepped up beside him, her nearly grown face unnerving him again with its pale, watchful beauty. Feenix came next, her coat and the ends of her wild mane of hair blowing wildly.

"Do you smell that?" Feenix exclaimed. "Am I crazy? I think I smell coffee and doughnuts!"

Now Eddie came panting up to join them. "Pinch me, please!" he yelled. "Do you see that, or am I dreaming?"

The others looked where Eddie pointed. There, on the opposite corner, was a warmly lit plate glass window. Danton wondered how he hadn't noticed it in the first place.

"It's a café!" Eddie said. "And it looks open. C'mon!" He plunged into the drifted snow of the empty street without looking behind him.

Danton hesitated. "Let's stay together, but be careful," he said to the two girls. They followed Eddie.

"This is so weird. I don't ever remember seeing this place before, do you?" Eddie asked as they came up behind him.

"It wasn't here last week. I'm sure of it," Danton said. The smell of freshly baked doughnuts nearly brought tears to his eyes.

"Something's not right about this," Feenix said.

Through the glowing window they saw a couple of comfy looking armchairs in the rear, and several tables arranged around the room, each one with its own shaded lamp and a small copper vase holding two or three red poppies. The frame around the outside of the window caught Danton's eye. It had been decorated with what looked like a crazy mosaic of different colored tiles, although he had the feeling there was some sort of pattern. He leaned closer and realized they weren't tiles but candies—butterscotches, Life Savers, and squares of chocolate. He reached out to touch one.

"Don't!"said Feenix sharply.

Danton drew his hand back quickly.

"Hey, look, there's someone inside," said Eddie.

Danton saw that he was right. The café wasn't empty after all. A man with a dark ponytail was standing behind the counter watching them all with a smile. He beckoned to them.

"Let's go in," begged Eddie. "Just for a few minutes. We can warm up. We can get some hot chocolate. Look, the bee things are nowhere in sight. We probably lost them."

They all looked behind themselves down the street and it was true. The snow was falling more lightly. The wind had dropped, too.

Danton hesitated. Perhaps it wouldn't hurt. Perhaps it would help give his troops a little boost. He took a step toward the café and was startled by a yank on his arm.

"No!"

He looked around to see Feenix staring angrily into his eyes. "No! We can't. How can you even think of stopping to eat when there's not a moment to waste? Tell them, Brigit! Tell them!"

Danton looked at Brigit. She nodded.

Danton shook himself. What *had* he been thinking? Of course. It was nuts to think about stopping now. "Right," he said. "We've got to keep moving. Just one more block up this way and we should hit the entrance. The cat pillars ought to be right there, if they're still standing."

CHAPTER SEVENTEEN
The Cat Gate

The wind, which had died down, seemed to rise up in fury at Danton's words. It came at them like a subway train rushing down a tunnel and tried to rip them apart.

"Stay with me! Stay with me!" Danton yelled. Brigit followed him, stumbling and fighting and panting. Feenix was up ahead now.

From behind them, Brigit watched Danton and Feenix plow with determination through the snow. They had both grown so tall and strong. When they had come through the last tear in the time fabric she had seen right away the great change in Feenix. It wasn't just in the balance of her face, how her eyes nearly lined up now. Something inside had shifted, too, as if she had come home to herself. Some of her meanness was gone, but she looked fiercer than ever. Brigit herself had only grown a little taller. And although she was apparently however many years older, there was still no sign of her voice. She was puny and mute and worse than useless. Danton would keep on feeling he had to protect her and what would she do except slow them down? Perhaps she should stay behind. She could go back and wait for the end of the world in the coffee shop. At least she would be out of their way.

She stopped where she was and was about to turn back when Danton—almost as if he could hear what she was thinking—wheeled around and peered into the storm. "C'mon! C'mon, we're nearly there. Let's not get separated!"

Up ahead, there was a shout. It was Feenix. Whatever she said was muffled by the storm, but Danton beckoned urgently to her and Brigit knew she couldn't really leave them now.

As she came up to him, he took hold of her hand for a moment and pulled her forward. She had this sensation in her ribs like her heart was a tiny elevator that had broken loose from its chains. Down it rushed toward her boots. Feenix shouted again.

They had reached the Third Street entrance to the park. It could not be a coincidence that here was another streetlamp still shining bravely through the storm. Brigit was sure now that these lights had been left burning to lead them where they needed to go. This lamp was an old cast-iron one with a glass globe on its top. It rose up straight and handsome into the night, and where it threw its welcoming rays of light into the darkness, you could see the snow spinning wildly through the air. It cast just enough light to show the opening of the trees into the park and the two pillars with the great bronze cats on top. Danton and Feenix were peering down the curving snow-covered road that disappeared into the interior of the park. A gust of wind blew past, and Brigit, looking up at the left-hand pillar, saw the shape of the huge bronze panther standing on its flat top. The swirling snow created the illusion that the panther had turned its neck to look down at them. Then the wind blew a curtain of snow across her vision.

Feenix and Danton were arguing about which way to go. Danton thought the safest thing to do would be to stick to the road, but Feenix wanted to cut through the playground. She said it would be shorter. On the other side they would hit the main drive and then, right across that, she was sure there was a little path that would lead them straight to the hill.

Brigit looked upward uneasily just as a gust of wind drew the curtain back again. The stone pedestal where the panther had just been was empty.

She opened her mouth to call a warning, but as always, there was no sound. She reached out to pull on Danton's jacket, but they were both distracted by Feenix, who suddenly yelled, "Hey! Where's Dweebo?"

Danton peered behind them into the storm. "Oh, drat

that dude! He's slower than ketchup. Where could he have gotten to? EDDDIEEE!" he yelled.

The panther was coming toward them. Only Brigit noticed it. It seemed to move effortlessly over the snow. Its head was low, its ears flat. She felt like she was in one of those dreams where you try to run and your legs won't work. She grabbed hold of Danton's shoulder and strained with every fiber of her being to get some sound out. Her mouth opened like a little bird waiting to be fed, but only silence came. The cat crouched playfully.

At this moment Feenix saw what was happening. *Her* scream was loud and bloodcurdling, but it was too late. With a single, elegant leap the cat pounced on Danton and ripped him out of Brigit's grasp. It held him fast in its jaws and shook him like a rag doll, then lifted him triumphantly into the air. The cat was—for the moment—merely playing with him. Danton wriggled and kicked, struggling fiercely to free himself.

Feenix didn't stop to consider. She jumped in front of the cat, yelling and waving her arms and stamping her feet. Her hair and her long coat flew out all around her.

God, she was brave, Brigit thought.

"Let go of him! Beat it! Shoo!"

The cat ignored her and merely continued tossing and shaking Danton playfully. Brigit now saw the other panther appear from out of the darkness. It came creeping up behind Feenix.

She knew that there was no way she would be able to get Feenix's attention, but perhaps she could draw this one off. She stepped into the path of the second cat, waving her arms wildly, and jumping up and down.

The cat acted as if she were invisible. It had eyes only for Feenix.

Brigit felt a rush of shame and frustration. What good was she to anybody?

Now the panther stopped where it was, a few feet from Feenix's back, and prepared to pounce.

It was then that a crazy thought came into Brigit's head.

The anchovy paste. Could Edward's aunt have known? Brigit lost no time reaching into her pocket. She pulled the tube out, then she wasted precious seconds yanking her mitten off with her teeth so she could unscrew the top. She took a deep breath and squeezed the tube, holding it aloft.

The smell that spilled into the air around them was way more powerful than it had any business being. Like a genie emerging from a bottle, the fishy, oily stink blossomed and unfolded around them.

Danton's panther froze where it was and opened its mouth to taste the air. Danton fell heavily into the snow.

The cat at Feenix's back froze, too. It turned its head toward the source of the smell.

Brigit waved the tube through the air. Both cats began to glide soundlessly in her direction.

"What do you think you're doing?" a voice yelled. It was

Feenix. Now that Danton was lying safely in the snow, she had turned to see what was going on behind herself. "Throw it! Throw the stinking thing now!"

Brigit took a step backward and then another step. She wanted to make sure she drew them well away from the other two.

"Throw it, Brigit!" yelled Danton. "Throw it as far as you can."

Brigit could see the panthers' yellow eyes fixed narrowly upon her. They looked very hungry. They probably hadn't eaten for a hundred years. She lifted the tube and flung it as far from herself as her strength allowed.

The tube went whirling end over end through the air and the cats were bounding after it in an instant. Because Brigit wasn't very strong and because of the storm, the tube didn't go very far, but dropped in a slow arc through the air and was immediately buried in the snow. The cats were on it in a few seconds, snorting and pawing at the drifts, digging for the treasure.

One of them had gotten hold of it.

Brigit could just make the cat out, standing there holding the foul-smelling treasure triumphantly in its mouth. The other one watched warily and then began to creep in, drawing closer and closer. The three humans stood transfixed, watching, afraid to move for fear of drawing them back again.

The first one paid no attention to anything other than

the problem of how to get at the anchovy paste. The cat dropped the tube and tried hold it down with a paw while trying to tear open the treasure with its teeth. The drifting snow made this almost impossible and the cat was too pre-occupied to notice the second cat before it was too late. The second cat dashed forward and snatched the prize right out from under the nose of its opponent. Infuriated by this treachery, maddened by the desire to get the anchovy paste back, the first cat flew after the thief and sank its teeth into the other's rump. A terrible scream rent the night. The sec-ond panther turned and raked the other's face with long, cruel claws and a smell of blood and raw flesh quickly min-gled in the air with the powerful, fishy scent.

The cats fell upon each other, biting and tearing. Soon it was impossible to make out one from the other, as if they'd had been thrown into a blender together with the ICE CRUSH button on.

Brigit couldn't bear to watch. She turned away and cov-ered her eyes. How long had they been up there on their pedestals, two silent princes, watching the seasons change, keeping guard over this entrance to the park? That waking them should bring them to this seemed a terrible pity.

The sounds of their battle were hideous, like the screech-ing of chalk over a blackboard, but turned up a hundred times. And then the noise of bones crunching and skin ripping.

When it was finally over, when the last piercing screech

of fury had died away, Brigit uncovered her eyes. There was nothing left to be seen but horrible bits of fur blowing through air.

Danton broke the silence. He sounded sad, too, but also relieved, and practical, as always. "All right then. Everybody okay? Let's get a move on."

"But what happened to Dweebo?" Feenix answered.

Brigit had almost forgotten, too, and now Danton was searching the darkness. "I don't think the cats could have got him. We would have noticed."

Brigit knew where he was. She was sure of it.

"Rat droppings!" hissed Feenix. "Don't tell me he went into that café?"

"Eddieee!" Danton called. But his voice did not carry far in the wind.

"I'm going back for him," Feenix announced grimly. "Don't look at me like that. He's . . . he's got dryer lint for brains. He'll never make it on his own. And there was something very sketchy about that place."

"No," said Danton. "No one goes anywhere by themselves now. It's insane out here. There's a blizzard and panthers and time-sucking bees, or whatever they are. We've got to stay together. We'll *all* go."

But the moment they turned and started back toward the café, they saw that it was too late. A mass of the foragers had come swarming out of the night. The individual sparks flickered and glittered faster than the eye could follow, while the swarm itself traveled slowly but steadily. As it moved along the street, eating without pause, the fabric of time dissolved wherever it went. It left behind a widening river of nothing. It was coming straight toward Danton, Feenix, and Brigit.

"Too late," hissed Danton between gritted teeth.

"But Edward—" Feenix cried.

"If you go through that thing now, first you'll turn into an old, old lady and then you'll turn into nothing along with everything else. We've got to keep going. We've got to find the Weaver's Hill."

Feenix just stood there, glaring angrily at the foragers and calculating the odds. At last she gave in, her shoulders slumping in defeat. She nodded.

"Let's get moving, then," Danton said, but he didn't move. Brigit felt him looking at her. "Listen, Brigit, maybe you should take my hand. It's not far, I think, but the snow is getting so deep and your legs aren't as long as mine and Feenix's." Again, he hesitated. "I wouldn't want to lose you, too."

It was true. Her legs were too short. She blushed as she held out her hand and he took it in his. It didn't matter. He couldn't see her face in this weather. How much more useless could she get, she thought miserably?

They began to plow through the snow. "Around that curve up there and then I think we'll hit the main road. Once we cross that, it's a little ways through the trees. I'm sure we can find it."

Brigit stumbled along bravely, doing her best not to slow him down. She knew that if she weren't there, he would be moving much faster. But his large strong hand held hers tightly and—she couldn't help it—his words kept going around and around in her head, keeping her warm. *I don't want to lose you, lose you, lose you.* Without her meaning to, they began to turn themselves into a little song. Now, where had she heard that melody before? Before she could remember, Danton interrupted. He had turned around to check on Feenix.

"Stop looking back there!" he yelled at her. "We've got to move faster!"

The melody slipped away. Danton led Feenix and Brigit past the playground. It was buried, now, under drifts of snow, an otherworldly little city of towers and slides. Then they were passing the old, abandoned toll-keeper's booth. For a second, Brigit could have sworn she saw someone standing inside of it, peering out at them. Then the face was gone.

It was only a matter of minutes—if minutes still existed—before they had reached what should have been the main road.

Brigit felt Danton's hand tighten on her own and pull her to a halt. Beside them Feenix gave a loud gasp and stopped, too. It took Brigit a moment to understand that the road had been replaced by a silent river of emptiness, a wide un-moving ribbon of nothing—a void without color or light or sound or smell. The foragers, for the moment, were nowhere to be seen; still the river was horrible to look at. It seemed to go against everything Brigit's blood beat for. Yet, as she stared at it, it drew her forward, irresistibly, with a power of its own.

Danton held on to her hand tightly.

The emptiness ran in either direction, as far as Brigit could see, and where it ran there was no snow or wind. It didn't rise high. You could see right over it, but it was much too wide to jump. On the far side she could make out the blowing outlines of trees, heavily shrouded in snow.

Beyond the trees was a softly mounded hill rising up to fill the night sky.

Brigit saw Feenix moving slowly toward the edge of the dark river, as if hypnotized.

"What are you doing? Not so close!" Danton yelled, and he reached out and grabbed hold of her. He pulled her back. "Now everybody hold hands. Don't let go, whatever you do. It doesn't seem to be so strong when we're touching."

Feenix gazed at the two of them for moment without recognition, then slowly came back to herself. "We're toast," she whispered hoarsely.

"There's got to be some way over it," Danton said stubbornly.

"Not unless you brought your wings," Feenix replied.

Danton didn't answer her. "What's that?" he said sharply. "I hear something."

Brigit heard it, too, or felt it. A thundering sound. It didn't seem to be in the air, but moved through the ground beneath their feet. It was coming closer.

"What?" Feenix cried. "What is it?"

The thing, whatever it was, burst from the trees to their left, running at them. It was four-legged and huge, and it blocked out the blowing night sky, gathering speed as it came.

CHAPTER EIGHTEEN
Hot Chocolate

When Edward stopped one more time to look into the window of the café, he saw to his surprise that one of the armchairs seemed to have changed positions. He could have sworn that just a few seconds ago it had been in the back of the room, but now it was drawn close to the window. It was covered in worn red velvet and looked deep and deliciously warm.

He turned and looked at the others again, and there was just the tail end of Feenix's long black coat flying out behind her. It didn't look as long as it used to be, maybe because she'd grown a few inches when they passed through the time rip. He wondered if he would have recognized her if he had met her on the street.

He wondered how much older *he* was. Would it just be

his body that had aged? Or had he actually jumped to some future point in his own life? He poked around in his mind trying to see if he had any new memories that he didn't remember having from before. Would he even be able to recognize memories like that if he had them or would they just seem like they had always been there? What if he had become something he didn't want to be?

What he needed was a hot chocolate and a moment to think. He took a step toward the café. The wind must have caught hold of the door, for it blew open as he approached, just wide enough to let one person through. The warmth curled out and around him and tenderly pulled him inside.

The door shut behind him. He wasn't much of a coffee drinker, but the rich aroma of ground beans lifted his spirits. A seedy, oniony scent of a toasted everything bagel filled the air and assured him that he had made the right choice. This was where he needed to be. He stamped the snow off his feet and looked around. A basket with a pair of red mittens and a red wool hat stood on the table by the door, but otherwise the place looked empty.

He approached the counter, feeling in his pocket to see if he had any money. To his relief he found a couple of crumpled dollar bills. The man behind the counter, however, had disappeared.

"Hello?" Edward called out, craning his neck to see if someone was back there. He could see an open doorway, which appeared to lead to a kitchen. "Hello? Anybody here?"

On the counter was a platter of muffins, cookies, and assorted brownies. Too many choices. A cup of hot chocolate was all he needed.

The silence was broken by a muffled sound of wailing baby. There were footsteps and then the crying stopped.

Edward called out another hello.

This time the man appeared. He was an older guy, wearing a white apron. He had oily gray hair pulled back into a ponytail and an earring in his ear. Edward wondered if he looked familiar. The thought of all those memories he couldn't quite reach made him feel slightly queasy. The man was wearing an apron and wiping his hands on a towel.

"Babies," the man said. "Now there was an invention. I'd give my two left thumbs to get hold of whoever came up with that one. Don't you agree?"

Edward was momentarily stumped. He'd never given much thought to babies one way or another. "Well, yeah. They seem like they would be a lot of work."

"Exactly!" The man paused and looked Edward over. "And for what? Why the grand campaign for everything to reproduce itself? Why all that furling and unfurling of DNA, all that winding and unwinding, all that Sturm und Drang, fuss and puss and bloody mess when everything ends up dissolving back into nothing anyway?"

Now, normally, Edward wouldn't have had much problem agreeing with a rant like this, but there was something about the guy that made him uneasy. "Does seem like an awfully big waste of energy," Edward agreed after a pause.

Ponytail smiled. "A man after my own heart. I knew it the moment I saw you walk in."

This was not, for some reason, information Edward was happy to hear.

"Hot chocolate?" the man asked, grinning.

Nor did Edward appreciate having his mind read. He hesitated. "Sure."

Ponytail disappeared into the back. Edward took the opportunity to examine his surroundings and was startled to see a tall, dark-haired young man standing at the far end of the counter, gazing at him curiously. Edward had been sure that there was no one else in the room when he came in. But he immediately liked the guy's face. It was the face of somebody who leaned on things and watched with friendly amusement.

Ponytail returned carrying two hot chocolates towering with whipped cream. He carefully placed the cups on the counter. "Hope you don't mind if I join you."

Edward said nothing. It came to him with a jolt that the guy watching from the other side of the room was himself reflected in a mirror.

Whoaaa.

"So you and your friends just out for a stroll in the breeze?"

Edward quickly tore his gaze away from his reflection. It

was too weird. He took a careful sip of the hot chocolate, feeling Ponytail's eyes on him.

"You saw us?"

"Why didn't they come in with you?"

Edward was startled. Why was that any of this guy's business? "They were in a hurry," he replied.

Ponytail shook his head. "It's lunatic, isn't it? Everybody rushing around. And then they all end up in exactly the same place they began."

Edward had so often had this exact same thought. We were nothing before we were born and that's what we went back to when we died. But somehow, he felt annoyed at the way the man was implying that the two of them were old buddies who shared a secret that everybody else was too stupid to see. He was also uncomfortable with the way the man watched him so closely every time he took a sip. Although, he had to say, the hot chocolate was good. Rich, creamy, and not too sweet. And something had been added to it that gave it a slightly peppery flavor. Cayenne, maybe.

"So where were they going?" the man asked carelessly.

Edward shrugged and took a quick glance at himself doing the same thing in the mirror. "What do you put in this?" he asked. "It's got an interesting flavor."

Ponytail smiled. "Out of this world, isn't it? Why don't you go sit down for a few minutes," he suggested, pointing at the red armchair. "You could use a little break."

Edward had to admit that the armchair looked really

inviting. He stole a glance at himself in the mirror again. The face wasn't bad looking at all. He saw with a flush of manly pride that it could have used a shave. As he turned away, he could have sworn that his reflection gave him a quick warning shake of the head.

"Well, I'd like to, but I don't think I should. I've got to—catch up with the others."

Ponytail lifted one eyebrow. "Really? Are you sure that's what you want to do? What harm would a minute or two do? Wouldn't you be more help to them if you restored your strength a little and then caught up with them?"

There was something confusing about this. How did this guy know that anybody needed any help? But it was hard for Edward to think. That armchair looked more and more inviting and the warmth of the café was beginning to make him sleepy. The guy was perfectly right. What harm would a few minutes do?

He allowed himself to be led to the armchair. From the corner of his eye he noticed his reflection following along. His posture had improved, he saw. In fact, he looked like he was in pretty good shape. Had he taken to working out?

He sank down toward the armchair and the armchair seemed to rise up to meet him.

Ponytail stood over him. He looked pleased with himself. "Don't worry. I promise you they won't get far on a night like this."

There was something creepy about having the guy loom

over him this way, but the chair was so comfy. It was soft and enfolding and cloudlike, yet it supported him perfectly, like an adjustable mattress from a late-night TV commercial. "Who are you?" Edward asked. In the back of his mind he knew this was not only a rude but also a weird question to ask, but he suddenly felt an urgent need to know.

Ponytail laughed. "I'll tell you who I am, if you tell me where your friends think they're going."

Edward tried to take a look at himself in the mirror, but he was too comfortable. He couldn't bring himself to move his head. "They're going to some meeting place."

"And where would that meeting place be?"

"The Weaver's Hill," he found himself answering. "Up past the Third Street entrance."

"Aahh. Yes. I know the spot well," the man said thoughtfully. "That gateway is certainly the closest, but hardly suitable for those of your nature. Getting past those cats requires skills your friends most certainly won't have."

Edward struggled to sit up in the chair. "Who *are* you?" he asked again. Some part of him was angry, but the rest of him seemed to have gone far, far away. He was having trouble even getting his voice to work.

"Does it really matter? When it is all just dancing atoms and mostly empty space?"

What? "Who are you?" Edward repeated.

"Well—I go by numerous names. 'Unraveler' would be most fitting for this occasion, I think."

Edward knew this sounded familiar, but now he couldn't remember why. "What does that mean?"

Ponytail shook his head. "Your lack of education is astounding. Don't they teach you people about entropy and order, about the warp and woof, about the forces that create and the dark energy that levels? I shouldn't complain, I suppose. Ignorance is one of my strongest allies. Would you mind giving me the Fetch now?" He held out his hand.

Edward stared at it. He noticed with a shudder that the man's thumb was on backward. "I don't have it," he said thickly.

"What? You must be lying. I can smell it clearly."

"I don't have it."

"Well, then, who's got it?" he demanded with impatience.

Edward didn't see why he should tell this guy anything, but found the words coming out of his mouth anyway. "Danton. Danton's got it."

"Danton is the tall one?"

"Yes." Edward made another effort to get himself up out of the chair, but his arms and legs were so heavy, and his brain was so tired.

Ponytail watched him with interest. "What do you think you're trying to do? Even if you were not such a sapless sort of fellow, even if you or any of your foolish companions happened to know the song to call them in, it would be too late."

Sapless? Who was he calling sapless? But Edward felt himself sinking. He managed to turn his head to look, one more time, for his reflection in the mirror. To his surprise, his reflection was gone.

In another moment Edward was asleep.

CHAPTER NINETEEN
The Spider

All three of them stood frozen. There was no escaping whatever it was that rushed toward them now. The creature was too big and too fast. As it drew closer Brigit saw its golden horns. They were so big, the beast would surely find a human being of no more consequence than a dandelion puff. Its hooves sent the snow flying up into the air.

With an unexpected grace for such a big creature, it came to a stop several feet away from the wide rip of nothingness that lay in front of them. Brigit saw that it was not some sort of monster, but a deer. A stag. A huge stag with golden antlers. It stood there, its great brown sides heaving, as if it had traveled here very fast and from very far away.

Danton hesitated only a moment before he stepped forward and stood in front of the stag. Brigit wondered, as always, where his courage came from. What a straight, clear line he moved in. How wonderful it must be to be like that. She went and stood beside him. The animal towered over them, but remained unmoving, merely gazing at them with its great liquid eyes.

Feenix joined them.

"What do you think it wants?" Danton whispered.

The deer continued to stare at them.

"I hope it's not hungry," Feenix said nervously.

"Well, it's not going to be interested in eating us." Danton said. "I'm pretty sure they're herbivores."

"Oh!" exclaimed Feenix. "Of course they are." She let go of Brigit's hand and stepped forward, plunging her hand into her coat pocket. She pulled out the red apple she had chosen for Edward's aunt. She held it out toward the stag.

The stag gazed at the apple with its unblinking eyes. Then it gave a short snuffle of pleasure. It stretched its great neck forward and opening its mouth, lifted the fruit delicately from Feenix's hand. For a moment it simply held the shining fruit in its mouth, then it bit down with a loud crunch. With one more crunch the apple was gone.

Brigit grabbed hold of Feenix's hand and gave it a squeeze.

"Now what?" Danton whispered.

The stag tossed its head back and gave a short snort of impatience, its breath steaming into the air. Slowly and a bit awkwardly, it lowered its hind quarters into the snow.

"What's it doing?" Feenix whispered.

"I have no idea," Danton said, puzzled.

But Brigit thought she understood. She had heard tales of the great winter stag from her grandfather, and she was pretty sure it must be here to help them. She let go of Feenix's hand and gathering the little portion of courage that was hers, she approached the deer.

It was a terrifying animal, but beautiful, as well.

"Hey!" Danton cried, following close behind her. "What are you doing?"

She ignored him and climbed clumsily onto the great animal's back. When she had seated herself as firmly as she could, she turned and looked at the other two.

"Seriously?" Feenix wailed. "Isn't this a bit much?"

"But of course she's right!" said Danton. "How do you always know this stuff, Brigit? You're brilliant. It wants to take us over the time rip, doesn't it? That's gotta be what's going on. Come on, follow me."

In a moment he had clambered up behind Brigit. Then Feenix, grumbling, climbed up behind him.

Danton wrapped his arms around Brigit's waist. How strange it was that a person could have room in herself for such different feelings. She was filled with terror yet also with a kind of yearning to lean backward into him. He had called her brilliant. Just the thought of it made her face go red.

"Are we ready?" Danton asked.

She was distracted by the feel of the animal's heart

against her legs, a deep, steady beating like a drum keeping time. And she could smell its strange smell—a mix of some things she thought she knew, grass and moss and cold water running over rocks, and then something else she couldn't name, something that made her blood race with anticipation.

The stag stood and turned to face the River of Nothingness. Brigit leaned forward and threw her arms around the creature's neck to steady herself. The others held on behind.

"Let's go!" Danton said loudly. Brigit felt him give the stag a quick kick with his heels.

They were off.

The edge of the emptiness wasn't far. The stag trotted slowly at first, then faster. The animal's muscles prepared for the jump. Brigit held her breath as it leaped into the air and sailed way higher than gravity would ever have normally permitted. On the stag, she somehow knew, there would be no question of getting stuck. There was hardly any of that fizzing, dissolving sensation, just a little in the fingertips and toes. It was only a matter of moments before they had reached the top of the arc and were coming down on the other side.

They landed with a soft *thump* and the snow flew up around them. Then the stag was off again, carrying them along the path through the trees. When they broke out of the little woods and into the open, Brigit saw, not far off in front of them, the earth rising up into a mound shaped like a loaf of bread. *The Weaver's Hill,* she thought, her heart lifting toward it. The deer did not hesitate, but raced forward. In another moment, they had begun the ascent.

From the base, the hill did not look big at all. It seemed to be just a gentle rise in the midst of the Long Meadow. But as the stag climbed, Brigit realized that the hill must be much steeper and higher than it appeared from the bottom. The path was rocky and bare of snow in some places and in other places the snow had drifted deeply. Thick stretches of woods passed by them on either side. The stag's heart beat steadily beneath their legs. When at last they reached the top, the animal stopped and knelt down, and the threesome tumbled off.

Brigit felt it right away—the thinness of the air. It took her a moment to catch her breath, then she straightened and saw that the snow had almost stopped. Overhead, the heavy darkness had begun to lift and turn to clouds, which drifted past each other like great white ships.

"Do you see this?" Feenix called out. She had stumbled a few steps away from the other two.

Brigit and Danton went over to where Feenix stood at the edge of the hill beneath the branches of a great bare oak tree. When they got to her they saw that beside her was an iron park bench. It was placed so that one might enjoy the view. Danton whistled softly.

They should have been looking out at the Long Meadow, rolling and stretching away in front of them. But that was not what they saw. They were so high up that what they saw was the whole of Brooklyn—or what remained of it—lying far below them. From here, it was easy to spot the vast swarms of glittering time foragers devouring their way through the streets. Wherever they traveled, they left behind a canyon or a rip or a river of nothingness, and as they moved from place to place the swarms grew rapidly in size. From where the threesome stood, they could see, too, the river that they had crossed over. It was rising swiftly and now lapped at the base of the great hill that they stood upon.

Brigit couldn't bear the sight of this and looked up and away. High in the oak tree, she spotted an old abandoned bird's nest wedged into the crook of a branch. Beyond it, she saw with despair that the stars were going out one by one.

"What happened to that deer?" Feenix asked suddenly. They all looked around. "Did anybody see which way it went?"

They listened for any sound, but there was only quiet.

"Well, now what?" Feenix asked quietly. "Anybody got any ideas?"

Nobody did.

"Who's got the Fetch thingie?" she asked.

Danton drew it from his pocket. Feenix reached for it, but he seemed reluctant to let it go.

"Well, are you going to let me look at it or not?" she asked impatiently.

He sighed and released it into her hand.

She turned it around, examining it slowly.

Suddenly something moved up in the branches of the oak tree. "Did you see that?" Danton asked, lowering his voice.

They all stared up through the branches, straining their eyes.

"There," Feenix hissed, pointing.

They followed her finger. Yes, there was definitely something up there.

Nobody moved. Very slowly they became aware of movements and shiftings along all the branches of the tree and in the shadows around its base.

"What's going on?" Feenix asked. "Something's happening, I think."

Brigit saw that it was like one of those puzzle pages in a children's magazine—the kind where there is a drawing of a beach or a classroom or a picnic in a forest. At first, you don't see anything except the picture in front of you, and then slowly you start to spot all the objects camouflaged in the scenery—all sorts of oddly floating things—teapots and hammers and shoes and whatever. That's the way it was here, only they weren't teapots and hammers.

Up in the branches of the tree, they were able to make out several small faces, wrinkled like dried apples, peering down at them. People, Brigit saw. Little people in woolen pants and leather jackets. Then she saw two much bigger people, sitting side by side. They had great wrinkled hairy faces and ear-lobes that hung to their shoulders. Trolls of some kind, she thought. On the branch above them was stretched a woman with a mossy, wet fish tail. Beneath the tree, Brigit made out a three-headed dog and a woman with six arms.

"Eddie's Christmas tree," Danton said in an awed whisper.

"Solstice tree," Feenix corrected him.

"Whatever," he answered softly.

Brigit saw that it was Edward's Solstice tree and more. There were several tall, thin, very *faint* looking people. You could actually see right through them, she realized. And then there were the heads sticking up out of the snow, large fierce godlike heads, whose bodies appeared to be still underground. Brigit spotted what she realized must be a minotaur—a thickly muscled man with the head of a bull. The man-bull was dressed only in some sort of loincloth and he glared at the humans and shivered in the cold. It occurred to her that what had happened here was like what happened when there was a flood or a forest fire. All the creatures went racing ahead of the disaster, looking for safety. Only now there was nowhere else to go. They were all in the same fix.

For a long moment, the young people stood staring into the shadows, while the solstice folk stared back at them.

Then Brigit felt someone pinch her arm through her coat. "It's them," Feenix croaked. "Over there by that lion with the woman's head on it."

Brigit spotted the sphinx and then she saw the two hags. They were young hags, but Brigit had no doubt they were Feenix's hags. One of them carried an awful pig-faced baby in a basket on her back. The other had only a single nostril. They seemed to be trying to stay off to the side of the crowd, as if they were not eager to be seen.

Brigit reflected that however terrifying they might once have been, they, too, had been brought low by this calamity. She didn't think there was much to fear from them now. She gave Feenix a brief pat of encouragement. Then Danton stepped forward.

He cleared his throat and stopped. Brigit knew he was trying to figure out how to address them.

"Friends—" he tried.

There was a low growl. Danton took a small step backward. It was the dog with three heads. Each head had its own long snakelike neck.

Danton tried again. "Ancient Ones, Most Honored and Powerful Beings—"

The dog stilled itself.

"As you all know, something terrible has gone wrong—"

One of the dog's heads, the black one with the white eye patch, interrupted him with a growl. *"Because of your ignorance and carelessness."*

Danton eyed the hungry-looking head unhappily. "Yes— we know and we are deeply sorry."

"Although, I'd just like to point out," Feenix interrupted,

"that your people have played their own part in this mess."
She pointed in the direction of the witches, but they had
somehow managed to shrink out of sight.

There was an angry buzzing in the crowd.

"You dare!" growled the dog. It shot one of its heads toward Feenix and bared its fangs.

"We don't have time for this," Danton said sternly. "We
have the Fetch. Show them, Feenix."

Feenix held the Fetch out for all to see.

There was a long indrawn breath among the watchers.
Then there was silence. No one shuffled a foot, no one rus-
tled a wing.

Brigit turned and saw how fast the river was rising. It was
halfway up the mountain. Brooklyn was gone. Everything
was gone. Where were her parents and her grandfather now?
she wondered fearfully. There were no lights or sound or
movement. The timelessness climbed steadily toward them.

A tall woman, cloaked in silver from head to toe, had
come out of the shadows. She floated toward them over the
snow, her feet not appearing to move at all. Brigit knew
from the stories that this meant she was of the Old Folk—a
fairy woman.

The fairy woman stopped a short distance from the
threesome. "What has happened here is, as you say, not the
fault of only one. All together must count their share of
the responsibility and then must bow to what will come.
The Fetch was not meant to be disturbed. At the end of its

season, its queen summoned her foragers back. She used herself up in doing so and the foragers fell into their long sleep, which is where they should have stayed until the Keeper came to collect the Fetch. It is our terrible misfortune that through some accident or carelessness the Fetch was moved from where it hid. Some of the sleepers awoke and were permitted to escape. Now it is too late. There is no one to sing the Calling In and our world is lost." She gestured at the rapidly rising river. "It would be best for each of us to use the time that remains in making peace with what must come."

Danton shook his head angrily. He looked at her and then around at all the others. "We've gone to a lot of trouble and come a very long way just to bow our heads and allow our world to get eaten down into a big fat nothing. Tell us about the 'Calling In.' What is it? Maybe we can figure it out."

"This is not a thing to figure out. The 'Calling In' is a song. The queen knew it. But for most beings—even of our order—it is difficult and dangerous even to listen to. I have made it my business never to hear it. There may have been a few rare humans who had the trick of carrying it, but that was in the old days. I believe there are none of those left in your generation."

Brigit suddenly drew in a breath and stood very still.

"What is it, Bridge?" Danton asked her. "Are you all right?"

She held up her hand, frowning at him. She needed him to be quiet. She was listening to something just beyond her memory. Everyone's eyes were on her. She could feel it, but she ignored them. It was so close. Maybe if she could hold the Fetch in her hands. She reached out and took it from Feenix, who started to object and then shut her mouth.

Brigit listened, straining to remember. And yes, there it was. She took a deep trembling breath and stepped forward.

"You?" said the fairy woman. She looked Brigit up and down critically.

"I don't think—" Danton began, but the woman ignored him.

"You carry the song?" she asked Brigit in a stern voice.

Brigit nodded.

The fairy woman continued to examine her closely. "You have the look upon you," she said at last. "You realize the danger?"

Brigit trembled. Whatever the danger was, it was probably better not to know.

"Everyone back! Back into the trees. She must stand alone," the fairy commanded. She pushed Danton and Feenix back. Danton tried to argue with her, but she was insistent. "If either of you tries to go to her before she is finished, she will be destroyed, and our chance will be gone. Stay beneath this oak tree. There is some protection here."

Feenix also tried to protest. "You know I don't think you realize but she doesn't—"

"Quiet! There is no time to be lost. If she has the song, let her begin."

A deep and expectant hush fell over the top of the hill. Everyone, Brigit knew, was watching her, so she held the Fetch out in front of herself. The song was as clear as a bell now in her head, and her voice, she could feel it, was waiting like a little bird right on the end of branch.

She opened her mouth. She took a breath.

And, of course, nothing came.

She thought about how Danton had called her magnificent and brilliant. She took in another big gulp of air. She opened her mouth and tried again and, still, nothing came. She was filled with fury at herself and in the heat of this fury, she pushed back her hood and lifted her face to the cold night. In doing this, she shook awake the gray spider that Aunt Kit had placed inside the folds of her scarf so many hours ago. The spider woke with a start and clambered along the difficult ridges of cloth until it reached the warm place in her neck where it could feel her blood pulse. It gave her a sharp little nip.

Startled, Brigit opened her mouth in a rounded O of surprise. Out tumbled the first notes of the song.

CHAPTER TWENTY
The Calling In

Edward slept a deep, dark sleep. For how long? It might have been hours.

But then, sometimes the space between two ticks of a watch can seem to drag on forever.

At some point, he began to dream. They were shapeless dreams, uneasy, mildly seasick things that he couldn't have put into words. They bumped up against him and floated away, and then came back in other unpleasant forms. He tried to push them off, but his arms were useless; he kept trying to lift them but they wouldn't lift. He tried to speak and his mouth was so dry nothing would come out.

I am dreaming, he assured himself. *I am in my own comfy bed at home and this is all just a dream. Very soon now, my aunt will come into the room and yank the covers off me.* But his aunt didn't appear. He struggled and struggled, but whatever it was that was pinning him down was too heavy. He could not open his eyelids, let alone move his hands or head.

After he had been in this place for what seemed several lifetimes, he heard a voice singing somewhere nearby, gentle at first, then more insistently. The voice, he knew, wanted him to follow it. But he had grown so heavy. It was the same voice he heard sometimes just as he was drifting off to sleep and his desire to go toward it was very strong. With the greatest of efforts he managed to lift himself up. But it was so dark, and when he felt for the floor with his feet, it wasn't anywhere to be found. The voice sang reassuringly. He took a step forward and although there didn't seem to be anything there, he found that he didn't fall. It made no difference if he opened his eyes wide or squeezed them tight. There was only darkness sliding by. He took another step and then another, and the voice kept moving, always a little ahead of him. After a while the voice began to climb and he followed it, walking on a stairway that wasn't there, either. Whatever was holding him up held firm, and the voice stayed steady in the darkness.

At last it began to grow lighter and he would have been encouraged by this, but at the same time, the voice was growing fainter.

"Wait!" he called out.

Suddenly to his surprise, the voice was right beside his ear. "Well, Sleepyhead, it is time." The voice was encouraging and sweet, but sad. "Wake up now. You are needed." He felt the soft brush of a kiss upon his cheek.

His eyes flew open and he was back in the café, sitting in the velvet armchair. He looked around eagerly for the owner of the voice, but there was no one there. The café was deserted. Outside, he could see the snow whirling and blowing past the lights from the window. The hands on the clock over the coffee machine said it was nearly midnight. Jolted by this surprise, he sat up. With a queasy shudder, he saw that his own reflection was still missing from the mirror.

Was it some sort of trick glass? Everything else in the room was reflected there—tables, chairs, coffee makers, the counter with the temptingly arrayed scones and cookies and muffins. Only he was not.

Who was this guy to go around stealing people's reflections?

Edward looked again at the hands on the clock. They were moving way too fast. He had to find the others. He stood up and buttoned his coat and pulled on his hat. He strode to the door and threw it open.

He knew he needed to get up the hill, but the wind seemed to know exactly where he wanted to go. It came roaring at him from the right and slashing at him from the left. He couldn't tell if it was still snowing or if the wind was only blowing the snow around. Sometimes the air would clear for seconds at a time. Then the wind would come whipping at him, blowing the snow up and blinding him.

He did his best to walk in a straight line, but he hadn't gone far when he nearly put his foot into one of those hideous cracks in the time fabric. Although it was dizzyingly without bottom or direction, it hadn't yet grown very wide. He was able to go around it before the bees noticed him, but when he had left it behind, another great gust of wind came raging at him from out of nowhere, and he was knocked to his knees. He rose quickly, thinking he heard voices and laughter. Could it be Feenix and the others? Or was it something else, something teasing him? He didn't know whether to go toward the sounds or away from them. So he chose a middle route, always aiming uphill, in the direction of where the park should be.

It was a terrible journey. Between the wind and the rips in the time fabric and the laughing voices, he despaired a hundred times. But whenever he would decide to pack it in and just lie down in the snow, he would hear the guy from the café taunting him—*why bother if it's all only dancing atoms and empty space?* Whatever unraveling doom the greasy dude had in mind for the world, Edward was not with the program. He needed to catch up with the others. He pushed and struggled and kept on going.

When he reached the Third Street entrance at last, he was so pleased and surprised by himself, he didn't even notice the missing panthers. He went right on through, and with renewed energy passed the snowbound playground and the old stone toll-keeper's booth.

When he reached the silent river of emptiness, the wide unmoving ribbon of nothing, he stopped in despair and knew himself for a fool.

There was no getting across this dark river. It all came down to the same old thing. Soon there would be nothing left to stand upon. Not an atom, not a quark, not a past, not a future. What difference if he dissolved now or a hundred years from now? It had all been empty space to begin with, and he was the same old bumblehead he had always been.

All he had left to do was wait.

He stood at the edge of the river and closed his eyes. He hoped it wasn't going to hurt very much. The wind had died down and it grew very quiet. He could smell the fresh cold smell of snow and the clean scent of pine trees somewhere nearby. He imagined it would have been a beautiful morning if it had ever come. He was surprised he didn't feel more tired.

Very gently, right next to his ear, the voice he knew and did not know, said, *"In your pocket."* He felt again the brush of the kiss.

He opened his eyes and looked around wildly. But there was no one there.

The snow had stopped. The moon had risen. The black timeless river threw back no light, but a little farther downstream, he thought he saw a swarm of time bees working hungrily away. Edward frowned and put his hand in his pocket. Something round and silky met his palm. He drew the object out and stared at it curiously in the moonlight.

He didn't recognize it at first and then he did. It was one of those little balls of spider thread. The ones his aunt kept on the windowsill. How had that gotten in there? Then he remembered how she had stuck her hand in his pocket, supposedly to find his gloves. The silky thread was slightly sticky to the touch and seemed to give off a faint light of its own. As he stared at it uncomprehendingly he noticed a stranger thing yet. Shooting right out from the side of the ball, stretched tautly, was a thread of silk. He could see it shimmering in the air in front of him and then vanishing into the darkness along the bank beside the river. He tugged on it lightly and it tugged back. He tugged on it again and it tugged a little harder. There was no mistaking what it wanted from him. Slowly at first, he began to follow where it led, rolling the thread up around the ball as he went. After a while he went a little faster, and then faster yet. The impossible thought came into his head that here, where he walked, there *were* minutes, but beside him in the river of nothingness there were none. He wasn't sure how long he went along like this, but then abruptly the thread changed direction.

If he followed it now, it was going to take him right out over the oily bottomless nothing.

"Why am I not surprised?" he said to whoever was listening.

Was it some kind of trap? Somehow he felt sure that the

voice that had awoken him would not purposely lead him astray. He peered into the darkness and saw that were no bees foraging here. He could see a swarm of them farther ahead, but for the moment, they had left this area behind. Still, what could possibly stop him from falling if he did what was being asked of him? He peered anxiously into the darkness and then he found what might be the answer to the riddle. There was something showing through the surface of the river. Something glowing faintly. A stepping-stone-sized, snow-covered island that the bees had missed.

He hesitated, but felt the thread tugging beneath his fingers. He took a breath. What was there to lose? It was all going to end the same way sooner or later, anyway. He put his foot out and stepped over the yawning dark and when his foot came down, to his great astonishment, it came down on something solid. He let out a gasp of relief. He couldn't see what he was standing on, but it felt like a rock—a slippery yet solid four-dimensional rock. Carefully, he brought his other foot along to join the first and he stood there and felt along the string. It gave another tug and he peered into the darkness. Was that another foot-sized island just ahead? Yes. He was sure of it. The string tugged beneath his finger. But this one was farther away. For this one he would have to jump. He hesitated. He bent his knees. He measured the distance. He hesitated once more and as he stood considering his own klutziness, the string tugged again and the silky ball slipped from his grasp.

"No!" he cried. Now, without thinking it over, he leaped from the rock, stretching, stretching his arm toward the falling thread. It met his fingertips and he snatched it out of the air. He closed his eyes as he continued to fall forward into the darkness.

Danton wanted, more than he had ever wanted anything, to go and stand beside her. Somehow, he understood that if he did, all would be lost. He made himself stay where he was, and it seemed to him that Brigit's voice was like a river dammed up in a narrow place until it had, at last, built up enough pressure to burst through. It came out stuttering and muddy at first, but as the leaves and twigs and stones got pushed out of the way, it came pouring into the air. If the song had words, it was in a language he didn't know, but his heart swelled with pride as he listened. Her voice was magnificent, bell-like, liquid, and strong. The melody was simple, but the song was commanding. He could tell that she was calling to someone.

The foragers began to arrive.

They moved more slowly now, almost drunkenly, like bees who have been feasting for a long, long summer afternoon. They came from all directions at once and, maybe because they were swollen and full, Danton was now able to get a better look at them. They looked like the tiniest of seed pearls and each one trailed a bright green comet's tail of light. Brigit held the Fetch out in front of her and the foragers approached it in lazy maneuverings until they were nearly home. At the last moment, each one woke up and shot forward, vanishing instantaneously through what might have been a tiny hole in the Fetch's side.

Danton watched closely, but the foragers seemed to ignore Brigit and only be interested in entering the stone. When the notes of her song had climbed so high they were nearly out of hearing, the song fell and began again. The melody returned almost to the beginning, although not quite. And now, from out of nowhere, Danton heard another voice join hers. An expression of surprise came over her face, but she hesitated for only the briefest of moments and then went on. He looked around anxiously, but he could not see the singer. The new voice didn't seem to be male or female or exactly human, either. Brigit kept the melody while the second voice held the harmony. They wound around and around each other, playful and quick. Now the foragers came pouring in. Once again, the song went up until it could rise no more and then dropped and began again.

On this third round there were more than two voices, but it was hard to tell how many. These were high and silvery and childlike, and in and around them there was the sound of laughter. The foragers were coming in fast and furious now. The air was full of them. They seemed to jostle each other merrily until they reached the Fetch and vanished inside. It frightened Danton to see how pale Brigit had grown. Her arms, holding the Fetch out, seemed to tremble as the throng of foragers grew. But so far as he could tell, she hadn't gotten any older and her voice remained steady. On the fourth round, the foragers were so thick, they clotted the air and had to wait for their turn to enter the Fetch. They seemed to grow angry and impatient with each other and the music darkened with their mood. A sound of pipes and drums joined the voices. The laughter faded and an undertone of urgency crept into the music.

Danton couldn't hold himself still. "I can hardly see her anymore," he whispered anxiously to Feenix. "Can you? Can you tell if she's all right?"

"She's all right," Feenix hissed. "You can tell from her voice. Be quiet!"

Danton fell back into silence. There was a sound of distant swords clashing, metal on metal, and the drumbeat pounded louder and louder, more like a battle call than a symphony. The music grew more discordant and confused but kept on. Finally, Danton could hear nothing of Brigit's voice in the noise.

"I've got to go in there!" he said at last. "She'll be trampled or killed." But Feenix grabbed his arm.

"No! You can't! Her only chance is not to move. You heard what the silver woman said. You have to let her finish it."

Danton shook his head angrily but stayed where he was.

At last a high whistle screamed through the air, and a moment later there was a tremendous bang.

Danton shuddered and felt Feenix reach out and give his hand a quick squeeze.

The singing voices could be heard again from within the still-thick cloud. No longer high and silvery, they filled the air with a solemn richness. There was triumph in the voices, and sorrow. Some were as deep as echoes in caverns and some were rich and golden as trumpets.

And through them all, steady and sweet, Danton was sure he heard Brigit.

"That's her!" Feenix said. "Can you see her?"

But he couldn't, not yet. The mob of foragers was thinning. They continued to vanish inside the Fetch. One by one the voices that accompanied Brigit's reached the sky and continued on up and did not return.

Then, at last only Brigit's voice was left and it rang out bell-like and true.

"There she is!" Feenix cried, but Danton didn't need to be told this. He had already shaken himself free and was running toward her.

Brigit stood as they had last seen her. She was very pale, but still standing with arms out, the Fetch in her hands. The last foragers disappeared inside and the final note of the Calling In song died away.

Danton pulled up short in front of her. He wanted to

touch her, but he didn't dare. She looked so still and far away. "Are you all right?"

She looked at him startled, as if she had forgotten all about him, all about everything that had come before. She studied his face carefully as if she were trying to remember not just who he was, but *what* he was. Then, at last, she smiled.

"Danton," she said. "It's you."

He'd been waiting for this voice for so long. It was an ordinary voice, a little shy, but with a ripple of gladness in it. He didn't think he'd ever heard anything nicer. He found he couldn't say a word.

"Yes, I'm all right," she assured him. "Are they all in?"

He looked around. The air was quiet and there was no sign of the bees. Danton also realized that the silver lady and the three-headed dog and the tree people and the witches and all the rest had vanished. Where could they have gone? He wondered if they had been frightened back into hiding. All that seemed to be left were the girls and him, the oak tree, and the very top of the hill where they stood, which seemed to give out a strange, faint light of its own.

"There's nothing else out there," Feenix said. "Everything's gone. But it's weird. Don't you feel like we're on a stage? Like there's something out there watching us?"

"Yes," said Danton. "Something's going to happen. I can feel it. Can't you? Something's listening to us."

"Do you think it's this Keeper dude?" she asked nervously.

"I don't know," Danton replied. "All we can do is wait."

So they waited. It was impossible to tell how much time, if any, passed as they stood there on the top of the hill. It was getting colder and they all drew closer together. When they were almost touching, shoulder to shoulder, they heard a noise. It was the sound of something moving toward them, a panting breath growing nearer and nearer.

"Where in this butt-faced blankety-blankety blizzard have you been? I've been looking all over for you guys!"

CHAPTER TWENTY-ONE
The Doorway

Feenix almost didn't recognize him now that he was however much older than he used to be, but she certainly wasn't going to show him she was impressed or anything. "That's what I love about you," she said. "The way you always manage to show up after everybody else has done all the work."

"What do you mean? Which work are you talking about? What happened?" Eddie asked.

"Nothing much," Feenix said. "We managed to fight off two panthers, cross a mile-wide bottomless crack in the time fabric, climb the equivalent of Mount Kilimanjaro, make small talk with the ornaments from your aunt's Christmas tree, and call all the foragers back into the Fetch."

"You were talking to the ornaments on my aunt's tree?" He looked around sharply.

Danton jumped in. "You should have seen them—there was a minotaur and Feenix's witches again and then a silver fairy lady. The Old Ones, I guess. I think they've camouflaged themselves again. They're really good at it. Something must have scared them off."

Feenix thought he was probably right. There was a lot to be scared of. So why was Edsel smiling?

"Let me see the stone," he said.

Brigit, Feenix noticed, hadn't moved since Eddie had arrived. She was staring at him weirdly. Now she brought the Fetch toward her chest protectively and stared at him.

"She was the one who called them in. She got her voice back," Danton said.

"That's great," Eddie said. He smiled at Brigit. "The stone must be very full. Could I see it?"

Now that Feenix was looking at Eddie more closely, she decided there was something else that wasn't right with him. It was more than the fact that he was a few years older. What could it be? "How did you get over that big rip at the bottom of the hill?" she asked him suspiciously.

"That's a crazy story. I'll tell you later. I think I've got an idea. Give me the stone."

"You look different," Feenix said. "What happened to you?"

"We all look different. It's been some night. C'mon," he coaxed. He held his hand out and took a step toward Brigit.

She took a step backward, her eyes fixed on his hand.

Now Feenix saw it, too. "What happened to your thumb?"

He pulled his thumb inside his fisted fingers and made a face of impatience. "It's fine. I twisted it when I was climbing up here. Stop fussing. We don't have time for this. Let me see the Fetch."

"You're not Eddie. Who are you?"

Danton had been looking back and forth at the three of them, seeming puzzled. "What do you mean he's not Eddie? Who else would he be?"

"Look at him. Don't you see? He's all—I don't know— backward."

"He's all backward? What are you—?" Danton peered at Eddie more closely and now he, too, must have seen something, because he fell silent.

"Whatever happens, Brigit, don't give him the Fetch," Feenix said.

Brigit nodded and took another step backward.

"Where's Eddie?" Feenix demanded. "What did you do to him?"

There was a short silence while Eddie-who-was-not-Eddie must have been considering his next move. "Not a thing," he said at last. "What was done, he did to himself. By now, he will be—gone."

There was silence while everyone took this in. Then Feenix said through clenched teeth, "You're that Unraveler guy, aren't you?"

Eddie-who-was-not-Eddie gave a small bow.

"Did you let those time bees eat him?" Feenix cried.

"The foragers are hardly under my control. Though I must say, I couldn't have done better work myself. By now, your friend will certainly have been gathered into the Sameness. Just as you soon will be. You will be returned to where there is neither time nor space nor light and you will rest, at last. It is what your wise teachers know we all seek."

"What?" Feenix shouted. "What do you know about what our teachers teach us?"

Not-Eddie gave a little laugh. "Think back. Did I not hear one of your teachers talking just the other day about the true and final state?"

"You're just blabbering," Feenix snapped. "Who would let you into our school?"

Now Danton spoke up unhappily. "Mr. Ross. He's talking about Mr. Ross. He got off on a tangent the other day about entropy, about how things always move toward losing heat energy and getting all disorganized."

Not-Eddie gave him a nod of approval. "Exactly. The wise among you spend their lives searching for the homeward path. The wise know that nothing is really solid. Things take on form and shape for the briefest of times and then return to dust. Everything carries within itself the means to its own return. I am only here to help things along. Why struggle so pointlessly? Aren't you tired?"

It was true, Feenix realized. She was very tired. The guy's voice was so soothing and hypnotic. Mr. Ross and everything else of their past lives seemed very far away. She made an effort to remember what it was she had left behind down there in Brooklyn, what it was that had seemed so important. But even as she struggled she found her memories were all dissolving. She started to turn toward the other two, hoping they could help her, but her arms and legs didn't seem to be following along.

"Now if you will hand me the Fetch, I will gladly dispose of it for all our sakes. We wouldn't want anyone getting hold of that honey and making more mischief, would we?" He held out his hand to Brigit.

Feenix was able at last to turn to face Brigit, but now she seemed to be looking at her from far, far away. It reminded Feenix of getting gas at the dentist while she had a cavity filled. *Yes, maybe it would be better if she just handed it to him.*

Brigit, however, made no move to hand the Fetch over. Feenix could see how she was staring at the Unraveler's backward thumb and how hard she was struggling not to give in to his voice. She managed to actually take another step away from him and then she shook her head.

The man's voice grew impatient. "You meek ones. I don't know why you're always the worst."

Brigit took another step backward.

Yes! Good for her, Feenix thought admiringly. She shook herself and suddenly another of Mr. Ross's schticks came into her head, the one about how wonderfully improbable everything was. How the odds were totally against their ever having come into being. Yet here they were. How they all ought to make the most of it and not waste their time. Would Mr. Ross want them all to just lie down and be dissolved back into the sameness again? No bleeping way.

Feenix came wide awake with a start and saw that the Unraveler was advancing upon Brigit in a smooth, rapid glide over the snow.

From the corner of her eye, she noticed that Danton had woken up, too. It was Brigit, she knew, who had broken the spell. Danton was moving quickly, running backward, his hands up in the air. "To me, Brigit!" he shouted. "Throw it to me!"

"Don't look in his eyes!" Feenix yelled. "He's hypnotizing you! Throw it to Danton."

Brigit took a shuddering breath and tore her gaze away from the man coming toward her. She threw the Fetch to Danton.

Danton caught it easily and moved off as far as he could.

"Now, children, you are wasting valuable time. And what's the point? Where can you possibly go?" said the Unraveler.

He looked around at the three of them, calculating something. Then he threw back his head and opened his mouth. It seemed to be hingeless, like a snake's mouth. The inside of it was very dark and much bigger than the inside of anybody's mouth ought to be.

Out of this mouth rose a spinning funnel of wind and dust. As the funnel twisted itself out of the open throat and thrust upward into the air, it began to pull the false Eddie inside out like a glove. Several seconds passed while the twister disposed of the Unraveler's body in this manner, but no sooner was the job done than the funnel began spinning over the ground toward Danton. The sound that came with it was a roar of white noise. The funnel grew rapidly wider and taller, sucking at him as it drew nearer.

Feenix watched in fascinated horror, then threw up her hands and yelled, "To me! Throw it to me."

The twister nearly upon him, Danton turned. He threw the Fetch up as high and far as he was able. Over it went, barely clearing the sucking vortex and then it dropped down, down into Feenix's waiting hands.

"I've got it!" she yelled.

With a roar of fury, the wind funnel began to turn itself around, looking for its opponent. It was clumsy and slow in this form, but all of them felt how its pull was growing stronger, like a monstrous industrial-strength vacuum cleaner.

"I'm open!" yelled Danton, but the funnel shifted its bulk to block him and Feenix threw the stone back to Brigit.

Back and forth they went, back and forth, but the twister kept growing in strength and seemed tireless. Feenix knew that she, Danton, and Brigit were not. Just as she was wondering how much longer they could go on like this, she saw that the funnel had slowed itself to one spot. It was turning like a top, levitating just off the ground, and its sound had diminished to a low, unpleasant grinding noise. The Fetch was in Danton's hand. He stood near the edge of the cliff, bouncing alertly on his feet, waiting for the funnel to approach him. But this time it didn't. Instead it turned sharply toward Brigit.

"What's it doing?" Danton yelled in alarm. "Watch out, Brigit! Get out of its way."

But where could she go? In the next instant, the thing swelled itself out again and with a giant snort of glee, sucked Brigit right into its interior. For a moment Feenix could see Brigit's pale, terrified face going around and around. Then she was sucked farther into the churning snow and dust. She disappeared from sight.

"No!" screamed Danton. "Let go of her!" He was already running toward the twister.

"Don't!" warned Feenix. "It's a trick. That's exactly what he's hoping you'll do, don't you see?"

Danton stopped and turned toward Feenix. "I have to go in after her. You take the Fetch and just keep moving. I've got to get her out."

Before Feenix had time to object, Danton had tossed the Fetch in the air. Feenix caught it in her hands and Danton dashed forward and leaped right into the heart of the funnel.

The whirlwind paused for a moment, listing a little to

the side, as if Danton's weight had sent it off-balance. Then it righted itself and began slowly to turn again, making an uneven grating and grinding noise.

Was it digesting Danton? It teetered slowly from side to side like a top again, then began to pick up some speed.

It now turned its attention back to Feenix.

She moved slowly backward, clutching the Fetch. She felt how it had lost a lot of its hardness. It had a fuzzy ripeness to it, like a peach with a little give to the touch. It was warm, too, and smelled sweeter than ever. She glanced down and saw that it was giving off a faintly rosy glow.

Anxiously, Feenix turned to see what was behind her. She was approaching the edge of the cliff. She looked back at the funnel and saw only spinning wisps of dust and snow, but the thing was making its grinding noise, stuttering and stopping. She wouldn't want to have Danton for dinner either. Was this demon sucker intending to devour her? Or just push her off into the Nothing? Feenix took another step backward. Probably either way would work just as well for it. She remembered the smooth and bottomless Nothing with a wave of nausea. No. She'd rather be eaten. At least she'd have a chance to fight. One more step and she'd be over the edge, but for now she could still feel the solid cliff beneath her feet. She dug in and stood her ground.

The wind rumbled gleefully as if tickled by her defiance. She felt herself being dragged inexorably into it.

"Eat my socks!" she yelled and held on tight to the Fetch as if its weight could keep her anchored.

Then she heard someone calling her name. The voice came to her only faintly through the screeching and rushing of the wind. Was it Danton? Or Brigit? The voice was saying something to her, but the wind picked up speed as if it were trying to drown out the words.

But now she heard it again, even louder. Someone was calling her name and whoever it was yelled, "Throw it to me! TO ME!"

Feenix stood frozen trying to understand where the voice was coming from, and then she saw a movement over to the right by the oak tree. She leaned forward peering through the dust and wind and blowing snow. She could just make out a figure waving at her, arms up in the air.

Was it possible? It looked like Dweebo—the non-backward semi-grown-up Dweebo.

"Throw me the Fetch. I see what we have to do!"

What did he mean? Was he trying to trick her? What if it was another fake?

"Look! Over here!"

He was pointing up in the direction of the oak tree, at what she had no clue. Its branches were bare except for a raggedy bird's nest with its bottom half fallen out.

"You see? It's got to be the doorway. My thread goes right there."

If it was him, he must have lost his mind.

But the funnel for just a moment seemed to hesitate and grow quieter as if it were listening.

"Are you working on your suntan?" the new Eddie yelled. "You are slower than cement! Throw it!"

She was slower than cement? How dare he? Now the funnel seemed to come awake again. As it moved toward her, its black mouth yawned open. For a second, Feenix thought she caught a glimpse of something or someone tumbling around inside, but she had no time to look closer. She lifted her arm back and blindly pitched the stone as high and hard as she could.

Up the Fetch flew. The funnel gave a roar of fury and jumped back, twisting to watch its prey flying into the air overhead. To Feenix's surprise, the Fetch cleared the top of the twister—just barely—and then came tumbling down the other side. She could hardly believe it when Eddie caught it neatly in his open hands. She thought again of Mr. Ross and his story about improbable odds.

Only now did the funnel seem to realize what had happened. It gave an ear-splitting scream of frustration and gathered itself together again, shrinking, but growing denser and tighter. Then it began to skim rapidly over the ground in Eddie's direction.

"Watch out!" Feenix yelled in warning, but he was paying no attention to her or the twister. He was staring upward. He held the Fetch lightly in his fingertips pulled close to his chest. He seemed to be waiting for something.

But what? What did he think he was doing?

Feenix followed his gaze up into the bare branched oak tree. Something was happening to the beat-up bird's nest, which hung out over the void. It looked like a ribbon of golden flame was racing around its rim. The twister was fast approaching Eddie, but he continued to ignore it. He kept his eyes fixed on the nest. In seconds the whole thing was engulfed in the white-hot fire, and soon the branch it hung from was burning as well. The twigs and mud of the nest seemed to melt with the heat, while the branch crumbled into ash and fell away. In a few moments, all that was left was a molten golden hoop suspended high in the darkness, hanging over the Nothing.

Eddie, of all the improbable klutzes in the world, bent his knees, held the Fetch out in front of himself, and sighted toward the sky.

The twister was right there on his behind.

"Go for it! Shoot!" Feenix shouted at him.

He took no time to turn around, but she thought she saw him nod. He bounced slightly, as if testing his knees, then he jumped nearly straight upward, launching the Fetch into the air. The Fetch flew toward the sky, glowing brighter and brighter, a small fiery tail shooting from its back as it approached its destination. Up it arched. Then down it came on the other side. It dropped effortlessly through the golden hoop and vanished.

There was an immediate and deafening silence. The

twister came to a stop right where it was. For a moment it shuddered and wobbled, and then it crumpled in upon itself. In the next instant, the little island they stood on grew as dark as the inside of a boot. Feenix couldn't see her hand in front of her face.

"You still there?" she called out to Eddie.

"Yes," he called out. "I'm over here."

The only thing still visible was the hoop hanging suspended in the air over their heads. It was shrinking rapidly. Soon it was only the size of a bracelet. Then a golden wedding ring.

The smaller it grew, the hotter and brighter it seemed to burn. In the next moment its rim was so shrunken that its sides had melted together. It was no bigger than a tiny golden bead, a bead that blazed so brightly it was burning a hole straight into the darkness.

"Watch out!" Eddie yelled.

Watch out for what?

The explosion that followed was unbearable—blinding and deafening and suffocating all at once. There was no time. Whether Feenix was thrown to the ground or up into the air, she had no clue.

CHAPTER TWENTY-TWO
Aunt Kit's Party

When Edward finally gathered the courage to uncover his head and open his eyes, the sun was just beginning to lift over the eastern edge of the world. The sky was flushed gold and rose in that corner. The rest of the heavens were a tender robin's egg blue.

He stood up and wondered why the ground looked so close. Then he realized, with a pang of regret, that he was shorter again. Feenix, not far off, was examining her arms and legs and grumbling.

"Rat crud," he thought he heard her say. She stamped her boots and brushed off her long coat. Her dark hair was wild, and when she caught sight of him staring at her, she glared back.

He looked away and, to his enormous relief, saw Danton

and Brigit untangling themselves from the pile they had landed in together. Danton unfolded himself and helped Brigit to her feet. She stood there, once again freckled and short, gazing quietly around.

Edward saw they were standing on top of a small snow-covered hill. The Long Meadow rolled away white and untouched in every direction. There wasn't a footstep or birdtrack to be seen. Along every tree branch ran a sugary ruffle of glistening snow. Beyond the trees rose the still sleeping buildings of Brooklyn. The air had that clean, bright smell that comes the morning after a snowstorm, as if the whole world were new again.

For a long time they all just stood there checking things out, getting used to themselves again. Then finally, Danton spoke up. "Well, we did it, didn't we? Looks like everything's back in its place. Everybody all right?"

"Hunky dory," Feenix answered.

"Eddie? You OK?'

"I'm good," Edward told him.

Edward noticed how when Danton turned to Brigit, he hesitated for just a moment. "Brigit? Are you all right?"

Brigit couldn't seem to take her eyes off the morning—the trees and the white-blanketed hills and the great arch of the blue sky, but finally she turned to him and she smiled.

Danton waited again, but still she said nothing. At last he smiled at her gently. "Well, let's go home then. I'm starving!"

Down the hill they went and then across the open

meadow, plowing through the deep powdery snow. It was slow walking. As the sun rose, the park glittered and glistened, but everyone seemed to be wrapped up in their own thoughts. Edward kept running over the night in his mind, trying hard to remember what it was that had happened.

At last, when they arrived at where the trees began, Feenix broke the silence. "Did you see—when that thing exploded—did you see that—?"

"Yes!" Danton exclaimed. "It was amazing, right? Like a giant circus tent without the tent. All those lights—"

Feenix interrupted in surprise. "No—that wasn't what I saw at all." She seemed to struggle with some thought. "It was a bird, I think, and it was on fire."

She turned to Edward. "Wasn't that it, Edward? Did you see the bird?'

Edward didn't think what he'd seen was either a bird or a circus tent. It had looked something like a giant glistening spider web, but this image seemed mixed up with all the other memories of the night, and as he struggled to un-tangle them, a big blob of melting snow fell from a branch and landed on the back of his neck.

"Hey!" he protested, shaking his fist at the tree. Then, while Feenix was laughing, another heap of snow landed with a wet plop on *her* head. Edward started laughing at *her* and she picked up a handful of snow and threw it at him and, in a minute, they were all running toward the

Ninth Street park exit, chasing one another and throwing snowballs.

When they tumbled out onto the sidewalk outside the park, they all stopped to catch their breath. No one seemed to look at anybody else and nobody seemed exactly ready to say good-bye and go home. It was then that Edward remembered his aunt's party.

"You're all coming tonight, right?" he blurted out, not knowing what had come over him. He had never invited anybody to this party before. "My aunt won't let me hear the end of it if you don't," he added lamely.

When Edward walked into the kitchen, the pots were already simmering on the stove. The air tasted of cinnamon and confectioner's sugar. His aunt stood with her back to him, stirring a pot. He had been working nervously on some reasonable-sounding story all the way home, but when she turned and he opened his mouth, she merely said, "Did you bring the vanilla beans?"

He stared at her in confusion for a moment; then he reached into his pocket and felt around. He pulled out the clear plastic tube with the two beans rattling around inside and handed it to her.

She took it with a nod. "Just in time for the custard. You're a mess," she said. "Take off your wet clothes and then come take over here. You'll stir the pot while I get the pie crusts going. When the custard is done, you'd better go out and shovel."

Edward was extremely relieved that she wasn't going to make him explain where he'd been. He wasn't exactly sure he knew.

She kept him hard at work all morning and afternoon—shoveling the sidewalks, helping in the kitchen, moving furniture around, bringing out plates, bowls, and silverware. It felt like too much effort to try to think about what had taken place, and he was actually glad to have so many little ordinary tasks to attend to. He kept expecting something to happen. But nothing did. Everything was back to normal. An hour before the party, she released him from bondage and let him go upstairs for a shower and a nap.

When he awoke, he could hear that things were already in full swing. The front doorbell kept ringing, and scraps of music came floating up to his room. His aunt always asked anyone who played an instrument to bring it, and he could hear someone with a fiddle and someone banging on the piano and a not very good harmonica player trying to keep up.

Halfway down the stairs Edward stopped, reluctant to go any farther. There would be all that chitting and chatting. He gazed at the scene. The house was filling up fast. His aunt kept up an exhaustingly busy social life. There were friends and neighbors from the block, students and cooking colleagues, people from her book group, her African Dance class, and the chorus she sang with. Probably half the Park Slope Food Co-Op was there, too.

Every spare inch of the house was hung with sweet-smelling pine boughs. The tree, with its bizarre collection of ornaments, was lit from top to bottom. Edward stuck his head out over the banister and saw the long table draped with the red tablecloth. Every inch was covered with platters and bowls and baskets of food. On this one day in the year, his aunt permitted friends to bring fish dishes and even roast turkeys or chickens if the proper thanksgiving prayers were made. These forbidden dishes were always tempting to Edward, but then there would also be the potato pancakes and the blintzes, the roasted pumpkin soup, blacked-eyed peas, and collard greens. On the table right beneath him he could see the plates of cheeses and hummus and jeweled arrangements of pineapple, berries, and sliced melon. Next to them were the loaves of homemade bread, the fresh butter, and the hot little puffed triangles of spinach and feta. And, of course, there would be the desserts, a mountainous bowl of whipped cream encircled by pies—cherry, apple, pumpkin, and pecan. Beside these were the pfeffernusse and the lemon squares and the plates of special solstice sugar cookies in the shapes of moons and stars, babies and kings, and reindeer.

Edward caught a brief glimpse of his aunt flitting and

bubbling, kissing and commanding. The mistletoe ball hung from the passageway between the dining area and the kitchen, so people were constantly stopping there to kiss and embrace, friends and strangers alike.

It seemed to Edward that everything was as it always had been. He drew a long breath of relief. It was wonderful to think tornadoes were not going to appear from out of nowhere and drag him in, that no rivers of darkness were going to open up at his feet.

When the doorbell rang again, Edward saw Danton come in and hang up his coat and begin to make his way through the mob.

"Hey, Danton, man! Over here!"

Danton spotted Edward and waved, then came up the stairs two at a time. He sat down on the steps next to Edward. "This is some party! Thanks for inviting me." Then he caught sight of the food in the dining room. He let out a gasp. "Don't pinch me, anyone. If I'm dreaming I don't want to ever wake up."

The doorbell chimed again and there was a rush of fresh cold air as a small group of people came in. Brigit was right in the center of them. *Must be her parents and her grandfather,* Edward thought. He remembered something about his aunt saying she was going to invite them. Brigit was holding what looked like a plate of fresh-baked brownies. They all stood there a little awkwardly and then his aunt went sailing over. She threw her arms around the elderly man and began talking to him excitedly, though Edward couldn't hear what she was saying over the noise. When she was done, she stopped and introduced herself to the other two, and then she took the brownies from Brigit and kissed her. She pointed up to where Edward and Danton sat on the stairs. Shepherding the adults in front of her, she left Brigit standing there alone.

Edward nudged Danton, who was still gaping at the food.

"What is it?" he said impatiently. "I'm very busy. This is going to require some planning. I'm wondering if I shouldn't start with a piece of that cherry pie, you know, just to get the gastrointestinal juices flowing. I'll want my digestion in peak form."

"Look who's here," Edward said.

Danton turned impatiently, but when he saw who it was, he froze.

"It looks like she brought her parents and her grand-father, but my aunt's already got hold of them," Edward said. "I think her grandfather sings in my aunt's chorus."

"Oh, yeah," Danton said uncertainly. "Don't I remember her telling us that? But when was that?"

"It was yesterday, I think," Edward said.

"Are you having trouble remembering stuff?"

"Are you?"

"Yeah, well, sort of. It all seems so much longer ago than yesterday. It was some night, wasn't it?"

"Yes," Edward answered slowly. "Yes, it was."

"Well, anyway, I guess everything's back to normal and that's the most important thing, right?" Danton said.

"Sure," Edward replied.

Neither one of them seemed inclined to say anything more on the subject, and this was fine with Edward. Danton hadn't taken his eyes off of Brigit. "All right, do me a solid. Let me go down to her by myself. You know how shy she is. I'll bring her over to the table in a few minutes. Meet us there."

"No problem," Edward said, trying to hide his smile. "You go get her and I'll find you by the food in a little while."

Danton unfolded himself from the steps and took a deep breath. "Okay. I'll see you in a bit."

"Right."

Danton crossed the room slowly, in his giraffelike way. Edward saw how when Brigit spotted him, she lit up like someone had switched on a little lamp.

She started to move toward him.

Edward was startled by a loud voice in his ear. "Well, here you are! Still sitting around like a giant tree sloth, I see."

Where had she come from? She was standing on the step below him in all her usual over-decorated glory. Today, she had her hair in some elaborate holiday hairdo with lots of sparkling barrettes. She had taken off her black coat for the occasion, but she was wearing her boots and something red and very short and all glittery with tiny black mirrors. The whole thing looked more like a costume than a party dress. Her strangely off-kilter eyes shone with excitement.

"Like it?" she asked and twirled around. "Very sixties, don't you think?"

"I wouldn't know. I wasn't born yet."

She sat down next to him.

"You know, Edward, I keep trying to remember, but I can't seem to—" Here she trailed off and stared into the distance. "I guess I'm just tired. It was a long night last night, wasn't it?"

He was staring at her. Something was different. What was it?

"Why are you looking at me like that?"

"Nothing," he said, shaking his head.

She gave him a puzzled once-over, then turned back to the crowd.

Danton and Brigit were standing there at gazing each other. The crowd just went around them good-naturedly as if they were some sort of natural scenic wonder that had appeared suddenly in the middle of the living room.

Brigit smiled. Danton smiled. Neither of them seemed capable of speech.

"They can't go on like this," Feenix said. "It can't be healthy. All those hormones backing up in their bloodstreams. It'll weaken their immune systems. KISS HER ALREADY!" she yelled down to the crowd.

Danton looked up, confused, trying to see where the

voice had come from. While he was searching the room, Brigit ducked and slipped away into the crowd.

"What is it with her, do you think?" Feenix asked.

Since Edward had no clue, he did not bother to reply.

"It's supposed to snow again tonight," she said.

"More shoveling," he groaned. But the thought was actually not unpleasant. Not that he wasn't glad to be here inside the warm house, with a fire going and people playing music and the table covered with food.

Beside him, Feenix let out a weird half noise.

He looked at her questioningly. Her mouth gaped open.

"Please tell me that is not what I think it is," she whispered finally.

When he followed her gaze, he saw she was staring down at the dessert table.

"What?"

"Where'd that gingerbread house come from?"

Without another word she stood and plunged down the stairs. When he caught up with her she was standing there, staring at it with the strangest expression on her face.

It stood on a silver platter sprinkled with fluffy snow-white coconut flakes. The house was, as always, a thing of awe-striking over-the-topness. The eaves of the roof were outlined in the glassy jeweled colors of Life Savers—yellow, red, green, orange—while the roof itself was slated with squares of chocolate. The chimney was built from bricks of caramel. The sugar icing walls were dotted with gumdrops and flower-shaped sucking candies. The windows were framed in red licorice. The path leading up to the door was lined with lollipops. The front door was frosted a bright raspberry red. It stood wide open.

"Did your aunt make that?"

"She makes one every year."

"I'm going to bend down to look inside. I want you to hold tight to my hand."

"What?"

"Just do it." Feenix grabbed Edward's hand and held on tight. She bent down and peered inside.

He knew what was in there already. He'd seen it that afternoon. Three marzipan witches. One was tall and thin as a broomstick, one was round and shriveled like an old apple, and one wore a bright red kerchief. It had given him the creeps. Feenix stared and stared and held on to him so tightly his fingers started going numb.

Someone else had bent down beside her to take a look. "*That* is a marvel," said a strangely familiar voice.

Feenix abruptly let go of Edward's hand and stood up.

It was Mr. Ross.

He was beaming at them. "Well, here you are, at last. My young seekers. That was quite a storm, wasn't it? What a night! Did you hear the wind? I was beginning to wonder if we were going to make it through. But we did. Now, with a little luck, the days will get longer and the spring will return."

"Luck? Won't that just happen automatically?" Edward asked.

Mr. Ross laughed. "Probably, but then again, you never know. Let us waste no precious time and hustle ourselves over to that table. 'Time and the world are ever in flight,' as Shakespeare said, and I hear our hostess is a wonderful cook."

He turned as if he didn't doubt they'd follow.

"Who could have invited him?" Edward whispered in an agony of apprehension.

"I did," Feenix whispered back.

"What? Why?"

"Your aunt said we could bring whoever we wanted. And I had a really fun idea. Now I want you to go with Mr. Ross to the table and, whatever you do, keep him there till I come back."

"Listen—" he began angrily, but she was already gone.

A fun idea? This was not a good sign. What was she up to? Wasn't it bad enough the way she always made a fool out of Mr. Ross in school? Now she wanted to do it in Edward's own house?

Nervously, Edward watched her disappear into the crowd. There was no way he was going to go along with one of her fiendish schemes, but he couldn't leave Mr. Ross on his own, either. What if he ran into Aunt Kit?

Mr. Ross wanted to taste everything, and he piled his plate high. Edward was afraid that he was going to have to distract him with chitchat about gravity and cell division, but there was no need. Mr. Ross was completely focused on the food.

"Spanakopita! The filo is so thin and crisp. Black-eyed peas! I wonder if she actually makes these blintzes herself. I'll have to see if she'll give me the recipe. Do you know who our hostess is? Could you introduce me?"

Edward hesitated. Edward hemmed. Edward hawed. There was that whole problem with the truth again. Although he knew that it was no more solid than anything else. "Oh, well, sort of. I mean I saw her earlier. She was very busy. Very busy. Strange lady. Better not to bother her. Probably in the kitchen somewhere."

"The kitchen? Now which way is the kitchen?" Holding his overflowing plate in his hands, Mr. Ross turned around. Edward turned with him.

He saw, to his horror, that Feenix was sailing toward them not only with a sly grin on her face but with her arm intertwined with Aunt Kit's.

Edward motioned to her desperately to back away, hoping Mr. Ross wouldn't notice.

Feenix ignored him and kept right on coming.

As she drew near, she said, "Why do you keep flapping your hand like that, Edward? You look like the Energizer bunny. Mr. Ross, this is our hostess, Kit Walker, Edward's aunt."

Mr. Ross looked at first delighted and then puzzled. "Edward's aunt?" He looked at Edward. "But you didn't mention—"

Edward was glaring at Feenix. "Oh, sorry, didn't I? Yes, this is my aunt. I live with her. Long story."

"Mr. Ross is our science teacher," Feenix announced to Aunt Kit.

At this news, Aunt Kit stopped where she was. She studied Mr. Ross's face as if she were trying to read something there.

Edward groaned inwardly, although Mr. Ross didn't seem the slightest bit fazed.

Edward held his breath, waiting for his aunt to say whatever fruit loopy thing she was going to say about the ignorance of scientists. Before this could happen, Mr. Ross reached out and took hold of Aunt Kit's hand and lifted it to his lips.

Whooaa, dude, was Edward's startled thought.

"May I say that you are a culinary genius?" Mr. Ross said. "May I tell you that I am transported? Everything is wonderful—the soufflé, the blintzes, the black-eyed peas. This rye bread—" he let go of her hand and raised the half-eaten slice, "this bread is pure magic."

At these words, Aunt Kit bristled. "Oh no, I assure you. I never use any outside enhancements like that in my baking. It's simply practice and more practice."

Mr. Ross looked puzzled for a moment. Then he smiled. "You are too modest. This is the work of an artist. Someone with a gift not bestowed on the rest of us mere mortals."

Edward saw that a faint blush had risen to Aunt Kit's cheek. "You are most kind. You're interested in cooking?"

"A dabbler. A mere dabbler. I hesitate to ask, but I wonder if—"

"Yes?"

"Are you one of those artists who prefer not to share recipes or might I inquire . . . ?"

"This recipe was passed on to me by my grandmother. I believe that passing knowledge along is one of the Great Purposes."

Edward saw Mr. Ross's ears quiver with excitement. "Well, of course! Sharing the knowledge we gather. We are of like minds on this! If there's a reason for being here, that's got to be it!"

Edward was dumbfounded.

Aunt Kit was smiling at Mr. Ross. "Well, one of them," she said.

"And food! What a wonderful area of study! I envy you. The great chain of matter and energy, each always transforming, one into the other. So fascinating. But how do you achieve this airiness in your bread?"

"Ahh," she laughed. "That's the great secret. You must use a flour with the correct level of protein. A hard spring wheat is generally the best. Those are the highest in glutenin and gliadin. Without the necessary amounts of these, the gluten will not form properly."

Mr. Ross was riveted. "But this is fascinating. You've studied chemistry?"

"Chemistry is one way to see the underside of things. Yes, I have studied it in some of its aspects."

This was mind-boggling news to Edward. Was she serious?

"Unfortunately, the labeling on store packaging is often inaccurate. You can, of course, call the flour company and inquire as to the protein content, but in my experience the answers given by customer service are often unreliable. Over time, I've learned which flours are likely to be most successful for which breads and pastries. I could also show you the water absorption test, which might interest you as a scientist."

"Really? You would be willing to do that?"

"Certainly. Why not? Hands-on is always the best way. And I could show you some kneading techniques, too."

"This is exceedingly generous of you. I would be honored and grateful."

"How would next Tuesday evening be for you?"

Edward felt a sharp poke in his ribs. "Am I a genius or what?" whispered Feenix. She was laughing. Not in a fiendish way. She looked happy. Had she actually planned this? "Come on, Edward. Don't be such a dork. Time to leave them on their own," she said into his ear.

Feenix grabbed Edward's arm and yanked him away from the table. He heard his aunt saying something about pie crust.

In the other room, the harmonica, the fiddle, and the piano were joined by a singer—a man's voice, a little quavery at first, but then more and more sure of itself as it went on. Feenix pulled Edward in their direction. "Come on," she said. "Let's go listen to the music."

A big crowd had gathered around the piano. Feenix shouldered her way to the front, not releasing her iron grip on Edward's arm. When she stopped, Edward saw that the singer was Brigit's grandfather. He stood there, a little white-haired man, his feet planted apart, a glass of punch in one hand.

> *The holly and the ivy, when they are both full grown*
> *Of all the trees that are in the wood, the holly bears the*
> *crown.*

Edward could see Brigit standing nearby with her parents, watching and listening. Then, as the old man got to the end of the verse, he stepped into the crowd and took hold of his granddaughter's hand. Brigit was so startled she didn't seem to know what to do. Her grandfather pulled her with him to the piano and her face first turned pale, then it was flooded with a rush of pink.

"Oh no, the poor kid," Feenix whispered in Edward's ear. "Doesn't he realize what he's doing?"

Brigit stood there in all her silent flaming misery.

"It's like watching Joan of Arc being burned at the stake," Feenix said.

It was true, Edward thought, but since when had Feenix cared about anybody else being burned at the stake? The musicians played on, and Brigit's grandfather kept singing and smiling away at her.

It was then that Edward noticed something else. Something that was out of place. Something that was seriously strange.

There was a piper playing, but where was he? Edward could hear him clearly. Maybe he was hidden somewhere in the crowd. Edward took a step backward to get a better look. As he did this, it was as if someone had taken hold of the volume knob and turned it all the way to the left. The music, and all the other sounds of the party, faded into silence. In the next moment, he felt the floor melt away beneath his feet. The walls of the house and the ceiling, too, appeared to expand and fly apart, revealing all the space between their gazillions of spinning atoms. There was nothing solid left to stand on. He was floating alone in the darkness. The clear, star-bright night went wheeling and turning around him. He could feel, more than hear, the faint cricketlike ticking of time. It came from everywhere at once.

How long he hung there, exhilarated and terrified, he wasn't sure, but then, from somewhere far off, he heard the musicians and Brigit's grandfather and a voice he was sure he recognized.

> *Oh the rising of the sun, and the running of the deer*
> *The playing of the merry organ, sweet singing round the fire.*

Edward took a step forward toward the music, and as he did, everything contracted and rushed inward. In another moment, the walls were coming back around him and the ceiling was lowering itself into place. To his enormous relief, the floor rose up beneath his feet.

Brigit and her grandfather were singing together, their voices climbing around each other, lifting up and up.

The crowd around the piano had grown bigger and the piper could no longer be heard. Feenix was standing next to him and over there by the fiddler was Danton, waving and smiling his big sunbeam of a smile.

Feenix gave Edward a sharp poke in the side, trying to get his attention. "Look at her parents, Edward."

He saw that Brigit's mother was crying. Her dad leaned over and dabbed at her tears with a crumpled napkin, but then he turned and kept his shining eyes fixed on Brigit.

Edward found he could only half concentrate on this scene. Something was bothering him about Feenix, but what was it?

Suddenly, he knew. It was like being struck—*ping*—right in the middle of the forehead with a pebble.

She had called him "Edward."

Everything was the same and everything was different.

He felt eager to begin. Although begin what, he couldn't have said exactly.

In here was warmth and candlelight and a richness of hours filling the rooms. Outside was the wind, tapping and rattling at the window, trying to get in.

Around them, the stars went wheeling through the night.

Edward heard his aunt's clear, triumphant voice somewhere in the crowd. Beside him, Feenix began to sing. She was a little off-key, but he made no comment. Taking in a long breath of the warm and fragrant air, he, too, lifted his voice.

ACKNOWLEDGMENTS

I would like to express my gratitude to Elise Howard, an extraordinary editor, who did so much to help make this story all I wanted it to be. Gratitude, as well, to all the amazingly energetic, cheerful, and hardworking folk at Algonquin. So many thanks to my agent, Edite Kroll, who has supported me with such saintly patience.

My sons, Mark and Charlie, inspired this book in so many ways and helped me remember things it is easy to forget about being young. I owe them. Thanks to my husband, Sam, for the precious gift of time; to Kate Hanenberg for the idea; and to my friend Erica Weissman for all the free therapy sessions. Mostly especially, I thank Dina Redman for giving me courage when my courage flagged.